## THROUGH THREE GENERATIONS— FROM TRAGEDY'S CURSE TO FORTUNE'S JOY

ARTHUR TRESIZE—The seaman whose dream of becoming a gentleman came true, even as three wives ruined his happiness.

SIMON TRESIZE—The handsome, spoiled son who squandered his legacy on pleasure, and nearly ruined his devoted sister.

LETTICE TRESIZE—Betrayed by her brother, and the one man she loved, she fought to raise the son who could never bear her family name.

ALAN HEATH—Denied his birthright, he struggled to protect his mother from the cruelty of those who would take all she had.

ARABELLA SHAWCROSS—The beautiful heiress who spurned her wealthy suitors out of secret love for Alan Heath.

# THE OLD PRIORY

# NORAH LOFTS

 AVON
PUBLISHERS OF BARD, CAMELOT, DISCUS AND FLARE BOOKS

AVON BOOKS
A division of
The Hearst Corporation
959 Eighth Avenue
New York, New York 10019

First Avon Printing, April, 1983

# CONTENTS

# PART ONE

# Narrative by
# Arthur Tresize

# CHAPTER 1

I began to build my house at Ockley, in the county
of Suffolk, in the year 1590, when I was twenty-seven
years old. A good many houses were being built at
that time by men who had been successful in piracy
or in trade. Mine has a story behind it, so fantastic
that sometimes even now—remembering, as old men
do—I find it incredible, but it happened. It happened
just as I remember....

Captain Briggs, master and owner of the *Sea Gull*,
decided that year to avoid Bristol, our usual port,
and go round to the east of England.

He was engaged in the Three Point Trade. The
*Sea Gull* left Bristol carrying trade goods—all things
coveted by the West Coast Africans—axes, nails,
saws, sets of scales, a few muskets, woollen cloth and
trumpery things like beads. On the coast, wherever
a landfall could be made, these things were exchanged for slaves. This sounds cruel, but the slaves

were men and women captured in the endless tribal wars or men who had got into debt and thereby forfeited their freedom. Most of them would have ended in the cooking pot, but for the trade. In the West Indies, the Sugar Islands, they had value; some masters were kind. The slave money was then spent on rum, sugar and tobacco, which were brought back to Bristol, the triangle completed.

For us it had not been a good voyage. Despite all care—and Briggs was a careful man—an epidemic had broken out and we'd lost almost half our human cargo. Other ships had done better, so the value of slaves was slightly down and the price of sugar up. So Captain Briggs, who had all his wits about him, thought it would be to his advantage to sail on to Yarmouth, where what he had acquired might sell better, facing less competition. And he said to me, because I was the one in charge of the ship's stores, "At least herring should be cheap in Yarmouth."

We approached the place on one of those spring mornings which only those who have seen and smelt other countries can fully appreciate. There was a time when the wind, blowing against us, brought the scent of the land, of green things growing, of flowers. Closer in, nearer the harbour, Yarmouth reeked of fish, fresh, dried, smoked and rotten.

In Bristol I should have known just where to go and should have made for it forthwith, a comfortable combination of lodging house and brothel which I had patronised many times. In this small but busy town, I was all at sea and set out to find myself a place beyond the stench of the harbour.

I dislike the theory of predestination, yet sometimes I am compelled to wonder. I think...if Captain Briggs had not decided upon Yarmouth...if I, seeking a sweeter air, had not walked inland...all would have been otherwise. As it was, I was walking along, keeping a sharp lookout for a suitable inn and just level with a great church and thinking that I was out of bounds when a coach came up behind me. It was very grand and drawn by four dapple-grey horses, perfectly matched. It was they, rather than the coach or whoever might occupy it, that drew my attention. Just then the coach seemed to be empty — and no concern of mine. It went by, and I, thinking that I was not in the neighborhood of cheap inns, turned and began to retrace my steps. The coach must have turned too, for soon it passed me again, travelling at a slower pace, and I had that feeling of being under observation, though I could see nobody in the coach.

Opposite the church I took a side road and soon found what I wanted—a neat but modest inn called the Sailors' Rest. No fish stench here. There was a little garden, full of gillyflowers, and a hawthorn tree in bloom. And there was a black and white mongrel dog, half friendly, half cautious. I shared my dinner with him.

After the meal I had a nap and then set out to walk about, avoiding both the harbour and the marshes, getting to know the town. Once, in a quiet street, I had the feeling of being observed from a window. I was accustomed to women's stares. I was six feet tall then—too tall for a sailor really—and brawny and tanned; also I had a wonderful head of hair, not red but a true, bright chestnut. Aware of being watched, I swaggered slightly.

In the evening I found a satisfactory brothel. Yarmouth was nothing like the port that Bristol was and the girls were not overused.

Next morning—another beautiful day—I began my survey of the places which sold ships' stores, not to buy yet, but to study and compare prices. A great deal depends upon the casks' quality and a great deal can be learned by just lounging about. Briggs trusted me absolutely; he once told me that I was too arrogant to be dishonest. All his judgements were like that, slightly on the sour side. And I had the advantage, not common among sailors, of being able to read and write and reckon a little. I owed that to my second oldest brother, who had had a little schooling and passed on some of what he learned, and to the teaching of my first captain.

I went back to the Sailors' Rest for my dinner. The landlady there knew what sailors ashore needed— fresh food, nothing salted or dried. I was enjoying a dish of beef and spring cabbage, and the dog was watching me hopefully, when I again became aware of being watched. You know, that sensation at the nape of the neck. This time it did not set me swaggering. I had a feeling that when I turned, if I turned, I should see somebody whom I had no wish to see. So far as I knew I owed nobody a farthing. So far as I knew nobody owed me a grudge, but everywhere there is the possibility of falling in with somebody, met long ago in some far place and now beached and craving for sailors' talk. Harmless but boring.

There was another possibility, too. Somebody might be measuring me up. Sailors ashore are supposed to be easy game.

However, when at last, prickled into doing something, I turned, there was nobody behind but a woman, old enough and dim enough to eat her dinner alone in a public eating place. She was very small and so muffled about in black that all I saw was a half-hidden chalky face and two hands, also dead white. Having caught my attention, just by staring, she nodded and raised one hand. I saw a diamond flash. And I thought to myself, One of those!

I had encountered her kind before. Perhaps to be pitied, I realise now; women in whose bodies the appetite gnaws long after the time for its satisfaction has passed. I had never lent myself to that trade. I was nobody in the eyes of the world, a common sailor, but in the matter of what company I kept, I was choosy and, where sex was concerned, the buyer.

This old woman came towards me and at my elbow said, "Surely such a pretty young man should be drinking wine."

She was not English. People from Germany and the Netherlands, given practice enough, can disguise their origins; the French and Italians cannot. It is a question of rhythm rather than pronunciation.

"I choose my own drink, madam."

But she was not to be put off. She dragged out a stool and seated herself with an air of purpose.

"I have a matter of importance to discuss with you. It is not what you think. Adonis could not stir me now. We will drink the red wine of Burgundy." She beckoned to the potboy, and the diamond winked. Apart from the jewel there was nothing to show of rank or wealth. Yet she was very assured. I thought that she might be in some way connected with the provision trade, a widow with no son. She could have seen me that morning making my preliminary rounds and decided to make a bid for my custom. So when the wine came I let it stand. I didn't cheat and I didn't take bribes.

"Would you like to earn two hundred pounds?"

I almost fell off the bench. Two hundred pounds was a fortune.

"Who wouldn't?" I asked. A thought struck me. A matter of importance involving so much money must be concerned with crime. Sailors, being here today and gone tomorrow, were sometimes hired as assassins—a staged brawl, a dead man and the killer safe aboard and away. But paid in shillings, not pounds.

Also, owners of vessels were sometimes paid to smuggle away somebody wanted by the law.

I said, "I am not prepared to kill anybody, if that is what you want. And *Sea Gull* does not belong to me."

She caught my meaning and laughed; not an old woman's cackle, a soft, velvety ripple of sound.

"How suspicious you are! No, nothing like that. No drama. No danger. You would merely be required to play a part and keep a secret. One might say—a masquerade."

To me that made a kind of sense. With the rich, masquerades were a passion and once I and three others of our crew had earned five shillings a head to man a boat on an artificial lake in the grounds of a nobleman in the West Country who wanted to give his masquerade some touch of reality. We'd eaten and drunk well, too.

But here the price offered was too high for comfort, and despite everything there was something sinister about the old woman herself. My mind took another turn and I thought, What she may want is a corpse of a well-grown fellow with bright chestnut hair.

I looked her straight in the eye and asked, "Does it involve danger? I should warn you, madam. To you I may seem to be of no importance, but my captain values me. He is in Norwich now, but he will be back here on Saturday morning and if I am not here then, with a list of stores ready to load, he'll raise a hue and cry of no small order. And he has friends in high places." It was true in a way. His brother was member of Parliament for Plymouth.

She counted. "This is Tuesday. Four nights." The sum seemed to dissatisfy her slightly and for a moment she looked not like an upper servant who had been given a costly ring by some chance, or a decent old woman engaged in trade, or a grand lady come in disguise to hire a man for a masquerade, but like a witch, muttering enchantments. Then she said, "I swear by the cross that no harm shall come to you. That nothing shall be asked of you that is not easy and pleasant and that you shall be back here on Saturday morning. What more can I say, except that the money is the price of discretion—that rare virtue—and that you can have half now as an earnest of good faith."

She fumbled about amongst her wrappings and produced a leather bag. She said, "Open it under the table." I did so and saw a jumble of coins. I picked one out and it was an angel with the Queen on one side and the Tudor rose of her family on the other. I was astounded. I thought how very easy it would be for me to jump up, give the old woman a punch that would keep her silent for some minutes and dash away to lose myself in the anonymity of the waterfront.

She said, "You see, I trust you. You should trust me."

In a fashion I did, for she had sworn by the cross; and she was French. The French were papists still and did not take the cross lightly.

Again she seemed to read my mind. "You will come," she said, and it was not a question.

"Not until evening. If I am to absent myself for four days I must be busy this afternoon."

"That suits me excellently. At sunset, walk along the road you took yesterday. I will come for you. And remember, not a word to anybody."

There was no temptation for me to confide in anybody; Captain Briggs was in Norwich, where he thought he stood a better chance of acquiring such trifles as beads than he would have done in Yarmouth, and my shipmates had scattered.

I tried to concentrate upon the ship's needs and

the quality of the goods offered me, but my mind kept slipping away to the rendezvous at sunset and what might come after. One minute I thought of it as a desperate enterprise, the next as a trivial adventure. Slightly before the sun began to decline I went back to the inn, washed myself thoroughly and changed my clothes. The terms "drunken" and "dirty" are often applied to sailors by people who do not realise that there are times when the amount of rum aboard exceeds that of the water.

I told the landlady that I should be back on Saturday—and immediately wondered if I were being overoptimistic. But a man who shied away from danger would never go to sea in the first place, or last long if he did.

I said good-bye to the black and white dog, who showed some disposition to accompany me.

Sunset is a vague term. In the tropics the sun vanishes suddenly; in hilly country it may be abruptly obscured; in this flat open land sunset might last an hour. I was in good time and was walking steadily into the fragrant countryside when I heard the sound of wheels and hooves behind me.

# CHAPTER 2

It was not a coach but one of those light, two-wheeled vehicles with a canvas cover across the seat and the rear. They are common enough not to be noticeable and the old woman, crouched low, could have been any farmwife bound for home at the end of the day. But, as the ring had done, the quality of the horse betrayed it. I notice animals, and this, though not one of the dapple greys, was a horse of quality. But it had not come straight from Yarmouth. There was enough lather to inform me that it had been driven fairly far and fairly fast.

And now we took a roundabout route, driving for a little while straight into the sunset, swerving off, travelling for some time through woods along a path where no larger vehicle could have gone. Going west, then due south, and once due north, and through a village which was like something out of a fairy tale.

On a slight, artificial mound stood a castle. Below it, sheltered as it were, was a church and a wide spread of village green bordered by a slow-moving stream on one side and some huddled cottages on the other. I thought I should know it again and looked for an inn sign as a landmark. There was none. It was a village without an inn.

Soon after that we were in the woods again and presently in a little clearing. The light was then fading fast and I could only just make out a little hut, the kind charcoal burners use.

"You wait here. I will come for you presently," the old woman said, breaking a long silence. In all the long journey we had exchanged perhaps twenty words. We were both busy with our thoughts. What hers were I could not guess; mine were of complete bewilderment. Now she seemed concerned for my comfort.

"Have you a tinder?"

"I always carry one," I said.

"Wise man. You will find a candle. And a simple supper." She drove quickly away.

It was as she had said: there was the candle, a loaf of white bread and one of those cream cheeses which I remembered from my boyhood. Delicious, but mouldy within two days—nothing like the cheeses I had earmarked that afternoon for *Sea Gull*'s next voyage.

Left alone and more mystified than ever, I thought of the half fortune I carried. I was still suspicious and I thought that if the bag of gold angels were bait which the old dame thought to recover, I'd fox her. I had my knife and I carried the candle to the doorway of the hut; it was such a still evening that the flame did not even flicker. By its light I dug a hole at the root of an oak tree, put the bag into it and trod it in, carefully replacing the moss.

Then I waited for what seemed a lifetime, the
treadmill of my mind going on and on, always stopping at one of the least valued of human emotions—
curiosity. I had in actual words promised nothing; I
was free to dig up what I had just buried and run
away into the woods. But, although I was a seaman
through necessity not choice and loved the land rather
than the sea, I shared in some part the seaman's
disease—the desire to know what lies beyond the
horizon. That itch has been responsible for many
remarkable voyages. And in a modest way, now that
I had embarked, I shared the feeling that had taken
Drake round the world. What next?

What next was the old woman coming for me. She
carried one of those lanterns with a shutter and
seemed, for the first time, agitated. She said, "Leave
your shoes. Here are slippers. Silence is of great importance. Follow me." In the darkness she was all
but invisible and she held the lantern very low.

I could tell that we went through a garden because
I could smell the flowers; then our feet were on stone
and the air was damp and stale. My guide halted,
listened and whispered, "Stairs. Twenty-two of them."
We mounted and were in a passage, then at a door.
I heard the old woman let loose a long, sighing breath,
as though she had held it for a long time. Then she
opened the door and said, "He is here."

After the darkness, the room seemed brilliant,
lighted by a small fire and many candles. It was
occupied by a woman who, met unexpectedly, could
have been taken for a ghost. She wore a white robe
of very fine lawn and some gauze was folded about
her head and face so that only her eyes were plainly
visible. Against the whiteness they looked enor-
mous, and dark and apprehensive.

She sat very straight and still in a high-backed

chair near the fire. Seven candles burned on a table beside her and slightly to the rear.

"You are welcome," she said. "I feel I have some explaining to do." She was nervous; her voice was breathy and jerky, and although she sat so still, her fingers writhed and twisted in her lap. "Sit down," she said. "I will be brief...." As the story unfolded I understood her nervousness. Bawds talk bawdy and there are some well-born ladies with foul tongues; this lady was not of that kind and what she had to say embarrassed her.

"I am a widow. My husband took a fall from his horse ten days ago. I have no child. Everything, the ti..." She checked herself. "Everything goes to his nephew. No provision was made for me—though two bastard sons were remembered in his will! The nephew is here now and has made it plain that he takes no responsibility for me. So I thought...if I could become pregnant, soon...very soon...paternity could hardly be questioned....I have seen no one, been nowhere....And the hair..."

I understood her predicament but at the same time I was deeply affronted. It was a more cold-blooded arrangement than any made by lustful old women. I thought to myself, Hired like a stud stallion, chosen for his colouring!

It reduced my manhood. In every way. In my own opinion of myself and in my ability to do her the service she asked. Through the fine lawn I could see slender, well-shaped limbs and body; her eyes were beautiful, and the fact that the rest of her face was hidden, the possibility that it was unworthy of the eyes, did not deter. In Jamaica there is a brothel— much patronised—where all the girls wear masks, some very hideous and all said to conceal the ravages of the pox.

I said, "I don't think I can do what you wish. I will give you back your money."

"You are married?"

"No."

"In love?"

"No."

"A lover of boys?"

"My God! No!"

"Then *why?*"

"I can give you no reason."

Now that would have angered most women, or set them questioning their own attractiveness. But this lady, after a little silence, laughed and said, "In ancient times, we are told, kings spent a lifetime looking for an honest man. Without looking I seem to have found one. Come, share the joke! No one else can. And to think that only this morning I made the heir presumptive turn pale with a hint that he should not yet count his chickens. I still had a few days then.... But life seems determined to cheat me. Has it cheated you?"

"Insofar as it made me the fourth son of a poor man who had done his best for three. And sent me, a landlubber born, to sea. And kept me poor—which after all is the common lot. And now this..."

"Yes, a grave pity. I hoped for a son."

"Daughters are born too."

"I know. But a pregnancy lasts nine months, and knowing what I now do, I could make some provision, given time, and a willing man with the fam...Oh, why do I bother? I needed a well-grown man with chestnut hair. And willing. I thought...a miracle. Or an act of justice. But since...well, at least you can take a glass of wine with me, Honest Man!"

She stood up and the movement sent waves of sweet scent wafting out from the white robe, and the firelight behind her outlined her figure. None of it mattered to me. What I was caught by, entranced by, was her courage, by the laughter in the face of defeat—surely the highest courage of all.

Suddenly something happened to me. The mule-like impotence drained away. I was master of myself—and of her. Her hands, recently so uneasy, were steady on the flagon and that too was admirable. Restored, my body just for once was governed by something that was not mere lust. I said, "Who needs wine? Come here!"

I'd heard about priest holes. Now I occupied one and can say with certainty that a priest hole compares very favourably with an ordinary seaman's accommodation aboard ship—this was before hammocks were common. I lay in a narrow space, but on soft down; an air vent led upwards and a drain downwards. The old woman brought me food of the utmost delicacy and hot water, soft towels.

I slept most of the days away, waking at intervals, and knowing with some sense for which there is no name whether my lady, my love, were in the adjoining room or not. My heart knew. Otherwise it was a time without time. It was an experience out of this world not merely because she was the best partner in bed that a man could ever hope for, but because we could talk and laugh together, both before and after the act.

She was candour itself about many things but careful not to give away anything which would allow me to identify her. Often she almost did, but checked herself in time and stared at me with those great dark eyes, appealing to me not to press the point. Once she said, "In our house in Warwickshire—the house in which we were staying, I mean."

At first I laughed and said, "Why so cautious? Who you are matters to me not at all." Then, as I fell more and more deeply in love, the lack of trust hurt until it was swallowed up in the greater hurt.

I was a fool, of course. I said, "Look, why bother with this masquerade? Come away with me. Two hundred pounds will buy and stock a farm. I'd make you happy, I swear." I thought briefly of a farmwife's life and rushed on, promising that she should never soil her hands but be treated like a queen all her days.

Her face set like stone. She said, "I have been poor. Once in a lifetime is enough." I could have argued that with two hundred pounds and a strong body no man could be called poor; but I thought of the coach and the four greys and all they represented, and though she had bitten off the word "title" I was sure she had one, possibly a resounding one. I said bitterly, "And of course if you can keep your hands on the money you can hire any number of red-headed sailors."

"Ah, don't," she said. "It has been so sweet a time."

"But you do not wish it to continue?"

"Dear God! If only it could! You and I...But there is so much to think of...this, for instance." She placed her slender hands on either side of her slim body and laughed. "I told you that for me time was short. You told Marie that you should be back in Yarmouth on Saturday...as narrow a gamble as there has ever been, I think. But it happened, I *knew*. A woman always knows...with a lover. And besides, for two days now it has not been with me as it should. You understand me? I have won. But at what cost!" And suddenly the laughter changed to tears. No contortion of the face, no gulping or sniffling, just the tears rising and spilling. She said, "I shall love you till I die. I shall miss you every day of my life."

I said, "Then why not come? Let everything go. Come with me and be happy." I kissed, I actually kissed some of the tears away, and then she drew away from me and changed, becoming again the great lady whom I'd been brought in—hired stallion—to serve. She said, "Life is hard, but I wish you well. You have my heart, my prayers and every good wish in the world."

How long any feeling she had for me lasted, I never knew; or if a child, boy or girl, came of our union. I only know what happened.

Marie came with her lantern and we made our journey in reverse. She was if anything more nervous than before, and now I understood. The great house was full of the dead man's kin.

At the hut she said, "I will come for you in the morning. You seem to have done well. Good night."

At first light I rose and disinterred my treasure, which now seemed...not worthless, to call it that would not be honest...but somehow diminished. So much diminished that I did not think about the other half or how and when, or if at all, it would be paid. I told myself that I had lived in Elfland for four nights and four days and had lost touch with reality. I had been marooned on a desert island and was presently to be rescued by an old woman in a covered cart. I tried to think of Captain Briggs, of the stores I had bespoken and what I must tell him, for even the half price would buy me freedom. He'd curse, but he'd easily find a man to replace me.

Marie came and I got into the cart and she took an even more devious route. We did not go through the village which had seemed so homely, nor did we cross the river again. I felt like telling her that it was a waste of time. If I'd wanted to put the finger on my love a day's sniffing about would have been sufficient. Within an easy or a hard drive of Yarmouth the number of great ladies, suddenly and recently bereaved, must be very limited. But I said nothing and she only mentioned the weather and clucked to the horse. I was not feeling talkative either.

Having left Yarmouth to the south, we approached from the north, along a causeway with marshes on either side, possibly the most dismal country that England can show. It matched my mood. Then the town loomed up and Marie reined in.

"I will set you down here," she said. "You can walk to your hostelry. This is yours." She fumbled and produced another bag, into which I did not even bother to look. "And here," she said, producing with a benevolent air a small napkin tied up by its four corners, "the little sweet cakes which you liked."

A kindly gesture. Having made it, she drove off, the better to confuse, to the south.

I am not a pious man but I do thank God that on my walk back to the Sailors' Rest I met no beggar child. At the entry of the inn I met the dog. He recognised me, yelped with delight, jumped about me, and I said, "Hullo, mate. Good dog. Good boy." I was coming back to ordinary life with such difficulty that even a dog's recognition had value. I said, "I have something nice for you," and opened the napkin, gave him one of the little cakes. He gulped it down, looked for another and then suddenly went stiff and fell over, dead.

I stood there trying to tell myself that he had choked, that perhaps he was old and that old dogs, like old men, are subject to fits. But it was useless. Somebody had wanted me to drop dead. And that was so staggering a thought that I could not accept it without further proof. I must be sure.

Men earn their bread in many ways and freeing ships of rats is one of them. Many rats are killed outright but there is a demand for live, uninjured

ones for rat-catching competitions. For this purpose
the big brown foreign rats were favoured as they
were more aggressive. The usual price is fourpence,
but I gave the man I finally found two shillings for
two rats in a makeshift cage. In a quiet corner of the
harbour I dropped a cake into the cage and both rats
died, as the dog had done.

As I was supposed to do!

I added some stones to the contents of the napkin
and dropped it into the filthy water. I did not wish
the gulls to be poisoned for though to landsmen their
greed and raucous cries make them unlovable, seamen feel differently. They speak of land nearby, they
shout their welcome.

All that day as I hurried about on *Sea Gull*'s business
I felt myself in danger. I even bought a hat to hide
my hair. I pinned the blame for the attempt to kill
me on Marie. I believed that because I wanted to
believe it. I wanted to believe that the woman I had
loved was incapable of such treachery. And yet, and
yet...I remembered her face when she spurned my
offer of marriage. She'd looked capable of anything
then. And the old woman would obviously do exactly
what she was told.

I thought the sooner I was out of Yarmouth the
better. I did not even feel safe aboard the ship, for I
had mentioned its name.

Captain Briggs arrived early in the evening, in-
spected the stores I had had stowed and approved of
everything. He was more offended than I had expected when I told him that I should not be sailing
with him on Monday. It was never his habit to praise
or to allow any man to feel more important than
another, so he only said that he would find it incon-
venient and that I should have given him more warn-

ing. "But," he added, "I always knew you were a landlubber at heart."

It was only then that I realised that the last few days had not been merely a visit to Elfland, a love affair and a narrow escape from death, but also a profitable exercise. The two hundred pounds lay snug against my ribs. I was a landlubber who might soon become a landowner! The thought was like a dab of ointment on a wound. It soothed, though it could not heal. Nothing but time could do that.

# CHAPTER 3

I came to Ockley by accident. I'd just walked aimlessly, taking side roads, avoiding the highway. I did not feel hunted, yet I was relieved when I was out of Norfolk and into Suffolk. I told myself that I was looking for a village something like the one through which Marie had driven me—it had had such a homely, settled air. And I must have tramped through dozens of them without feeling that here was the place. I walked to divert my mind by fresh scenes and to exhaust myself so that I slept at night. And so I stumbled upon Ockley, just before noon on a high summer day. Something within me said, Here is the place!

There was the village green, bordered on one side by the slow-moving river, on the other by cottages. On the other side of the river stood a tiny church, and beyond it, on slightly higher ground, were ruins set in what I can only call wasteland, though a different kind of wasteland from that on the border between the two counties.

I walked slowly, looking for an inn, but there was none. I reached the bridge, very old and humped, that separated the church, the ruins and the waste from the cottages and the green, and there turned.

My arrival had not gone unmarked; several women had clustered about one cottage door and one asked me what I was selling. I carried my spare gear in the ordinary seaman's bundle. The woman took me for a pedlar and seemed disappointed when I said, "Nothing. I am a stranger, looking for a bite and something to drink." I added that I could pay. One oldish woman said, "Better call Enoch," and a younger one ran to the rear of the houses and shouted, the name echoing.

Enoch came, scythe in hand, and other men appeared, too. It would be wrong to say that at this point they were hostile; simply wary of a stranger who was not a pedlar. To an extent they were hospitable enough, but I was not invited to enter any of the open doors. A meal was brought, ham, which most seamen avoid when ashore—but this was different, sweeter and less salt—fresh bread, a mug of beer. But I was to eat and drink on a bench under a crooked apple tree and Enoch—I thought waiting for payment—sat too. Finally he asked, "What is your business? Why are you here?"

I said what I was to say again and again: "I am a sailor with a bit of money saved. I'm looking for a place to settle—to farm."

"Know anything about it—farming, I mean?"

"I was born and worked for the first thirteen years of my life on a farm. In Devon."

"Ah," he said, "a foreigner." I did not then know that for real Suffolk people foreigners begin at the parish boundary. "And around here there's no land to hire that I know of, unless..." He moved his gaze from my face to the land across the river. "There's the Priory," he said, "but I wouldn't advise it."

"Why not?"

"It's been waste too long. I'm fifty and in all my years the land across the river never did anybody a mite of good. My father—he's dead now, pity you can't talk to him—he was full of tales. Mostly sorrowful about how in the old days of the Priory there was work for everybody and help in hard times and care in sickness. All long ago. But what I do know is that nobody has flourished there in my time. According to my father, when the monks left, it went to a man called Parkyn. He tried sheep. They didn't prosper. Tom Thoroughgood—he's a horse breeder—hired it for his son. His horses didn't breed, or they broke their legs. And his wife died. That sort of thing, over and over, as though there was a curse on it."

Sailors as a breed are very superstitious, perhaps because they are so much in the hands of luck. Even Captain Briggs, a hard-headed character, would never dream of setting sail on a Friday, or a Sunday, or with a priest, a donkey or a corpse aboard; and to change a ship's name for however good a reason was an open invitation to ill fortune. I was no more immune from superstition than the next man, yet Enoch's talk affected me in a contradictory fashion. I thought that a place with a bad reputation should be cheap.

"Whose is it now?"

"I can't say. Parson'd know."

I had already felt a little surprise that no parson, inquisitive and omniscient, had yet appeared. Parsons in England, priests on the Continent, witch doctors in Africa, all take interest in newcomers.

"Where can I find him?"

"Nettleton. We share."

"And how do I get there?"

"By road or through Layer. Layer'll save you a good three miles."

I was to learn that sooner or later everybody in this district was to make that statement, with a slight difference as to numbers.

"And what is Layer?"

He almost managed a smile. "The wood. Layer Wood. 'Lay' is an old word for a pool and there's a good many in there." He made a vague gesture that seemed to involve all points of the compass. He laid his big hard hand palm uppermost on his knee. "There's the wood, and here and here"—he touched the tips of his fingers and the places where they joined the palm and reeled off a lot of village names, Clevely, Muchanger, Greston, two Minshams named after saints—and of course Nettleton, and slightly into the palm of the hand, Baildon. I could see that almost any journey in this district could be almost halved by taking to the woods.

I offered payment for my meal but it was not accepted. "It was nothing," Enoch said courteously.

"I'll go across and take a closer look at the land," I said. "Do you know the acreage?"

"It was about a hundred and fifty, but the woods have crept in." With the suddenness of a summer storm the atmosphere between us had changed. Become cooler. I attributed this to the fact my continued interest in the wasteland went contrary to his advice.

I crossed the bridge. Between it and the door of the church there was a faint trail and then lush, overgrown grass, poppies, wild oats, scabious, this-tles, nettles and young trees, shoulder-high. Ruins cumbered the ground, too. A long cloister had evidently once joined the main building to the church; some stone piers and a broken archway or two remained and at its far end there was a kind of stone honeycomb, large cells and small, all roofless and with walls varying from knee height to ten feet.

I'd seen ruins in many places, deserted buildings gently decaying, and it struck me that here the damage had been deliberate and violent, less the work of time and weather than of human malice.

Even in the bright noon sunshine it was a scene of desolation, yet it did not dishearten me; on the contrary I had again that unaccountable sense of having found my place in the world and the comfortable feeling that I could afford to buy it. The ache I'd been carrying about with me eased off. I even thought cheerfully of the future: of owning a hundred and fifty acres and seeing them prosper; of building a house out of these ruins and taking a wife whom I should love and respect though I could never share with her the ecstasy I had known with my dark-haired enchantress who might, or might not, have planned my death.

In this jubilant mood I set out for Nettleton. I found the parsonage easily and was kindly received at table by Parson Ambrose, who either took his dinner very late or had lingered over it unduly, though he looked as though he had never had a square meal in the whole of his long life. He was a little thread of a man, but his eyes, despite the milky line around the pupils, were lively. He offered me food and, when I said I had eaten already, insisted upon pouring me a glass of wine. Lifting his own, he said, "And now, what brings you here?"

"Some land at Ockley—the Old Priory." He gave such a start that his wine slopped.

"What about it? You wish to hire part of it?"

"I should like to buy it—if the price is right. In the village I was told that you would know who owns it just now."

27

"You have been in the village? Talked to the people?" He sounded quite incredulous.

"But of course. A man named Enoch gave me some dinner and talked to me as I ate it."

"And what did he tell you?"

"Not to have anything to do with it. He spoke of a curse and repeated misadventures."

"God give me patience! And them forgiveness! Well, having heard the lies, listen now to the truth! The last prior at Ockley was a saint—Alwyn was his name. Within the community he was so strict that the numbers dropped so it was one of the first to be dissolved, and the buildings destroyed. It broke his heart, but even so, even when he was dying, his one care was for the people of Ockley who had worked on the Priory land and to whom he had been father and mother. He came of a great family and he appealed to his brother, saying, 'I want nothing for myself; I have vowed myself to poverty; but I beg you buy some land to the east of the river so that my people shall not become beggars.' The brother took *some* heed. Did you notice the layout of that village?"

"Not closely. The man Enoch had a scythe in his hand so I imagined he had hay to cut."

"Exactly. To each man his plot. That was Prior Alwyn's wish. And what is his reward? To be reviled, most blasphemously reviled, well on into the second generation."

"I heard nothing said against the prior. I was told that several people had suffered misfortunes so that the land was said to be cursed."

"Pure coincidence mingled with a lot of folly. A man called Parkyn made a sheep run there. Any thickhead could have told him that it was not sheep country, lying as it does between woodland and river, and lush, well-tilled land at that. Naturally their

feet rotted. Then Tom Thoroughgood hired it for his
son..."

"So I was told," I interrupted, not wishing to hear
that story again.

But there was no stopping him. "He never had
any intention of living there, but his horses were
valuable so he kept fierce dogs, running free. One
went mad during a hot summer, bit the others and
they went mad too. They stampeded the horses who—
sensible creatures—tried to take refuge in the ruins,
stumbled and broke their legs. Nothing remarkable
about that; nor in the young wife dying; she came
from a family riddled with consumption. It is a disease that makes women fair to the eye but they never
breed well. I've noticed it often enough. Now, who
came next? Dear me, I grow forgetful! Oh yes, a
Clevely man, not content with what he had—but
there may be some excuse for him, he had four lusty
boys—he bought the Priory and before he could do
anything about reclaiming the land or building a
house all his sons were dead of the sweating sickness,
which was bad that year. He was then past the age
when a man begets children. After that there was a
man called Burgate..."

I interrupted again, this time more firmly. "Can
you tell me who owns and might be prepared to sell
the land *now?*"

"I cannot. The last I heard—and it is, after all,
my parish—was that it had fallen into the hands of
some great landowner who already had more than
he or his agents could handle. Some talk, I believe,
of making a hunting lodge...and when I think of
what it once was! Top Field, Nether Field, Ten Acre
and Eggar's Piece and the teams coming home in
the evening—all the oxen wore bells, attuned so that
they chimed in a small way, like the bells in tall
steeples. And Alwyn never allowed a goad to be

used.... That should show you what manner of man he was and may explain how I feel about the people who perpetuate this scandal and say that on his deathbed he cursed that beloved place and all who set foot in it!"

He recovered from his fit of rage and told me the man who had the handling of the Priory land was an attorney, Master Turnbull in Baildon. And when I said I would go there straightway, he said it was a long way by road, but a short way through Layer.

So I came to Baildon, a neat compact town, not unlike Exeter, and there I found Master Turnbull, who plainly expected me to drop dead when he said that his client had empowered him to sell the land at Ockley but not at less than four shillings an acre. "A total of thirty pounds," he said, almost challenging me to produce that sum.

The truth was, of course, that I did not look a buyer of land. I'd come ashore as all sailors did, with two outfits which differed only in that one was more worn than the other and that the better one would eventually replace the one worse for wear. Aboard ship there was no room to store fine clothes. Also, sailors are notoriously poorly paid and on the whole improvident; so a sailor with thirty pounds in hand was a rarity indeed. And there was always the likelihood of any large sum being the proceeds of piracy or other ill-doing.

However, as soon as I produced my shining angels, Master Turnbull became affable.

"I shall be heartily glad to be rid of that business," he said. "For years there has always been somebody interested and then some excuse for withdrawal. A waste of valuable time." He took from a cupboard a dusty bundle of parchment and paper, gave it a cursory glance and then wrote busily.

"Do you write?" he asked.

"I can make shift to sign my name." In fact I had cultivated a fine clear hand in the new Italianate style, far superior to his crabbed script or that of the two clerks called in as witnesses.

"My client will be able to buy himself a new ornament for his hat," the lawyer said drily. "And you— I would advise against sheep. Here are your deeds."

I took them and went out into the still-sunny street. I was a man of property, my dream of the impossible had come true. A dream fifteen years old. I'd been twelve when my father told me that naturally Edgar would inherit the farm, Stephen would continue with his education and Henry would be apprenticed to a saddler in Exeter. "For you, my poor boy, I can do nothing." Now here I was, sole owner of a farm twice as large as the family one and, if I knew anything about it, potentially five times as productive.

I looked about for and found a comfortable hostelry. It was called the Hawk in Hand and it overlooked a large open space on which, I was told, there was a weekly market. Market day was Wednesday and this was Tuesday, so I stayed on, listing in my mind my immediate needs. A horse, a wagon, a cow, stores of food, tools. I thought of geese, which can keep down grass and the weeds that grass shelter; and I thought of goats, which can destroy even well-grown trees. I needed pigs and fowls, too, but I imagined that they could be found at Ockley.

I also needed labour, and that I also imagined could be found in the village.

It was almost dusk when I reached Ockley, for the wagon would not travel the narrow woodland rides and we went at the pace of the cow tethered to the wagon's tail. The scent of fresh-cut hay was strong on the air, interspersed here and there with the smell of supper cooking.

As it had done before, my arrival attracted attention. Enoch—his full name was Enoch Bowman—came forward from the group, looked us over and said, "So you're stopping!"

I said, "Yes. I have bought the land and what you can see here. But I need much more stock." My stores, four geese and two goats filled the wagon.

It is always amusing to watch two differing emotions at work in people. Here cupidity warred with a distaste for having anything to do with an ill-fated man. A kind of dumbness fell, broken at last by one bold old woman who said she had a goat which she intended to send to market very soon. That encouraged others to offer pigs and geese and hens; but nobody came really near me. They all, even Bowman, held off as though I carried some contagion. I lost patience and said, "What you have to sell, bring across tomorrow and I will give a fair price."

"At the church door, sir," Enoch said, and they all nodded and clucked.

Once across the bridge and on my own ground I loosed the cow, the goats and the geese and drove on towards the ruins. There was what had plainly once been a room some twelve feet square, with three of its walls still standing high enough to give me clearance, and with a hearth. This, I thought, would be my centre, covered by a tarpaulin should it rain, until I could find masons and carpenters.

I unharnessed the horse and almost immediately, while I was beginning to unload the stores, he threw himself down and rolled. Now that is supposed to be a sign of good health in a horse—every roll worth a pound was an old saying. My horse rolled four times and then got to his feet and began to graze. I knew nothing of his history but it pleased me to imagine that he was a town horse, unaccustomed to pasture, and his pleasure added to mine as I unloaded, ate my bread and cheese and bedded myself down on the bare earth, my head on the bundle of spare clothing.

In the morning I found the horse dead.

He'd looked all right in the market. I'd looked at his teeth and judged him to be about five or six years old. He had not died of excessive eating; his belly was not blown up. Inevitably my first thought was about the curse, about all the mishaps which Parson Ambrose had dismissed so airily. My second thought concerned the village people and what they would make of this. They'd add my name to the list of unfortunate fellows and say, "Then there was Arthur Tresize, whose horse died before it had been there for twenty-four hours!" I walked down to the bridge, looked back and was pleased to find that the carcass was invisible. I determined to say nothing about it, to go on foot to market next week, buy a similar horse and ride home.

The cow, the geese and the goats were all right.

As though they had been waiting for signs of my existence, the villagers began to muster with what they had to sell. They huddled together as people do when danger threatens, hesitated before crossing the bridge, crossed it and stood on the little path that led to the church door. I went no nearer to them. I thought, I'm the buyer, you come to me! But in the end I went to them and without quibble paid what was asked for the spare goat, various pigs, a calf and a dozen hens. I overpaid and I overpraised, scattering compliments right and left, trying to establish a friendly and unsuspicious atmosphere before I made mention of work. Finally I said, "As you can see for yourselves, there is a great deal of work to be done on this place. I'm prepared to give twopence a day to any man, a penny-halfpenny to any woman and a penny to any child who will come to work for me."

This was a ridiculous offer; fourpence a week was an average wage for a man.

Nobody spoke; they huddled even closer, looking not at me but at Enoch Bowman. I thought, I've overdone it!

"I'm offering such high wages *for a time* because it is not a straightforward job. The land must be cleared before it can be cultivated."

"We're all busy with our own," Enoch said at last. "Yesterday nobody even went to market on account of getting the hay cut. Next week it'll be strawberries. Then cherry picking. Then oats. You see, sir, we're all busy with our own."

He was speaking for all and they all eyed him with approval. I'd failed and through my disappointment shot the thought, This is Prior Alwyn's curse on me; giving every man his own plot has made it impossible to hire anybody! I thought, idiotically, I'll do it with my own hands. I knew many a Devon farm run by one man and his wife. But this was not a Devon farm; this was a hundred and fifty acres, most of it arable land.

I concealed my feelings and said, "Since you are so busy, there is no more to be said. I must get busy too."

The man who had sold me the calf said in a bashful way, "I hope the beast thrives, sir." But he plainly had no confidence in its ability to do so, on this side of the river.

They hurried away and once over the bridge burst into a clamour, congratulating themselves and each other on the prices I had paid, no doubt. I took an axe and worked off my fury on four sturdy saplings; but felling them was not enough. I needed grubbers to pry and pull out the roots. And curiously, I had no doubt that I should find them, given time. I recognized this confidence as a money-bred thing. I could afford to wait.

I had expended my rage and my energy when I saw movement at the bridge. My heart leapt up; I thought, They have talked it over and seen sense. But it was Parson Ambrose on a rather fine mouse-coloured mule. I went to meet him.

"Ah," he said, "so you were not deterred. I am so glad. And I congratulate you." He dismounted, slightly stiffly, and looked about with—I thought—content. "You seem to have acquired a fine show of livestock."

"Yes. But the horse I bought yesterday in the market died in the night."

"Horse dealers are notoriously wily. They have ways of making a poor beast look lively, an old one young."

"I know. But this was a sound horse of no great age and loosed from the wagon he rolled."

"Thereby twisting a gut most likely."

That was a possibility that had not occurred to me, and absurd as it may sound, some little knot of discomfort deep within me was loosened. I said, "Can I say come in to a house that has no doors, no roof? But I have good ale."

"Could we then drink it in the garden?"

"The garden?"

"My good man, do you mean to tell me that you have not seen the garden? So beautiful. Come, follow me."

He led the way through a maze of walls and broken doorways—things I had just thought of as ruins—and into an enclosure which I had not investigated. It had once been a garden close, and although nobody had plucked or pruned or weeded there for many years it had somehow retained something of its cultivated look. Perhaps the height of its walls had protected it from wind-borne seeds; the paths were still faintly discernible and some rose bushes, reverted to the hedgerow variety in shape but not in colouring, bore flowers, red, white and striped. Against the south wall, espaliered trees, grossly overgrown, gave promise of cherries, plums, apples and pears.

Lowering himself onto a moss-encrusted stone bench and struggling visibly with some emotion, Parson Ambrose said, "He loved this spot. It was his favourite place."

"The prior?" He gave a little choke and a nod. I saw that his eyes were moist with the tears of old age. None fell, however, and after a moment he looked towards the far end of the garden and said, "They grew herbs there, healing herbs. He was his own infirmarian. But there was no remedy for the disease that killed him—a broken heart."

"Did he die here?"

"Oh, no. Like others, he was granted a small pension and evicted. He died in a little house in the Saltgate at Baildon. But not before—as I told you— he had provided for his people. And in return they call him a warlock!"

"That I had not heard. Why?"

"Because there was nothing else to be said against this community; there had been no accumulation of wealth, no lechery, no sodomy. But the numbers had dropped to thirteen, which the king's commissioners considered significant—thirteen makes a coven, you know. And they knew that after the sad affair of Anne Boleyn, witchcraft was anathema to the king. That is why the Priory was so totally dismantled, not merely stripped of its roof and left to decay. Total demolition was ordered and would have taken place— not one stone standing on another—but for the fact that plague broke out among the destroyers. That also, of course, was laid at Alwyn's door."

I said, without any disrespect or frivolity, "I also laid something at his door only this morning." I told him about my failure to find any labour. Immediately and with an ease surprising in so ancient a man, he switched his mind from past to present.

"You must hire help from outside. Not from any village nearby, the vile story has spread, and even if you found a man from nearby who was unaware, he would soon be informed. Hire men from Essex— they speak what is almost a foreign language to Suffolk ears. And pamper them. Pay, feed and house them so well that envy is engendered."

I thought this an eminently sensible suggestion, though perhaps not one quite in keeping with his calling.

"Do that," he said, "and persevere, even if there are discouragements. There may be losses. Hide them! There will be triumphs. Flaunt them! Give this ugly story time to die a natural death."

I told him how I had already planned to conceal the death of the horse. He looked at me closely and then asked a strange question. "Are you, by any chance, Jesuit trained?"

I laughed. "Me? I had no formal learning at all. My brother went to school and passed on the elements; and at thirteen I went to sea. I chanced to fall in with a captain who had been dismissed from Cambridge for unseemly behaviour and taken to the sea. A pedagogue born, he had me as his sole pupil." I also took a backward glance, recalling those three painful but most profitable years. Some sort of learning had been beaten into me, with intervals of great pampering, a state of things which I did not understand at the time but came to do later. "Whom the Lord loveth, he chasteneth" is true of ordinary men.

Parson Ambrose said, with a kind of sigh, looking round the garden, "To a man of your understanding I have perhaps betrayed myself. Is that so?"

"I suspect that you were one of the thirteen."

"'Deduce' would be a happier word. Yes, I was. Not professed, not even a novice. Young enough, at sixteen, to go to Cambridge and presently to be ordained. I had a parish in Sussex, but I always hoped— and prayed. And when the living of Nettleton with Ockley fell vacant and was within the gift of my college, I took it gladly—little knowing. I must ask you to keep my secret. To be thus closely associated, in the minds of the vulgar, would do me and the religion I represent a grave disservice."

"I understand that."

So he trotted away on his mule and I turned my attention to the dead horse, about which flies and carrion crows had gathered throughout the day. I began to dig a grave, but the spade struck stone; strength and time failed me, so I built a cairn of the stones that were lying around and which children could have gathered if the villagers had been more amenable.

Next day I walked, through the woods, to Nettleton and bought myself a rather splendid saddle horse. On it I rode to Colchester and there engaged with no great difficulty seven stout men and eight women, one pregnant. There were five married couples, most with children, two hardy-looking widows and a single woman of plain aspect, and two single men, both elderly but able-bodied. I deliberately avoided young single men who might gravitate to the village in search of female company. I promised not only a summer's occupation but a permanent job to any man who would throw in his lot with mine. They should be well paid; they could build their own houses, own their own plots. I visualised another Ockley taking root on my side of the river and putting the people who had refused to work for me to shame.

I also engaged, while I was in Colchester, a mason named Samson and his team to come and make, out of the ruins, a house for me and for all who wished to live under my roof. Since he said that the earliest possible moment that he could come to Ockley would be the back end of August, I decided that what was needed was a quantity of tarpaulin which stretched from standing wall to standing wall and weighted down with stones would shelter us should the rains come.

I rode back to Ockley well content.

# CHAPTER 4

I had imagined a kind of communal life, with the pregnant woman and the two older ones taking turns at making meals for us, but the idea was not workable. Petty quarrels broke out. Every woman said she had expected a hearth of her own and as one man said of his wife, "She may not be the best cook in the world but she knows what I like. A soft egg I can't abide." So they split into families or groups, spreading tarpaulins from ruin to ruin, making what had doubtless been a dignified building look like a tinkers' camp. The oldest of the widows, without consulting anyone, appointed herself my housekeeper. She'd been employed by a widower who had suddenly remarried and that was why she was unemployed, she said.

They all had some similar story to explain why they were available at the busiest season of the year

and doubtless some of them were true. Even of lies
I could not be critical for I had told them a thumping
one about the Ockley people. I said they all wanted
to come and work for me but that I wanted more
continuous labour than they with their own small
holdings could offer; therefore the Ockley villagers
were unfriendly and they would do well to keep them
at arm's length. I said that in this part of the country
strangers were resented.

We met at church. Parson Ambrose explained his
system to me. Nettleton was by far the larger parish
and the services there were attended by a number
of people who, because parish boundaries took no
note of shortcuts through Layer, found it easier to
attend church there than in their own villages. So
there was morning and evening service at Nettleton
every other Sunday. Ockley was served by a morning
service each alternate Sunday in winter, by an evening one each alternate Sunday in summer. It was
not only wise but necessary to attend church whenever a service was available. Not to do so led to the
suspicion that one might be a secret Catholic or, even
worse in the Queen's eyes, an extreme Protestant of
the kind beginning to be called Puritan.

I had been so long at sea, or when ashore so much
part of the drifting population of a port, that I had
to have these things explained to me. The fines for
not attending church were very stiff ones. So every
other Sunday evening that summer I and my work
force went down to the church, dressed in our poor
best, and the village people, far better clad because
when generation succeeds generation in one place,
things like good clothes accumulate, came in in a
huddle and took up a position on the other side of
the aisle.

Our parson was the kind that all rather unwilling
churchgoers would envy; his sermons were ex-

tremely brief. I had heard of—but never been called upon to endure—those that lasted two hours. Ten minutes was enough for him.

Afterwards, leaving his mule on my side of the bridge, he would go and visit Enoch Bowman's mother-in-law, who had, he said, been dying for two years and would, by the look of her, go on dying for another five, accept hospitality as it was offered and then pay me a hasty visit, always asking how things were going.

I tried to give cheerful answers, realising how much he loved the place which I now owned. And certainly the clearance of the land was going on apace. But I had mishaps to report too, all, or almost all, trivial things.

My pregnant cow aborted and that was against the rule of nature which holds that when cows run with goats they never abort because whatever it is that causes abortion in cattle—some herb—is gobbled down by the more lively goats. Then the calf, so sleek and lively, fell away to skin and bone, racked by a cough which, before it died, had communicated to the plough oxen which I had bought in anticipation of the ploughing season. There had also been the quite unnatural behaviour on the part of my male goat. I had bought only one, knowing how prone males are to fight. But my one male turned upon a female and gored her so that she died.

Nor were the mishaps confined to animals. A man who, in the Colchester hiring market had said he was a skilled woodman, sliced into his foot with an axe. The pregnant wife—spared, by my order, all heavy labour—suffered a miscarriage, too late, and became an invalid.

I did not myself escape.

Two days before the masons came I was walking round, planning that the first piece of ruin to be restored and roofed should be that overlooking the garden. The cherries and, hard after them, the plums had ripened and we had all eaten our fill, and my housekeeper, Jenny was her name, had shown her ability to turn even overripe, even bird-damaged fruit into a liquor far more potent than ale. I stood there, thinking about the masons' arrival tomorrow or the next day, the back end of August being a vague term, and a stone fell from the wall and hit me fair and square on the shoulder. I heard my collarbone crack.

I did not take the injury seriously. Collarbones and ribs are very vulnerable but also swift-healing. Lacking other medicament, I dulled my senses with the cherry liquor and went about with my arm in a sling, fretting over my uselessness.

Samson and his gang—five stalwart men and a frail, gangling boy—arrived with their wagonload of ladders and the other tools of their trade and all their personal belongings and spent the rest of the day setting up what they called their lodge.

They were an odd, self-contained group and I felt it was unnecessary to warn them to keep away from the village; they even wanted to keep away from us and installed themselves in the most distant of the half-habitable places—the Priory dovecote, a large octagonal building whose walls were virtually intact.

In the morning I took Samson to look at the section of ruin out of which I wished my house to be built. He surveyed it dubiously and then denounced my choice. "The facing has all gone; this is nothing but rubble core, sir. Look." He carried a rod marked off in feet and inches and shod at the tip with an iron spike. With this he prodded the wall and saw it penetrate with a kind of gloomy satisfaction. "Rotten as a pear," he said. "Must it be here? There're places where the walls are still faced with good ashlar."

"I wanted it here because of the garden."

"Then if you don't mind my saying so it'd be quicker and better to start afresh at the far end." He indicated what Parson Ambrose had said was once the herb garden.

"But I wanted to restore and live in part of the old building."

"You'd still be doing that if we used the old stone."

He prodded the apparently solid-looking rubble again and the spike sank in; a few flints showered down. Dodging them, I said, "It was a heavier stone that hit me the other evening."

"Just proves what I say," he said with a glance at my sling. "Ruins can be very tricky."

"Very well," I said, looking across the garden and telling myself that it would be folly to hire an expert and then reject his advice; telling myself also that a house built at the far, western end of the garden would catch the morning sun.

We tramped through the garden—I noticed some hardy marigolds holding their own in the wilderness, and rosemary and lavender bushes and some white poppies, far larger than the red ones.

"Brick," Samson said when we reached the boundary wall. "Used a lot in gardens where it was available. Being red, you see, sir, people thought it was warmer." He lunged at the wall with his staff and made no impression at all. "Sound enough." He half turned his head and then I realised that the frail, pale boy had been in attendance like an acolyte upon a priest. "Try it," Samson said.

The boy held in his hand a Y-shaped twig, not unlike a catapult except that it lacked a string. He took the arms of the Y in his hands, the leg held forward, walked towards the wall and was almost immediately involved in what looked like a struggle between him and his twig. It writhed like a live thing, twisting and turning.

Samson grunted, reached out and grabbed a handful of the boy's shirt, pulling him backwards. "It's all right, Fred. Let go! We know now." The boy came back, the catapult thing dropped, motionless, from one hand, and Samson said, "I make it a rule not to build over water. Bad for my reputation and for the health of the people who live in the house. Nothing more productive of head colds and stiff joints than a damp dwelling. So we must start again."

I'd lost, momentarily, interest in everything except that twig which had come alive in the boy's hand. This was not something reported; I'd seen the thing happen.

I said, "What is all this?"

The master mason said, "Nothing much. Just a thing I'm careful about. Fred, here, is a water diviner. And never wrong. He's been with me, now— damn, I shall forget my own name next—how long, Fred boy?"

"Ten years come Easter, Master."

"Ten years! Yes, he was using his gift as a trick to gain farthings or buns. I found him at a fair." He spoke as though the boy were a stray dog and the boy looked at his master with a doglike devotion. And like a well-trained dog he fell to the rear again, coming forward when called upon to do so to prove to Samson's satisfaction, if not to mine, that all the garden walls stood with, as the mason termed it, "their feet in water." It was almost midmorning before we found a section of the ruins which was not mere rubble or built over some hidden waterway. When we did it included the room with a hearth in which I had temporarily camped.

"And that'll mean turning you out, sir," Samson said with no note of apology in his voice. But about the lack of garden in that particular area he was soothing. "You can make a garden anywhere. Come to that, knock down a wall or two and you can extend the present garden right up to your front door. Now, to get down to business. What size of house are you wanting?"

I had thought about that. Several things had gone wrong for me lately, but I still had money and I still looked hopefully to the future. I thought of a wife, two children at least, a guest or two now and then.

"I want a sizable room and smaller one and a kitchen. Above stairs, four rooms, each with its own doorway." I thought I was being very up-to-date and grand, for in most of the houses I had known—including various inns—the sleeping chambers led out of one another.

Samson said crushingly, "A mite on the small side, for a family house. I take it you'll need servants. Time was when servants slept in the kitchen or even in the dining hall. But things are changing. All the better class of house nowadays, sir, has accommodation for servants above stairs and with a separate staircase. Which reminds me, have you engaged a carpenter? We only do the stonework, you know."

By this time the good strong draught of the cherry liquor which I had taken to fortify me was beginning to lose its effect. The pain in my collarbone gnawed and I bowed my shoulder forward to ease it. All I wanted at the moment was another dose and the chance to lie flat, the only position which gave any real ease. And it irked me that I had been so simple, thinking that all I needed for my house was the site, the material and the builder. I said, in what for me, a self-controlled man, was temper, "Very well, Master Samson, I leave it to you. Do your best for me." He never knew how nearly I came, in my irritation, to saying, "Do your worst!"

\* \* \*

I should remember him more kindly. He built me a four-square house. To say that he served me in another fashion would be to lay oneself open to the charge of undue credulity. I can only relate what happened.

The masons continued to hold themselves aloof; they even resented being watched at work. I, whose house it was, was not welcome on the site. They behaved as though every move, every process, must be carefully guarded from the uninitiated. My collarbone was healing, but very slowly and lumpily, pulling my shoulder forward and downward, so that I, always proud of my shape and posture, acquired in a short space of time the appearance of a hunchback. I tried to work one-handedly, but my efforts were limited and always provoked pain; so having made my miserable little contribution and supervised everything, I should have liked to watch my house grow. The men sang and whistled and called to each other as they worked, but as soon as I appeared, the noise and the work seemed to stop. "You want Master, sir," a man would say, and he'd shout. Samson would appear, wearing his cap and apron, and usually holding some kind of tool. Obviously forcing himself to be patient, he'd ask what I wanted, adding the perfunctory "sir." I'd find myself making some vague excuse, all the time conscious that time was being wasted because nobody did much while I was there. So I'd turn away and full activity would be resumed.

Then on one of those brisk September mornings when autumn seems to be a season on its own and not the sad prelude to winter, one of the masons, a young man, fell from a ladder and landed not on the bare ground but across a heap of that dressed stone which Samson called ashlar. I think he broke his back.

He did not die immediately and before he did—in the evening of that beautiful day—he said that he had been pushed, though there was nobody within ten feet of him at the time.

That evening Samson did an unprecedented thing. He came to visit me and he was extremely grave, refusing all offers of refreshment, refusing even to sit down though my now temporary dwelling was furnished with stools. I, forced to be unmannerly, did sit, holding my left elbow in my right hand and thus slightly relieving the pain.

"Timothy Brake died," he said.

"I'm sorry."

"So am I. One of my best men. And a careful man. A good mason." He hesitated. "I know there's an old belief about every house needing a sacrifice and I was prepared to sacrifice a pair of doves, or a kid. But not a good man. I wonder if anybody ever made so bold as to tell you, Master Tresize, that there's something seriously wrong with this place."

I said flippantly, "Do I need to be *told?* From the first day, when a good horse died, minor misfortunes have beset me. But I prefer not to blame the place."

"Well, I do. I reckoned on a good straightforward job and there's been nothing but trouble—and now a death. And you're not the man you were the day you hired us. What I want to know, and I hope you'll give me an honest answer, is this—did anybody, to your knowledge, ill-wish you?"

I wondered what he would say if I told him that somebody had wished me dead. As it was I chose to act as though I were offended and said, "I am not in the habit of giving dishonest answers. And the answer is no."

"Then there's a mystery and one I have little taste

for. Timothy Brake said he was pushed and a man about to meet his maker wouldn't say such a thing 'less it was true. *And* there's the boy. Eating like a team of horses and dwindling away before our eyes."

"I have never seen him at his food," I said. "And I've never seen him ill-treated—had I done I should have interfered; but I don't regard his as a happy life."

When not exercising his gift as a water diviner the boy was servant to them all. It was he who collected the food rations which I dispensed daily; it was the boy who cooked, fetched water, chopped wood and did the washing, no light task since every mason seemed to have a clean shirt, cap and apron each day. And so far as I had been able to observe, except when serving, he was not allowed into the lodge. He certainly didn't sleep under cover. More than once, made restless by pain, I'd gone out on a fair night and walked about and almost stumbled over him.

"The boy knows his place," Samson said. "A mason he can never be. Not the strength for it. But that doesn't fret him....Well, sir, if you can't enlighten me I must look elsewhere or leave a job ill-finished. And that is against my principles. Good night."

Adjacent to the little church there was a burial ground, full of humped graves under which lay monks and village people. Priors had been laid to rest inside the church, under flat slabs, inscribed with Latin and now worn smooth by trampling feet. The graves outside had been, at one time, marked with crosses of wood or stone, now decayed or destroyed during that time when a cross was regarded as a Catholic symbol. Timothy Brake went to his last rest there under a massive stone with deeply chiselled words: "Here lies Timothy Brake of Edmonton; Good Friend,

Good Mason, dead of an accident. September 19th, 1590."

Except for the essential work of tending the livestock, no work of any kind was done that day. None of the Ockley people attended the funeral, but they hung about on the safe side of the bridge and I could imagine how they were thinking. Our minor disasters could be concealed, a death could not, and since the coffin was carried by four masons it was obvious that death had not struck at the old or the young— always the most vulnerable—but at a man in his prime.

On my side of the village all that day there hung— palpable as mist—a sense of foreboding, an expectation of further disaster. My old Jenny summed it up: "Everything go in threes, sir. Even death."

I woke in the night and the pain was waiting. In my sleep I had turned onto my left side. I moved over onto my back and lay waiting but the pain did not recede, so I got up and went out. The harvest moon hung low in the sky, coloured like bronze.

I saw earthly lights in the dovecote, extraordinarily bright, and on the now goose-grazed, foot-trodden smooth space in front of it figures moving, into the light for a moment, then engulfed again. I remembered Samson's ominous words about leaving a job unfinished. The masons, I thought, were preparing to steal away in the night. I thought angrily of the power superstition wielded even over people like the masons who in every way regarded themselves as superior to ordinary people. I thought of my unfinished house and the fact that in law I should have no redress. Master Samson and I had no formal contract; he and his men worked by the week and were paid by the week. He could easily say that due to circumstances beyond his control, work at the Priory had been delayed and he was due at the next job.

And think, I thought, of the talk it would cause. My future was dependent upon my being able to sell my stock and my crops—when I had raised them.

I went forward, intending to argue, to plead, if necessary to bribe. Then it struck me that these men were not engaged in so ordinary a thing as packing up their goods. About their movements there was a kind of stylised formality; they took measured steps, bowed, turned, gestured as though engaged in some ceremonial. I went towards them, got nearer, near enough to hear a kind of chanting, near enough to see, in the uncertain light, a flash or two, as of metal or jewels on the clean aprons they had donned for the funeral.

Then it was as though a giant hand had reached down and gripped my crippled shoulder, wrenched the ill-knit bones apart. Clenching my teeth against the agony, I let loose a sound, half a groan, half a hiss. Audible enough to alert them. The almost ceremonial activity ceased. A man scuffed his foot across something on the ground. In the same instant another man turned and asked me the old question: "You want Master, sir?"

I said, "Yes," and he called and Samson came out. I went forward to meet him—at that moment unaware that I was walking upright again, no bowed shoulder and no pain.

I said, "What is going on here?"

"Going on? A little drinking, to take the lads' minds off their grief. I regret that you were disturbed, sir."

Then he, too, moved his foot, but not before I had seen in the dust some scrawled symbols already half obliterated; part of a circle, part of a triangle and part of what looked to my ignorant eye almost like a bit of the backbone of a fish.

"You look to me to be standing better, sir," Samson said. Then I realised that I was. I put my right hand to my left collarbone and there was no lump. No pain, though I kneaded at the spot where the knot had been. I was cured.

Old Jenny's theory about death going in threes seemed to be justified. Parson Ambrose, taking the woodland path home after the funeral, had fallen from his mule—or alighted and lain down to die. There was no mark on him and the animal was quietly grazing near the body. Then just before my house was finished and ready to be moved into, the pale boy coughed blood and died.

After that everything went well, very well, and the ploughs with their ox teams were at work on Plough Monday.

# PART TWO

# Narrative by Lettice Tresize

# CHAPTER 1

By the time I was fourteen I had had two stepmothers. My own mother died when I was six, but I remember her well. She was gentle, soft-spoken and pretty, but always so low-spirited that she affected everybody around her. I understood, even then, that she hated Ockley and always felt lonely and isolated.

She was a daughter of the attorney Mr. Turnbull of Baildon and was one of a large family, most of them settled in or around the town—but on the far side. She could have visited them easily had she learned to ride, but she came to it rather late in life. And there was some mystery about travelling in the jolting cart. I did not understand it at the time, but did later. After one such journey she had had a miscarriage. The child she lost would have been a boy—the son both she and my father craved. So she could go visiting only when Father went in on horseback and had time to go at a slow jog trot with her on the pillion behind him. Such times were rare; more often he took the cart or the wagon, laden with stuff to sell and bringing back stores; or riding at a fast pace so that he had time to make a visit to his sheep run out at Stratton Strawless, which he had bought the year after I was born.

And of course Mother could venture forth only on fine days, riding pillion being no occupation in bad weather for a woman generally agreed to be delicate.

Sometimes when she went she would stay for a week and her absences were highlights in my life. Jenny took charge of me then and allowed me to do much as I liked, with no consideration about the state of my hair or my clothes. She let me make gingerbread men in the kitchen, or took me into Layer Wood where we gathered blackberries or hazel nuts and came home looking thoroughly disreputable.

Then there were the evenings when I had Father to myself and he would tell me tales. He'd been a sailor when he was young and could tell tales of far places and of people born black—no amount of scrubbing could make them white. He'd crack jokes, too, another thing he never did in Mother's presence. Once, to lighten the interminable sewing, I tried to tell her one of his jokes. Probably I told it badly for afterwards I heard her rebuking him in her die-away voice—so much more deadly than a shout. She told him to be careful what he said to me and remember that I was a girl. Father said, "Am I likely to forget that?" And Mother wept.

On one occasion I made her cry, too. It was all the Queen's fault! She was then an old woman but apparently when she was only three she'd made a very elegant shirt for her little half brother. Generations of girl children not handy with the needle must have suffered because of that story, and hearing it for the twentieth time, I said, "But I haven't *got* a little half brother who needs a shirt!" Whereupon Mother wept and took to her bed. What was worse, Jenny scolded me and said I was old enough to mind my tongue.

"But I only said..."

"I know what you said. I heard you. And you must learn not to say the first thing that comes into your head."

That is the kind of thing which stays with one down the years. From that day to this I have very seldom—except in temper—said anything without examining it first.

At rare intervals my various aunts and uncles with their husbands and wives came to visit Mother. In her sad way she enjoyed such visits, but was more melancholy afterwards. All the men of the family were what is called "professional," lawyers, physicians, parsons and—as I now understand—regarded themselves as superior to a farmer who, though successful and becoming rich, worked with his hands rather than his head. I was watchful, as children are, and I noticed the faint air of patronage....

I often wondered how they—feeling that my mother had married beneath her, if only slightly—regarded my father's second marriage.

My mother died in 1599. The plague was bad that year and had reached Baildon. But my Grandfather Turnbull was celebrating a birthday and Mother wished to join the celebration. "The house stands apart and I promise I will not go into the town, even to look at the shops." She also mentioned the fact that her father's house faced north—the plague was supposed to be borne on the southerly wind.

Actually the plague was already in the secluded, north-facing house when she arrived. She died, together with her father, two sisters and a brother.

They shared a common grave, and when I was still young enough to be sentimental I was glad to think that after seven years of exile, she might, in her last moments, have felt at home with her kin.

My father waited a decent year and then made a most extraordinary marriage. At least everybody regarded it as extraordinary. The fact was that he was extremely good-looking—I'm very like him, but what is right and handsome in a man is a drawback to a woman. Possibly I was the one person who understood why Anne Hatton fell in love with him.

He was past his first youth, but tall, and hard work had kept him spare and he had the most beautiful hair. Since I have inherited it, perhaps I should not say that, but it is true. Real chestnut—not carroty red, which goes with pale eyelashes and freckles—is very rare.

Anne Hatton was as different from my mother as it was possible for a woman to be. She had a wealth of black hair, which, let down, fell well past her waist; she could sit on her hair. Her eyes were exactly like a hawthorn leaf in autumn, green and brown in patterns, like daisies. She was one of a family that had been at the great house of Mortiboys for unreckoned generations; and she had money of her own; not a dower conferred upon her by her father and passing to my father, as her husband, but real money, left to her by a widowed aunt.

Stepmothers are notorious and I had dreaded her coming, but in fact, when she noticed me, she was invariably kind. She taught me to ride by the simple hit or miss method of stay on or fall over. Sewing was never mentioned except scornfully: "What are sempstresses for?"

I think that for Father as well as for me that was the happiest time. Anne entertained a great deal. The big room, seldom used before, was always full of men, eating, drinking, throwing dice or playing cards. And since gentlemen who had drunk and gambled an evening away often needed beds for the night, I was obliged to give up my bedroom and go to sleep in an alcove in Jenny's room. That was no hardship. As for being called in from time to time to act as lady's maid, that was positive pleasure because she never talked to me as though I were a half-wit because I happened to be young. I learned a great deal about everything, but especially about elegance and the niceties of a lady's toilet during the two years between the time I was seven and the time I was nine—very impressionable years.

Amongst the other things I learned was the importance of sons. People married, apparently, in order to have boys to inherit their property and carry on the family name. Girls were definitely inferior beings. A daughter or two was welcome, to make advantageous marriages or to cheer one's old age, but only boys really counted.

"And unless I have a baby soon—and that baby a boy—I shall be in sore disgrace," Anne said one evening. I found that hard to believe, for Father was so enamoured with her that he was even talking of adding to the house, the better to accommodate her many friends and relatives. It was nothing for some to come for a night's play and stay for a week or a fortnight, and Father was far more at ease in their company than with the townsfolk. They, grand though they were, were at ease in our house, being interested, before the gaming started, in the pigs, the cattle and the crops.

Our house was sometimes called the Old Priory and sometimes the Stone House and by comparison with some it was small, but compared with most it was large. It had four bedchambers upstairs, two rooms, one large and one small, on the ground floor and behind it a warren of kitchen, larder, buttery, brewhouse, bakehouse, laundry, with servants' quarters above them. When Father proposed adding to the house, he and my stepmother had one of their amicable disputes. She was always so eager to pay. Even for wine. "It was my people who drank it," she would say. And Father always said, "Any man who drinks under my roof is my guest and I pay for his wine."

Her having money of her own never led, as it might have done with couples less attuned, to any acrimony. It was a subject for jokes. Father would say, "Since you are so rich, my dear, buy up half Bywater and become richer. It is a port with a future." Or he would advise her to invest in some sheep to run along with his at Stratton Strawless. And over the extension of the house they came to what seemed to me a most sensible agreement. Father should pay for the building and she would provide the furniture.

Then what happened? Suddenly she veered about and was against the plan to enlarge the house. "You don't want to end up with something like Mortiboys, do you? It takes one man there all his time to clean the windows! This house is very well as it is. It is sound—and snug."

It was autumn when she said that and the wind was lashing the trees in the orchard and howling in the chimney and somehow that made a house that was snug seem desirable. Father said, "So long as you are happy, I am content, Anne."

And she said, "Dear Arthur, so long as you are content, I am happy."

It was on that windy evening or another much like it that I was called in to brush her hair. It had a life of its own and, brushed down, sprang up, encircling my fingers and the handle of the brush. As I struggled with it our eyes met in the glass and she said abruptly, "And what will happen to you, Lettice?"

"What is likely to happen to me? Why do you ask?"

She said, "Because God pity women! My Aunt Agnes...Never mind. Hand me that casket." It was the one in which she kept her jewels. She fingered the contents and then said, "Put the brush down. Hold out your hands.... This and this and this. They are yours. Remember that, they are your very own." She pushed into my hands a ruby as red and as big as a cherry on a golden chain, a pair of emerald earbobs and a ring set with what they call a table diamond.

I said, "It is too much."

"No, too little. Dear child, remember me kindly."

I do to this day, though my heart, not then hardened by circumstance, was torn apart by divided loyalties. I loved my father, I'd been entranced with his second wife. And she ran away. Two or three days after she had given me such valuable presents she ran away with a Frenchman, some kind of distant relative, a descendant of a Hatton who had gone to France and settled there long ago.

I was sad and upset but not tearful, taking, as children do, example from Father, who bore his surely much greater loss with fortitude. My Uncle Thomas, who had taken over my grandfather's practice, came out to Ockley and talked about divorce—easier now than it had been in the old days. However, no proof of desertion or adultery was needed in this case. The ship in which Anne and her lover had embarked went down in a storm off Bywater and their bodies were washed up at Dunwich. To this day I do not know how they were identified: the whole affair was hushed up and I never heard Father mention Anne's name again. Apart from this silence and the fact that he changed from the room he had shared with her, he gave no sign of anything untoward having happened.

There were no more gay, noisy parties. Life returned to the way it had been during Mother's absences and during the year that followed her death; but now that I could ride I saw more of Father than ever before. It was almost as though he had accepted the fact that he would have no son and that at some distant date I should inherit everything, the Priory, the sheep run and some other parcels of land which he bought up as they came onto the market. But Jenny said darkly that he would marry again, and he did, once again choosing a woman as different as possible, a coarse, totally uncivilised creature whose parents kept a little beerhouse called the Evening Star out on the marshes.

I had seen her because Father had bought some marshland, as an investment, he said. One thinks of the land and the shore as a fixed thing but seemingly it is always changing. To the north of us Dunwich was slipping into the sea; to the south of us the Slipwell marshes were rising and would, in ten years or so, make tolerable pasture. On the day he had gone down to Slipwell to view the land we'd turned aside a little and eaten bread and cheese at the Evening Star and Kate Shillito had served us, if that is the right word to use for dumping bread and cheese and beer down on a dirty table with about as much ceremony as though she were feeding pigs.

Once when I said to Jenny that I simply could not understand Father marrying such a creature, she said gruffly, "She has seven brothers!"

Going around with Father as I had done for almost two years, I'd picked up some information about breeding animals, characteristics to be courted or to be avoided. So I was willing to accept Kate purely as a female from a family whose record for boys was good.

It would have been all right had she been able to accept me on any terms at all. But she hated me, and Jenny, and in fact everybody who had been close to Father in former years. Me, of course, most of all.

# CHAPTER 2

I can look back now and see that there was some reason for Kate's treatment of me. I'd grown very close to Father during the interval between his marriages and we had interests which she could not share. She could not ride and Father did not encourage her to try; she knew nothing of farming and had no wish to learn. She had no conversation, was completely illiterate, so that she felt left out of our talk. I would have been more tactful and concealed my possessiveness had I liked her the least bit, but I'd taken against her at first sight and her behaviour to Jenny converted a mild dislike into something like hatred.

Jenny had been the mainstay of our household since before our house was built. My mother, like a good housewife, visited the kitchen every morning, distributed stores and supervised menus. She'd go again if anything required her presence, but ordinarily the kitchen was Jenny's kingdom and with the help of two young maids she saw to all domestic matters. In Anne's time she became even more powerful, for Anne behaved as though the house were run by benevolent fairies and regarded the kitchen as a shortcut to the stables. Jenny had managed perfectly, even when she did not know for certain how many people would come for supper or stay overnight.

Kate, perhaps to show that there was something she *could* do, seemed determined to change all that. She spent hours in the kitchen and found fault with everything, doing her best in unsubtle ways to reduce Jenny in her own eyes and in the eyes of Margery and Maude—our current maids—and of anyone else within hearing.

She began by attacking Jenny on the subject of extravagance. This was not entirely without justification. Father liked to eat well and, unlike many people, fed his servants much as he fed himself. Jenny, accused of wastefulness, said in a perfectly civil way, "I'm only carrying out the Master's orders, madam."

Kate said, "Don't back answer me!" Jenny then answered only direct questions in the shortest possible way and Kate said she was sulking and complained to Father, who said mildly that Jenny had always managed very well and was a bit old to get used to new ways. He sounded almost placating.

"She is too old to do anything but waste," Kate said. "We must get rid of her."

"She has no home but this. She has been with me for fourteen years. Where could she go?"

"Back to her own village. Paupers are taken care of."

It is impossible to describe the coarse, callous way in which Jenny was thus dismissed. But Father said, "No. If she is too old to be useful to you, let her keep

to her room. And be fed, of course." By adding those
extra words he showed that he understood his new
wife very well. Then how could he—I asked myself—
go on allowing her to have her way, taking her into
Baildon in the cart, giving her money to spend, treating her as his wife? It diminished him in my eyes.

I should have understood it better had she been
pretty, but she was not, apart from her hair, which
was yellow and very coarse. I thanked God that she
never demanded that I should brush it! All her fea-
tures were coarse: broad flat nose, fat cheeks, fleshy
chin, a mean mouth. My mother had been pretty in
a frail, pale way, and Anne had been beautiful—at
least to my eyes—and very elegant; both had been
dainty in their habits; this one was not even that.
With her what showed was washed, nothing else.

Through all the misery of the time I used to think
to myself, Very well, she has seven brothers, she
comes of a boy-breeding family... *but what will her
boy be like?*

I remember the first time she hit me. I had reached
the age of eleven without ever being physically chas-
tised. It was while Kate was still ousting Jenny.
Jenny was still feebly, but stubbornly, refusing to
accept retirement; and perhaps, pushed away into
premature senility, was becoming a little senile. It
was in October—the marriage then almost three
months old—and it was time for the making of the
Christmas puddings, a comestible that I have never
since enjoyed.

A tedious business, all the chopping of suet, taking the pips out of dried fruit, the heavy job of mixing, the tying up into a bag-cloth and boiling for
twelve hours, the removal to a fresh cloth and hanging up in the airy larder to be taken down, heated,
soused with brandy and brought flaming to the table

to be eaten on the day that celebrated the birth of a man who was poor—or so we were told—and never tasted such a dish in his life.

Just for once Kate was not sure of herself; Margery and Maude denied all knowledge of the niceties of making Christmas puddings—a certain amount of carefully measured spice was involved—and what I knew I kept silent about, so poor old Jenny was called upon to come back to the kitchen to give advice but to have no hand in the making. I knew exactly what Kate wanted—to be able on Christmas Day, the day of peace and goodwill, to say that she had made the pudding herself and to ask Father was it not the best he had ever tasted.

I felt sorry for the old woman who had ruled in the kitchen for so long and who now was told to sit there and touch nothing, just give advice when she was asked for it.

I had been given the job of chopping the suet, which had to be, Jenny said, reduced to the size of fine bread crumbs. Kate went out of the kitchen and Jenny said, "Not fine enough yet."

"You take a turn. My wrists ache," I said, and it was true—all my bones were very thin and delicate and, fond as I was of riding, I could never ride a hard-mouthed horse. Jenny took my place with eagerness and was chopping away vigorously when Kate returned and yelled, "Didn't I tell you not to touch anything, you dirty old crone?"

Jenny was actually cleaner than Kate but she looked dirty because her skin had darkened with age and her hands particularly were blotched with liver-coloured patches. My temper flared and I forgot all about thinking twice before I spoke. I jumped up and shouted, "How dare you say that to Jenny? Remember the filthy place you come from!"

Unforgivable, of course. Had my own mother heard

me she would have died of shame, and Anne...what would she have thought or said?

Kate turned and slapped my face, her palm on my left cheek, the knuckly back of her hand on my right. I was incapable of returning such heavy blows, but I could claw! Beside myself with fury and outrage, I would have done so, but Jenny jumped up and put her thin, wiry old arms about me, holding me as though I were in a cage. She dragged me into the sleeping chamber which we still shared and there she said, "Child, breeding women take strange fancies *and they must not be provoked.*"

I understood then and bore myself meekly, though there were things hard to bear. The Christmas dole was one.

It was time-honoured custom for men who could afford it to give lengths of cloth—varying in quality—to the females of their family and to servants. Anne had had many dresses, but Father, being punctilious, had given her green velvet for a riding habit one year and some silk, tawny orange, another. I had received some fine cloth, the colour of a dove's neck, for a riding habit and some ribbed silk from France, greyish blue.

The silk weavers in a town called Lyons had come to realise that the silk strands from which they wove their shimmering lengths sometimes had little uneven knots in them and had cunningly adjusted their looms to bring the nubs into alignment; that was ribbed silk, only very slightly cheaper than the smooth.

Even Jenny had one year received silk—a singular honour—but Father said that in the days when she was taking care of him with no proper kitchen he'd vowed to himself that if she stayed with him she should one day have a housekeeper's black silk dress. She kept it for church and for occasions when we had guests, which in Anne's day had been often, so it was now growing rather worn, despite the care she took of it, sponging away any small mark and always putting it in a bag before hanging it in the cupboard.

At Kate's first Christmas I was in need of new clothes, having grown so rapidly, and I rather hoped that, since Kate was growing rather bulky, Father would take me with him to Baildon and allow me to do the buying, but Kate insisted upon going herself. She jibed at the story of my mother having suffered a miscarriage after a journey in the jolting wagon. "She was always a poor ailing creature," she said offensively. "Nothing would make me miscarry." And indeed she seemed designed for childbearing, her torso as broad as it was long.

For Margery and Maude, upon whose goodwill she depended, Kate bought red cloth for cloaks; for Jenny, some hanks of drab wool, "So that she can knit herself a shawl," she said, but it proved insufficient even for that; and I received instead enough very coarse unbleached linen for an apron! Breeding women must not be provoked, so I accepted this humiliating gift without complaint and set my wits to work to find a way in which to replenish my wardrobe.

I thought of the dresses Anne must have left behind when she ran away so suddenly and with no preparation. I know now that rooms which have not been inhabited for a long time acquire a desolation of a peculiar kind. Father had abandoned that room, and despite Kate's show-off activity in the kitchen she was not the kind of housewife who would see that unused rooms were dusted and aired. I had avoided the room because of the memories. But they must be braved; my skirts were halfway to my knees, my sleeves halfway to my elbows.

The air in the room was cold and heavy and dank.

It smelt of desertion. I crossed hurriedly to the cupboard and opened the door and was immediately aware of Anne's scent. My mother's clothes—how disposed of I do not know—had smelt faintly of lavender and rosemary; Anne had used headier, more exotic perfumes, and now, assailed by them, I remembered the times when I had brushed her hair and she'd treated me as an equal and made jokes.

With her black hair and eyes that were neither brown nor green and her very white skin she had looked well in every colour but blue. Apart from that lack it was a rainbow collection. I chose the least obtrusive, a mulberry-coloured gown with a good deal of creamy lace about it. I measured it against myself and it was about right. I thought that I must strip off the lace, in case Father should be reminded; and I thought that Jenny must take in a few tucks, for Anne, though slender, had been curved where I was not. My mother's needles and mine were no doubt rusted into the flannel which was supposed to protect them, but Jenny's were still bright.

"And what do you think you are doing?" Kate's hateful voice!

"Finding a gown for myself." Surely that was not provocative.

It was one of those very clear winter afternoons, the forerunner of a frosty night, and the cold light slanted in at the window. The cupboard door—open—revealed to her the treasure which, in her carelessness and her obsession with the kitchen, she had completely overlooked.

"They are mine. Mine," she said in her possessive way. "Everything in this house belongs to *me*."

"They would none of them fit you. My—the lady to whom they belonged was very slender." Less tactful than true. It sparked off one of her wholesale denunciations. She called me a saucy bitch, taking

things without asking permission and making rude
remarks when caught out. Then she veered off into
an attack upon Anne. "What was wrong with her
that you dare not take her name in your mouth either? Did she bewitch you, too?"

I had by this time learned that the best and quick-
est way was to stay silent, so I stood clutching the
mulberry gown and waited for her to run out of
breath. Finally she said, "Put it back."

"But I need a new..."

"Are you arguing with me?" I saw the blow coming
and put up my arm to shield my face. The blow fell
on my wrist. Something cracked and a terrible pain
ran to the tips of my fingers. Great black waves
swirled all around me but I fought them down with
the thought that if I let myself go she'd snatch away
the dress, which I was now more than ever determined to have.

The crack had been quite audible and I think that
even she was momentarily taken aback by what she
had done. Slapping—even flogging—of children by
parents was an everyday thing but few bones were
actually broken.

I staggered away to Jenny, who at first did not
believe that my wrist was broken. Her examination
hurt almost more than the breaking, but when she
was satisfied she made a stiff paste of flour and water,
soaked linen in it and bound it about my wrist, where
it hardened into a kind of case, within which, we
learned later, the bone healed crookedly, disfiguring
my arm for life.

I told Jenny what had happened and she said,
"How can we keep it from your father? Poor man,
he has enough to bear."

"He married her."

"Out of desperation. And bitterly he must be regretting it. It's aged him by ten years already."

"She won't always be breeding," I said. "Then we can get our own back...."

"She's carrying it high," Jenny said. "It'll be a boy. So that might be the end of it."

I explained the bandage and the sling, upon which Jenny had insisted, by saying that I had slipped and fallen on the stairs. For that Kate should have been grateful to me, but she was not. If anything, it intensified her hatred and some time before the child was born she managed to get me banished from my own father's table and sent to eat in the kitchen, where the food was far worse. Kate now ordered the meals; Margery did most of the cooking. Kate had often commented unfavourably upon my leaving bits and pieces on my plate. The truth was that I could not stomach fat, and one evening, struggling one-handedly to separate the fat from the lean, I sent the whole plateful skidding. Kate claimed that the resultant mess made her feel sick. She pretended to retch, recovered and began shouting that the sight of me picking and pingling over the good food was enough to turn anybody's stomach. "Go eat in the kitchen," she ended. Father looked miserable, but made no protest, and my opinion of him diminished still more. I realised how important the coming child was to him and tried to make excuses for him, but it was very hard.

However, he was not so blind or indifferent as he pretended to be. Some few days later, after he had gone into Baildon alone, he returned with a pressing invitation from my Uncle Thomas Turnbull and my Aunt Margaret to go and stay with them.

"Must I go?"

"It would ease matters. And you would get some education. Your cousins have a tutor."

Like many people who have a little learning, I

considered myself educated already. My mother had taught me my letters and *almost* how to read. Father, in the midst of all his busyness, had continued the process, and living with Anne, who could barely write and never took a book in hand, had given me a wide vocabulary. Like many of her kind, she knew and used words which she could not possibly have spelt.

"I don't mind eating with the servants, if that is what worries you," I said bluntly.

"But it is not suitable, my dear. And it worries me."

By this time the stiffened bandage had been hacked off my arm and the bumpy, ill-set wrist was plain for all to see unless I were very careful with my sleeve. I was growing so fast at the time, lengthwise, but not in bulk, that in a short time I should be in need of another new dress.

I looked Father straight in the eye and said, "Will you promise me something? When all this is over and your son—Jenny assures me it will be a boy— is born, I may come home. If only as nursemaid. I understand," I said, "that you crave an heir and wish to establish your name, and to pamper your wife through this difficult time. But promise me that I shall one day come home."

He promised, and in order not to distress him I went with feigned cheerfulness to Baildon and submitted myself to a way of life alien to me but useful in later years.

# CHAPTER 3

My half brother was born in May, just when I was
beginning to think that unless I got back into the
country for the summer I should die.

Everybody—my uncle, my aunt and all four cousins—was extremely kind to me. I was poor Elizabeth's poor daughter. Poor Elizabeth who had died
of the plague, poor Lettice whose father had married
again, not once, but twice.

My uncle had hired a tutor, Master Grattan, to
prepare my elder boy cousin, who had passed through
the grammar school, for Cambridge and my younger
boy cousin for the grammar school. Education was
becoming more and more a competitive business. My
two girl cousins and I were allowed to sit in and gain
what knowledge we could. My uncle was an enlight-
ened man and saw no harm in a daughter being
educated. My aunt concentrated more upon clothes

and domestic matters—always with marriage in view.

Coming up to the age of twelve I was already, in her view, too tall to be quite eligible, so she made me go about for three hours a day with a brick on my head, held by a scarf tied under my chin. As a deterrent to growth, it was quite ineffectual. In fact, I think it worked contrariwise; pressing against the weight, my neck grew longer than any neck should be.

It was all well meant and I resented nothing, but I longed for home and for the freedom I had enjoyed there. My girl cousins and I were never allowed out unaccompanied; if my aunt did not wish to walk she sent a maid called Nellie, whose idea of a nice walk was a gentle amble across the marketplace—though never on market days—into the churchyard where my mother was buried, along Honey Hill and so home again. My uncle kept a horse, but purely as a means of getting from client to client. As the spring advanced I found myself longing for Ockley and for the long, solitary rides I was in the habit of taking, or the even more delightful ones when I could go with Father.

During my exile Father came twice to see me and reported that everything was as usual at Ockley; and once my uncle, visiting a client nearby, called at Ockley. He said all was well there but as he spoke he cast a significant look at my aunt and I guessed that he would have a different tale to tell when they were alone.

Then—and I remember the moment as well as though it were yesterday—a servant came from Ockley bringing a great basket of asparagus, which grew well in our garden, and the news that the baby was born and was a boy.

Well, that was what Father had set his heart on

and I was glad for his sake. I imagined that now the reign of tyranny would be ended and I could go home, but I was not recalled for another three weeks. Then Father came for me himself—with my pony on a leading rein. I noticed that although his hair was now almost completely white, he'd lost his harassed look.

My aunt had, well-meaningly, given me a few hints on how to behave when eventually I went home. "I know," she said, "that your position will not be easy, but by treating the baby as your brother and thus pleasing your father, you will increase your chance of a good dower."

A good dower was the most that any female could ask of life in my aunt's view.

So, glad to be riding again and sorry to see that the hawthorn was already fading, I said to Father, "I hope my brother is well."

"He's splendid. But there have been changes. That is why I waited before fetching you home. You may as well know. She went lunatic."

The pronoun was enough. Between ourselves Jenny and I had always said *she* when referring to the woman who was my stepmother and Jenny's mistress. Now here was Father using the anonymous term.

I thought twice and then said, very cautiously, feeling my way, "She always was—a little queer. At least, that was the excuse I made for her in my mind when she was horrid to me."

"I have not forgotten," he said, his voice harsh. And then, on a different note: "The boy will make up for it all."

Father had been right about the changes. The big bedroom, which had been the connubial chamber, was now a nursery, shared by my half brother and a woman from our village who was his wet nurse. The cradle was a very fine one, made of oak and richly carved. It had a satin cover and lining and everything else was of the finest linen.

He was asleep when I saw him first, dark lashes curved on flushed cheeks. I thought he was beautiful and loved him straightaway.

Father had prepared for my homecoming, too. I was no longer to share Jenny's room; my old one was restored to me with the bed newly furbished.

In the kitchen Jenny ruled again with all the power of renewed authority, and Margery and Maude had been joined by another, younger girl whose sole function was to wait upon the baby and his nurse.

Kate was nowhere to be seen but that did not surprise me; after even an ordinary childbirth women who could afford to stayed in bed for a month, and one who had turned lunatic might be expected to be confined to her room for rather longer. I was surprised that she, always so noisy, should be so quiet in lunacy. But perhaps she was asleep.

The three maids bobbed but Jenny embraced me. "I'm happy to see you home again. Come in here. I have a minute to spare." She drew me into the room which we had shared, and there were changes there, too. A comfortable padded chair, a table and an open cuboard with flagons and wine cups, a covered dish of cakes, a rug on the floor and curtains at the window had transformed a servant's sleeping place into a room any woman would have been glad to occupy.

"Your father," Jenny said, pouring wine and uncovering cakes, "overlooked nothing and—forgave nothing."

"In what way do you mean?"

"Look from the window."

From the window nothing much was visible except

a stretch of pasture and the dovecote, a relic of the monkish days. It was octagonal and of fair size. At ground level it had a door so that, when doves were needed for eating, somebody could creep in and take them, sleeping, from their perches. Much higher up were the narrow apertures used by the doves in their comings and goings. It had always been roofless for as long as I could remember; now it wore a conical thatch and built out from the doorway was a low wooden building, a kind of shed, with a chimney from which a thread of smoke rose into the sunny air.

Jenny said, "She is there. With a keeper, a deaf mute from Nettleton." Jenny's voice was gloating, but absurd as it was a faint shadow fell across the pleasure of my homecoming. I had a sharp feeling of what it must be like to be mad and locked in with a deaf mute for company. On the brightest day in summer the interior of the dovecote would be sunless and dim, the doves' entrances being so small and high up. Perhaps she was too mad to notice. I hoped so.

"Jenny, how mad is she? What form did it take?"

"She's no madder now than she was when she broke your wrist."

"That was temper."

"Call it temper then. Your father bore it, hoping for a baby, and we all bore it because we had to. So then the baby was born, a fine healthy boy, and the master set about doing over the dovecote, roofing it in and adding to it. He gave out—and we all believed him—it was for the poor thing we all call Dummy that he'd taken pity on. That'd be like him, wouldn't it? And he was thorough. He asked me to go over and see if the kitchen was workable. It was and there was a new little room. I didn't wonder much about that but I thought the new door on the dovecote itself a bit funny. Very strong, and bolts on the outside and in the middle a kind of little hatch, with another bolt. None of my business..." But a happy, spiteful glint showed in Jenny's old eyes. I could imagine it all, the hatch in the door just big enough for food to be pushed through.

I remembered Kate, big and strong and rough.

"Getting her in there must have been difficult."

"There again she worked against herself, the silly bitch! Always on the nag. People like Dummy should be in the poorhouses. Why else did people pay rates? Mind you, given *her* way I'd be in the poorhouse myself! So one evening your father said, 'Let's walk across and you'll see that I haven't wasted money.' And she went, and there was Dummy waiting, no size to speak of but strong as an ox! And understanding what to do because her mother had found a way of making her understand and passed on the knowledge to your father."

I thought of the wretched food the servants and I had eaten during Kate's reign and said, "What about food?"

"Nothing but the best. I see to it and I obey the master's orders. What sort of cook Dummy is I can't say. Maybe bad—there's screeching to be heard at times."

My own petty schemes for revenge once the baby was born—answering back, complaining to Father—shrank into nothingness. I seemed to be the only person who spared Kate a thought, even when she screamed in the night, mostly at full moon, a sure sign that real lunacy had set in.

And I loved the baby, who was very beautiful and amiable. His name was Simon, in memory of Father's father, and when I looked at him I was glad of my few accomplishments because presently I could hand them on, gifts to him. I could read and write and reckon; I rode well and could teach him. Youth is so flexible and buoyant that I was able to forget that he was not my true brother, only my half brother, and that his mother was a screaming lunatic, locked up in a dovecote.

# CHAPTER 4

During the next few years there must have been some days of bad weather, some small household upsets, but I remember Simon's childhood as a perpetual summer, all unbroken sunshine with peace inside the house and prosperity without.

Jenny died when Simon was eight, but that was a natural event. She had never known exactly how old she was, but she always said that she was old when Father first hired her and certainly before the end she looked very old indeed, but she remained active until the last. Then one evening, just before supper, she said she felt tired and would go to her bed early and leave Margery to manage. She did not appear first thing in the morning, but that was not unusual, and having had my own breakfast, I looked in to ask what she would like for hers. She was dead. To all appearances she had just died in her sleep.

There was no cause for grief, except in a general way—the thought that life must end, that all men must die, and when I thought that I naturally thought of Simon and was glad of my twelve years' seniority since it made it more likely that he would grieve for me than that I should for him.

I loved him with a passion only just short of idolatry, he was so extremely beautiful, more like an angel than a child born to ordinary human beings, one of them handsome enough, the other coarse-featured. His hair was true golden, not in the least like his mother's fairness, which was, so to speak, a negation of colour, and his eyes were blue. There are many shades of blue—my own eyes were blue; Father's eyes were blue, so were Jenny's, so were Kate's. Simon's were different—the dark, soft blue of bluebells in bud, just before they break into flower, and his lashes were darker than his hair. And his complexion was extraordinary—pale, yet creamy, as though some of the gold of his hair had drained into it, with a flush of rose in his cheeks.

I can remember thinking that he really was too beautiful to live, and when, at the age of six, he had smallpox, I was distraught. I was afraid he would die, or that he would emerge with that apricot skin marred. However, Jenny being in charge, he emerged unscathed. She had a sheep killed and skinned and Simon wrapped in the skin, still warm, and she hung his bed and his window with red stuff and spread a red flannel blanket on his bed.

After that I felt easier about his delicate look; only the strong survive the pox.

I taught him to walk—taking a mother's place. Presently I taught him to ride on a pretty little pony as safe and comfortable as a chair. I taught him his letters, and how to count, and how to write. I played with him, too, shedding my extra years. I'd had no

playmate when I was a child, and although I had not
been aware of the lack then, I found it a disadvantage
during my exile to Baildon, never winning a game
of marbles or fivestones and inept at all bad games,
even cup-and-ball, where the ball is tethered.

Father—and Jenny too in her day—doted upon
Simon and indulged him, but they both warned me
against letting him grow unruly by invariably giving way to him. I could no more help it than I could
change the colour of my hair. Father was capable of
saying "No boy," and Jenny could say "That will do,
Master Simon," but if I said "No" when he wanted
me to say "Yes" the look of displeasure which replaced his sunny smile would hurt me like a physical
pain and I'd say "All right then. Just this once."

In our walks and our rides we never went near
the dovecote, though I was always uneasily aware
of it. The deaf mute presented herself regularly at
the kitchen door and carried away provisions, and
the smoke rising from the little hut, which rather
resembled the church porch, something tacked onto
the main building, was evidence that some cooking
was done.

By concentrating upon Simon I managed to push
the thought of Kate aside, but one day, when he was
seven, he himself reminded me sharply.

"Lettice, who lives in that tower?" He called it a
tower because towers featured in the fairy tales with
which I had amused him.

"A poor woman."

"And why does she live there?"

"She is afflicted."

"How?"

Thinking myself very clever, I said, "She cannot
hear or speak." I elaborated this tale, falling back
upon something Father had once said. "When she

lived in another place the villagers were unkind and made mock of her. She is happier here."

We were riding towards Layer at the time and I urged my horse on, as though mere distance could help. Simon brought his pony alongside and looked at me with a peculiar expression, as though he were the elder and I the child.

"Is that all you know, Lettice?...Then just for once I know more than you do! The woman in the tower is my mother and she is as mad as a March hare."

"Who said that?"

"Margery."

I said, feebly, "She was teasing you."

"No. I was teasing her. Not much, just a little. I crept up behind her and untied her apron strings. Then she told me and said that if I didn't behave myself, the same thing would happen to me. But you wouldn't let anybody put me in a cage, would you?"

"Of course not, darling. And you must not believe what Margery says; she is an ignorant servant girl and what she doesn't know, she makes up. In fact you would do better not to talk to the servants at all. You're too old for that now."

"If you say so," he said, conceding a point. I made up my mind to speak very sternly to Margery, gossiping fool!

I said, "If you can drag yourself out of bed early tomorrow morning, you will see the poor afflicted person at the kitchen door."

Later that day, after Simon had gone to bed, I tried to talk to Father. I said, "He must know one day. I've fobbed him off for the time being but he cannot remain in ignorance forever."

"Forever, my dear, is a long time. If my luck holds, she'll die before he comes to an age to understand."

"You believe in luck, Father?"

"Why not? It has served me well so far. Today I bought a holding across the river. A man called Enoch Bowman died and his widow had no mind to work on. She wanted a cash payment and she will go and live with her married daughter in Muchanger."

I knew that Father had always been land-hungry and desired most of all the land in the old village, all small holdings owned by men who had in the past just managed to remain independent. But they had no reserves and taxes rose every year. I had little doubt that sooner or later the land across the river would be joined to our village and make one compact property, like the old manors which lay all about us. Father never felt quite the same way about Stratton Strawless and the Slipwell grazing grounds as he did about Ockley, though the two outlying places were the sources of his wealth.

London was growing fast and London was hungry, and although Ockley, at almost seventy miles from the capital, could not be said to be within easy distance, it was within reach. Cattle and sheep, not overdriven and given regular halts for grazing and watering, reached the London markets in good condition and fetched far higher prices than in any country town. This was a trade for big producers since the drovers, who must be capable and honest, earned high wages and to send six animals safely to London cost as much as sending sixty. The travelling flocks and herds were always accompanied by large fierce dogs trained to be unfriendly to all but their own masters.

The Priory acres were mainly ploughland apart from two pastures, one for grazing all the year round, the other a hayfield. When he was small Simon delighted to get out into the fields for the haymaking and the harvesting, and I often went too to see that he did not overtire or overheat himself, so there, as with the games, I enjoyed things denied to me in my youth. Neither my mother nor Anne Hatton would have thought it seemly for a girl child to go into the fields.

Ockley did not during this period see the parties it had known in Anne's time, yet we entertained moderately. One of Simon's godfathers, Richard Grantham, being related to the Hattons of Mortiboys through his mother, was a notch in the social scale above us, but his inheritance—an ancient house and a hundred acres at Minsham All Saints—was smaller than the estate that Father had acquired when he retired from the sea. He visited us quite often and brought his son Henry and his daughter Mary. He admired Father because he was successful in the way he wished to be. And of course in choosing my cousin Tom as the other godfather—temporarily at odds with my uncle—Father had been not only foresighted but cunning. My uncle and cousin soon composed their differences and we were all friendly again.

So it happened in the winter when Simon was ten, when the snow came, all unheralded and with great severity, an inch falling while we ate dinner, we had more people under one roof than could easily be accommodated. My uncle looked out of the window and said, "It is too heavy to last." But by the time we had reached the sweetmeats it was heavier and blinding. There was my uncle, my cousin Tom and his wife, a good rider, Richard Grantham, his son Henry, his daughter Mary and Mary's best friend, Frances Stokes, whom everybody hoped would marry Henry. Ten of us of all sorts and sizes in a house with four bedrooms. Small wonder that as soon as the snow cleared Father said, "This house is too small. I must build bigger."

Well, in the Bible there is a story about a man

who said exactly that but about his barns, not his house, and died, the story told as though death were a punishment upon him for building bigger, which, if he had grain or hay to store, seemed to me to be only sensible. In fact, I never did understand the Bible and sometimes wished—when I thought about it—that I'd been born when only the learned could read it and explain as best they could to themselves all the contradictory orders.

Since we'd all, during that cold season, lived cramped and disorderly, I was in favour of Father's determination to build on, especially when he said, "The time is coming when Simon will need a tutor— and a schoolroom."

I said "Yes" and "Yes" agreeing with Father and the men he hired, although, to be truthful, the word "tutor" and all that it evoked struck a feeling of fear into me. I knew that I was about to lose Simon. I had seen what nigh almost complete power Master Grattan had wielded in my uncle's household—not over me and my girl cousins because we did not matter, but to the boys he would say, "This is ill-done. You will forfeit your supper." As policy it worked. Places at Cambridge and at the grammar school had been secured. My uncle had thought his money well spent and Master Grattan had vanished to do a similar service to another ambitious family. I was probably the only one who remembered his name, and that ungraciously, not wishing one of his kind to take charge of Simon and deal with him strictly, saying that he must forego a meal or a ride or a walk.

But, unlike most people who lived off the land, Father set great store by learning. He'd acquired some himself in a haphazard way and had encouraged me to learn what I could—a little from Mother, more from himself and then more from Mr. Grattan. For Simon he was even more ambitious, and since the alternative to a tutor was a boarding school, I was in favour of the former.

Our house had been built by masons out of the stone of the ruins; it was square, like a box. Father said frankly that it had been built for use not ornament and at a time when he had to consider expense. Since that time he had seen Merravay and Mortiboys and Muchanger and even more farms which were not so deliberately plain, so he now wanted something more ornamental, with timbering and plastering and twisted chimneys. When the first new wing was added the house looked lopsided, so Father said, "In for a penny, in for a pound," and had a similar wing built at the other side. This made the original house look plainer than ever, so Father thought a deep porch would improve it. This porch was of stone and made as far as possible from the carved pieces which had been lying about since the Priory was demolished. The masons who built the first house and the villagers who had built their own had avoided the carved stone as being difficult to fit in. Or perhaps because they feared them, for there were gargoyles amongst this stone debris, and when our porch was completed a very well-carved but hideous devil looked down on all comers.

The tutor arrived while work on the second wing was still in progress.

# CHAPTER 5

I suppose it was inevitable that I should fall in love with Philip Wentworth, Simon's tutor. I was twenty-two and so far had loved only three people: Father, Anne and Simon. I was still fond of Father, but he had changed—or I had. I could understand his treatment of Kate, both the besotted indulgence and the terrible revenge, but I no longer thought him perfect, as once I had done. Anne had simply walked out of my life and was dead—somebody to be remembered kindly. Simon I still adored but he was already moving away from me and the day would certainly come when he would take a wife. When Philip arrived at Ockley my emotions were rather like strands of honeysuckle, groping about for something upon which to fasten and to cling.

All my former loves had been pleasing to the eye: Father, before his marriage to Kate aged him, had been remarkably good-looking; Anne had been beautiful, and Simon was angelic in appearance. Philip was tall and straight and may have been handsome when young before some discontent with life, or unhappiness, or even ill health had grooved his face. But that settled look of displeasure gave him a special charm; when he smiled—as he did when there was cause for it—it was like the sun coming out on an overclouded day.

My Aunt Turnbull, fastening the brick to my head, had warned me that men did not like girls who were too tall, and urging me to eat the fat which nauseated me, she had spoken of the necessity of developing curves. Despite the brick, I'd grown up and up and now was a bare inch shorter than Father, and I was flat-figured. Jenny had been concerned about that years earlier and insisted that I drink at least a pint of milk a day. I drank it obediently, but it made no difference and in the end I dismissed her theory as a kind of superstition, milk being drawn from cows' udders and full breasts on a female being udders in their way—and in due time.

Of my face I had nothing to deplore except that I had inherited Father's rather high-bridged nose, which showed only in profile. My complexion was good and my eyes—Father's eyes—bright blue. I had his hair, too, thick dark chestnut. And so curly that I never had to resort to curling irons. But such trivialities were not sufficient to give me confidence in the presence of a strange man. Confidence in women shows in two ways: Anne's—Look, I can do anything, outride you, outwit you; or in the other way, quiet as a mouse—Look, I have secrets, come and see. Neither role suited me and I think that we should probably have remained on purely formal terms but for something which happened one June evening.

Out at Stratton Strawless the shearers were at work—for sheep produced wool as well as meat on the hoof, and Father had gone out to oversee the operation. Simon, to whom anything was preferable to the schoolroom, had asked if he might go with him and Father had said, "Yes, but only if Master Wentworth chooses to release you." So Simon set off on his pony—his second, but already rather too small for him—and, apart from the servants, Philip and I were alone in the house.

I went in the evening into the garden to gather flowers for the table.

Philip came out and joined me. He said, "This is a place with a long history. Tell me about it."

I said, "I really know very little. It was a priory, dissolved and left derelict until my father bought it and built a house and reclaimed the land. He restored the garden, too, and added to it. But these are some of the old roses." They were the striped ones, the sweetest of all. I held the bunch towards him and he bent his black head, sniffed and said, "Sweet indeed," glancing up as he spoke so that a woman with more confidence or vanity might have thought that he was alluding to her. I did not so delude myself, and he went on to talk about the remains of the ruins which stood about. He said that it was unusual to see so much stone remaining. "Generally a demolished religious house serves as a stone quarry for all the district round."

"Nobody would have ventured here. There was supposed to be a curse on this place. When my father first came here nobody would come beyond the church, even for work. He had to bring in strangers. That is why we are really two villages. Even now, though some of the women are friendly and visit across the river, no one from the old village ever comes here."

"How very interesting. What form did the curse take?"

"I don't know. Father never speaks of it. I only heard from a maid."

And then the howling began.

Father had told me that Kate had screamed day and night when first incarcerated. Then, after a long silence, she had taken to howling at irregular intervals. Jenny had said that it was a sign that she was mad at last and that meant that God had forgiven her.

It was a terrible sound, the very voice of desolation, not unlike the noise dogs sometimes make at full moon or where there is a bitch in heat and out of reach, but there was a human element in it, too.

Philip looked startled. "What is that?"

"An idiot woman..."

With Father, with Jenny, with Simon and the maids, I had always had to pretend that I cared no more than they did, but I did care, and the fact that the outbreaks came at no given time made me worry about that keeper. Did she sometimes lose her temper or ill-treat the prisoner out of sheer boredom, as idle children will mistreat animals?

If the howling began when I was out of doors I simply went away until I was out of earshot. Indoors I'd rush to the virginals and make as much noise as I could. If she howled, as she sometimes did, in the middle of the night, I invariably woke and had to pull the covers over my head. Now here I was, trapped in the garden with a virtual stranger. All I could do was to put my hands over my ears and speak very loudly and rapidly.

"A lunatic," I said. "She has been kept in the dovecote for eleven years. I *know* she is well-fed and cared for." But as I almost shouted the words I wondered again. Who knows? The deaf mute might eat most of the food herself, giving Kate just enough to keep her alive. Perhaps the irregular howling fits were the result of hunger.

"I can't bear it," I said. "I can't bear it. I shall have to speak to Father." But I had already done so and he'd treated the matter with a bitter jocularity. "You of all people should be the last to worry. Who broke your wrist?"

*And who stood by pretending to see nothing?*

Philip cupped my elbow in his hand and said, "We can get out of range of the sound." He had already got his bearings and realised that to get into Layer Wood, the obvious place for a walk on a June evening, we would have to pass, not necessarily close by, but level with, the place from which the dreadful noise was coming. So he steered me downhill towards the church and the bridge and either Kate stopped or we were out of range.

He said, "It's a sound rule not to fret overmuch about things beyond your control."

"I know. Lame horses, overladen donkeys, the drovers' dogs, trained by cruelty to be ferocious. But this is—or was—a human being, one I had small cause to love but about whom I feel a sense of guilt. Quite inexplicable."

"Try," he said. "I admit that there is too much idle talk in this world, but sometimes to put a thing into words helps. Tell me."

There'd been a time when I could talk freely to Father but that time had ended when Anne ran away. Jenny had been my confidante to an extent, but she had never felt as I did about Kate, except when we were both being ill-treated, which made a bond. Now, having warned Philip, "My father would be extremely angry if he knew I had told you this," I told him a great deal. I even pushed up my sleeve and showed him my lumpy wrist. And he said, "That is not something, as children say, a kiss will make better, but it will do no harm." He kissed it. Lightly, almost playfully, but it set my blood afire.

I had not, like my girl cousins, been brought up in that state of ignorance that is called innocence. I'd lived among animals and understood about mating. It had never held any mystery or charm for me, and my aunt's words about men not liking tall girls had struck no chill to my heart. I'd never entertained daydreams that ended in the marriage bed. Nor had I desired children, largely because, just at the time when such desires might make themselves felt, I'd had Simon, ready-made, as it were. On the other hand, I was susceptible to love stories in books, things that had absolutely nothing to do with ordinary life. They were even in the Bible: Jacob slaving away for seven years for love of Rachel, David so much in love with Bathsheba that he arranged to set her husband in the forefront of the battle so that he would be killed, much of Shakespeare. None of these had seemed to have anything to do with Lettice Tresize of the Priory at Ockley.

Until that evening, even my future seemed clearly mapped out. Simon would marry; I should inevitably be jealous of his wife, but I should manage to conceal it. Father would leave me a good dower and the house was now big enough to have room for me. If Simon married some young woman like Anne Hatton with no knowledge of housekeeping, then I would continue to run the place for her. If he married a managing sort then I would keep to my room. I should have my horse, my dogs, the garden, my books, the woods and the countryside.

One kiss, lightly given, put an end to all this.

Father and Simon rode in, clattering over the bridge. Something must have shown in my face for Father shot me a keen look and dismounted, looping his rein over his arm. Philip went and walked beside Simon. I thought that if anything showed in my face, I could explain, so I said hastily, "She began that howling. And it was difficult to explain."

We never used her name.

"I no longer bother," Father said quickly. "Everybody now knows that I had the misfortune to marry a madwoman who would be dangerous if left at large." He gave a brief, nasty laugh. "A good many men I know wish that their wives would give them cause to take similar action."

As much as anything that last sentence illustrates that attitude of Father's which I found uncomfortable, different, unlovable.

I had intended to go on to speak about my fears that the Dummy might be unkind, but I was different, too.

I said, "So long as people don't get the idea that she was *my* mother." For who would consider falling in love with a young woman whose mother was a howling lunatic?

"Quite unlikely! My marriage to your mother caused stir enough. A man from nowhere, and still making his way marrying a daughter of Master Turnbull. And my second marriage was even more spectacular. It took a lunatic to give me a son."

"And for that reason, if for no other, I think...I mean, Father don't you think...that you...that we should make certain that she is not ill-treated?"

"We've covered this ground before, Lettice. Dummy understood what her mother told—conveyed to her. So far as I know she has kept to what she was told. The noise, I admit, is distressing. And having a lunatic mother may count against my boy. That I regret. But he will be rich.... What did you tell that fellow? About the howling?"

I lied. I said, "Just that it was an idiot, for whom

you made provision." I disliked Philip being referred to as "that fellow."

"Then you did well. Not that it matters much. Sooner or later, idling about, he will hear gossip."

It occurred to me to say that with Simon out with Father, his tutor could not be otherwise than idle, but I thought silence best. Something at Strawless might have put Father in a sour mood, or the talk about Kate upset him. It never occurred to me that finding me alone with a man had displeased him; he had always allowed me complete freedom and never treated me as so many parents treated their daughters—as a marriageable commodity. I'd seen my Uncle Thomas and my Aunt Margaret get to work on possible suitors for Marian, my cousin, extolling her domestic virtues, her smattering of education, making her sing or play the virginals. And my uncle was not above mentioning the fact that he was working himself to death in order to provide good dowers for both his daughters. There was nothing like that about Father and I was thankful for it—it smacked slightly of the slave market.

Men whom my Aunt Margaret would have called very eligible had come to our house often enough; Richard Grantham had two sons and they had friends. If it came to that Richard Grantham himself was an eligible man, a widower in his forties, Father's friend, just the kind of man who might settle for a girl who was no great beauty, was that fatal two inches too tall, but who was young and who had, as the vulgar saying went, "more than her leg in her stocking." But in our house, if a dish were praised, Father never said that I had overlooked its preparation and I was never called upon to play the virginals unless someone actually asked for music. In fact, now that I was grown, Father treated me as he had done when I was small—more like a son than a daughter—and it had suited me well.

That night I redressed myself before supper and greatly regretted the fact that I dare not wear any of the trinkets which Anne had given me just before she ran away. I never had worn any of them for fear that Father should notice and remember and be sad. Tonight the earrings would have gone well with my dress, which was of a greeny-blue colour, and the diamond ring would have drawn attention to my hands, which were long-fingered and slender as the old Queen's were said to have been. However, I resisted the temptation.

His place at table was opposite me, and contriving not to stare, I looked, looked away, looked again. Nothing of beauty there, little of youth, nothing to catch the eye. And yet already so dear, even the carved hollows in the cheeks, the scowl marks between the eyes. I thought, You have been unhappy; I could comfort you; I love you, I love you, I love you...

Simon said, "What I should like to be is the tarboy, with somebody to bet against. Master Wentworth, have you ever been at a shearing?"

"No, that is one thing I seem to have missed."

"The shearers compete to see who can take off more fleeces, with the fewest nicks. They bet against each other, and the tarboy, who has to dress the nicks, bets against everybody," Simon explained. "He made fourpence today."

"More likely eightpence," Father said. "They all bribe him beforehand. Several wounds would have gone uncounted—and therefore undressed—had I not been there and watchful."

I was glad of the ordinary table chatter though I took no part in it. I just sat and watched. Philip's hair was black, his eyes dark grey under the taut brows. For a man with an indoor occupation his skin was dark. His mouth was rather wide and thin-lipped; when he smiled, the crease on one side was deeper than the other. In repose, it was a hard mouth. I longed for him to kiss me properly....

Presently Simon said something about going to Strawless tomorrow and Father said, "You're not coming. I shall take Lettice. If you have too many holidays Master Wentworth will become bored. And boredom leads to mischief. Is that not so, Master Wentworth?" The question was asked in jocular style but the hostility was unmistakable. So was his purpose in suggesting that I should go with him next day. Even before Jenny's death I had gradually dropped into a housekeeping role while Simon took my place as Father's companion in field and market. At first I had resented this and felt displaced, but use had accustomed me. And now, though Father's design was quite obvious—to keep me and Philip apart—it did not displease me; it hinted that he did not regard me as wholly undesirable though I was too tall for most men, too flat-chested and had an ugly wrist.

Hindsight is very cruel. In its harsh light one sees the mistakes that others have made, the mistakes one has made oneself, sees how narrowly happiness was missed and disaster invited. One thinks, If only...if only...

# CHAPTER 6

When Philip had been with us for about six weeks he asked Father to lend him a horse for the day on Sunday.

"I have an old relative who lives at Summerfield," he said. "And he might take it amiss if he heard I had been so nearby and not called upon him."

"Summerfield," Father said. "Sir Vernon?"

"Yes. My great-uncle."

"Take the bay," Father said. "It has more stamina than mine and Summerfield is quite a distance."

If Philip had hoped to impress Father by this mention of good connections, he had miscalculated. Afterwards Father said to me, "If old Sir Vernon *is* actually his great-uncle, there's something wrong somewhere. People like that don't leave their relatives to take posts like this. They set them up in business or invent jobs for them."

Next day at dinner Father did what he seldom did—he asked a personal question; in fact two. "Did the bay carry you well?"

"Very well indeed, sir."

"And was Sir Vernon pleased to see you?"

"Alas, no. He finds it hard to forgive me."

"Forgive?" Over the food he was lifting to his mouth. Father gave me a what-did-I-tell-you look.

"Summerfield's living is in his gift," Philip explained. "He wanted me to be ordained and settle down to be a country parson."

"And you preferred to teach blockheads like Simon here?"

"With all due respect, sir, Simon is no blockhead. And yes, it suits me better. I live better for one thing." He cut into the beef that was tender as butter. "And I'm free. If a post is disagreeable I can walk away and find another. Livings are not so easily come by."

There was here a veiled threat. If Father continued to maintain his attitude of disapproval and a kind of scorn, Philip would leave, and then where should I be? The poets all say that the heart is the seat of the emotions, that it rises with joy, falls with despair. My feelings seemed to centre lower down, and at the thought I felt a yawning emptiness between my lower ribs and my navel, as though all was dropping, dropping away.

For by this time we were lovers in very truth.

It was all done surreptitiously, but the arrangement of the new house made it easy. Father valued his view over the garden, and I liked the garden too, so we occupied matching rooms in the gabled wings. The old rooms, built of stone, whitewashed, and cold even in summer, now comprised the hall downstairs, the kitchen behind it and, above the schoolroom, Philip's bedroom and a great chamber should space ever be scarce. We now had three stairways. I stole down one, Philip down another, and we met in the garden. And when I say met, I mean the real, the ultimate meeting between an ardent raw girl who nevertheless knew what she was doing and—I see now—a man set on seduction.

I see exactly how I looked to him; a girl well over marriageable age and not even betrothed, with a father who doted on her. Get her with child, face the first outburst of rage and abuse and then settle down to serious business. Who else will marry her now? Hurry, hurry, pay me to marry the wench, keep her and me in comfort for the rest of our lives.

That is how I see it now, but at the time it was all mixed up with the scent of roses and honeysuckle and nights of soft darkness, nights of bright moonlight, a night of heavy rain when I said, "Come to my room." I was so mad with love—or lust—that I gave no thought to the consequences.

It was October. A hot August had scorched the roses and the honeysuckle, the harvest had been cut and I was overdue by a fortnight. That brought me to my senses. I had been indulging in fantasy, never looking ahead further than the next surreptitious meeting, the next climax of joy. And now that I was pregnant I felt no real dismay. Father, I knew, would be furious and rail at me for deceiving him and behaving like a slut, but in the circumstances he could hardly forbid Philip to make an honest woman of me, and in the end he would forgive us both and find some kind of employment for Philip. After all, Father was fifty and his estate was not compact; to run it meant a good deal of riding; it would be years before Simon could be really helpful and I should be busy with the baby. Father would be sensible enough to take all these things into account.

I joined Philip in the garden, and because it was bright moonlight we stayed in the deep shadow of the wall. We kissed and embraced with—I have often thought about this since—a little less fervour on my part than usual. It was almost as though the inner hunger, which one kiss had started, had been satisfied.

"I have something to tell you"—and I suppose that because to me the matter was already so important, I sounded serious.

"He knows?"

"No. But he must be told. Darling, I am going to have a baby." He made a little sound and held me tighter for a second, then released me.

"He'll be very angry," he said.

"Furious. But he'll get over it. Always supposing," I said lightly, "that you are prepared to marry me. Are you?"

"There is nothing I wish more. It is the desire of my heart."

I'd been sure enough, but it was nice to hear it said. We then talked about who should tell Father. Philip said he was willing to, but I thought it might come better from me. Since the night when Father had found us together, the night of that first kiss, Father had been cold to Philip and at times positively hostile. His manner to me had never changed. I thought that I would bear the first brunt, let his fury exhaust itself and give his good sense a chance to come uppermost. I was prepared to behave in an abject manner—as was only right. I had broken all the rules, acted slyly, and since the night of that first kiss gone directly contrary to Father's will, which if not exactly expressed in words had been made plain enough.

I wondered what to wear—the greeny-blue dress, which made me almost pretty, or the plain grey, more suitable for a penitent. I decided upon the grey.

I ordered one of his favourite dishes—rabbit pie

and baked apples, cored and stuffed with chopped
raisins. Then when it came to the point I couldn't
eat, the very smell of the food nauseated me. I knew
a good deal about breeding and being pregnant had
caused me no actual shock, but I did not connect my
state with the feeling of sickness. The only breeding
woman I had ever come into contact with was Kate
and she had never been sick. Indeed she had attacked
her food with even more than her usual voracity,
saying, in her coarse way, that now she must eat for
two.

I sat there, pushing the food about on my platter
and now and again, when chance favoured, slipping
a bit to the hounds, which somehow always slithered
in at mealtimes.

The omens were not good. Father chose this moment to attack Philip about Simon's lack of progress.

"You yourself said at this table, Master Wentworth, that my son was far from a blockhead. Then
why does he still count on his fingers? I had no
schooling. Lettice spent a little time listening while
a tutor taught her cousins. *We* don't count on our
fingers."

Poor Simon looked downcast and Philip began to
say something about being able to count in one's
head not being the be all and end all of education. I
interrupted, beginning my penitent role untimely. I
said, "Father, the fault may be mine. I first taught
Simon to count—with *things*—marbles and pebbles,
fingers and toes."

"Within limits you did very well. But now I am
not satisfied. No, far from satisfied."

It was an inauspicious beginning to a vital talk
and it made me feel even more sick. But I knew that
the truth must be told so I slipped out and was sick
behind a rosemary bush and felt much better. Then
I went in and found Father, who was smoking his

pipe and looking more amiable, and I said, "Father, Philip Wentworth and I have been lovers since June and now I am pregnant with his child."

I knew it had to be said and I'd gone the shortest way about it and I had been prepared for anger and abusive recrimination. But not for what happened. Father let his pipe fall and sagged sideways, his face the colour of a plum.

I'd never seen an angry man suffer a rush of blood to the head, but I'd heard about such strokes. Something of a similar kind happened to many of my Uncle Thomas's elderly clients. I knew roughly what to do—raise his head and send for the blacksmith. I yelled for Philip and sent Simon running for the blacksmith. In Baildon, of course, I would have sent for the physician and he would have sent for the barber surgeon. In Ockley we were dependent upon the blacksmith, who came at once and, after a moment's consideration, bled Father from just below the ear. Most successfully, the plum colour drained away, leaving a ghastly pallor, but he was conscious again and presently made an attempt to rise from his chair, but he couldn't manage it. He fell back and said, "Weak, malaria does that to a man," which sounded as though he were not quite back in his right mind. But within minutes he was, and when Soames, the blacksmith, said in that way which humble people often use to their betters if chance gives them the upper hand, "Into bed with you, sir. A good night's sleep and you'll be right as a trivet," and Philip went forward to help with the getting to bed, Father said quite distinctly, "Not you!"

Soames said, "Take ahold of me, sir. I can heave you." He heaved so well that at that moment I hardly noticed Father's dragging leg.

I trailed along behind them, feeling guilty and miserable and yet in a way relieved that the words had been said and need not be said again. Soames began to unfasten Father's boots, but Father said, "Leave them. I want Carter." Carter was our horseman and lived over the stables and in the old days, when Anne had her gay parties and men overdrank, Carter had often been called in to put them to bed, so to ask for him now seemed natural enough. Then Father noticed me, standing attentive, willing to do anything, and said quite kindly, "I must have given you a shock. Go to bed. Good night."

Nobody hearing him would have dreamed that anything had happened. And nothing had happened except that Father had dropped and broken his pipe, had a rush of blood to the head and had to be bled. It was almost possible for me to imagine either that he had already forgiven me or that the stroke had begun before he took in what I had said. In which case I should have to say it all again.

I wanted to talk about these two possibilities with Philip and should have done so had he been hovering about the stairs or the passages, but he had evidently taken the "Not you" as dismissal and gone out, and I was now in the grip of such lethargy that I could not go in search. I was pregnant; I had been very sick and I had seen Father have a stroke, which, whether I was the cause of it or not, was a distressing sight. I went to bed, and although it was a warm evening the sheets seemed cold, and I started up a shivering fit which I could not control and which lasted a long time. My teeth chattered as my mind went over and over again the various possibilities and wondered if I had done wrong in being so blunt, if this, if that...Finally I fell asleep. Once I half-wakened and thought I heard hoofbeats and knew that I had been dreaming, and went to sleep again. In the morning I woke completely, with the sunlight lying across my bed.

I rose hastily, put on my robe and my slippers, ran a comb through my hair. I was going to see Father. To do that I passed through the old core of the house where Philip had his room. The door stood open and the room was empty.

# CHAPTER 7

I never saw Philip again. I never knew for certain what happened to him. I only knew what Father said to me that bright morning and of its truth I could not judge.

I went in and I said, "I came to see how you were feeling."

"I have the equivalent of a wooden leg and I think..." He put his hand to his left cheek and I saw that it looked as though it had slipped, only slightly, the lid of the eye, the corner of the mouth out of alignment. "But I will not reproach you, for you, my poor dear girl, are in a far worse plight. Your lover has deserted you!"

"Oh, no! I cannot believe...Father, as soon as I told him that I was—as I am—he spoke of marriage immediately. He said...he said it was the one desire of his heart."

"Last night he sang a different tune. Very different. Sit down. When I felt better I sent for him and was frank. I must be frank with you, too. I told him that he could marry you—with my blessing if he wanted it—but with no worldly goods. I was testing him, Lettice. God Almighty, if he'd taken up the challenge, I'd have respected him. If he'd said that so long as he could earn a crust he'd share it with you, I'd have seen that that crust was well buttered. But he played the craven. Talked about the difficulty of finding posts and people's preference for unmarried tutors. He was *despicable*. And I knew it from the first. And now he has run away. Like a thief in the night."

I felt sick again, my stomach heaving up, all my vitals dropping away. I said, "He will come back," but uncertainty showed in my voice, which was no more than a faint mew.

"I think not," Father said and gave a short laugh. "And if he does I'll have the hide off him."

I tried to excuse Philip in my mind. I myself had told him how Father—in cold anger—had treated Kate; what might he not do in hot rage? Father might be temporarily weak himself, but he had Carter nearby and the whole of our village to call upon. Even murder was not unthinkable; who'd miss a humble tutor? In this isolated half village? An ice-cold hand fingered my neck.

"I knew from the first," Father said again. "That night I found you together by the church. He'd had time to take stock of the situation—an only daughter with a fond father. And a deceitful wench into the bargain. I'll say this now, Lettice, and then be done with reproaches. I respected your feelings. I never tried to force any man upon you, or you on any man. If you'd shown even a slight preference, said a word in favour of one or the other, I'd have broken

my back to get him for you. You never gave any man
a second look till that rogue came along. A slimy,
sly fellow hired to teach blockheads. I tried to make
you see him as I saw him but you were deliberately
blind. I tried to guard you—but a man must sleep.
And now we have this on our hands."

I sat, bowed with sorrow and shame and, now,
with terror, for during Kate's rule I had spent most
of my time with the servants and had heard things
which I did not understand then but which now came
back vividly. ("Old Mother Warden got rid of it for
her and she's back in the field today...")

I said, "Father, please—not an abortion." I placed
my hands about my waist, inside which the seed of
love had taken root; and I realised that I was helpless.

"Of course not. Far too risky; seven out of ten die.
And undutiful and ungrateful as you have proved
yourself to be, I do not wish you dead. There is plenty
of time, a girl as long and lean as you... And presently I shall consult with your Aunt Margaret."

I was so stunned that I could only repeat the name.

"Aunt Margaret?" The most prim and proper person I had ever had contact with, the least likely to
sympathise.

"Yes," Father said. "Your cousin Marian was in
the same plight, but your aunt managed admirably."

Surprise can strike through sickness and sorrow
and despair. I heard myself saying, "Not Marian!"

"I have it on the best authority," Father said. "Your
cousin Tom told me. And your uncle does not know
to this day. Marian grew bulky—they said it was
dropsy and she went to drink the waters at—oh, I
forget the name of the place, I never thought that
*that* could concern me! But there is a regular trade
there and your cousin came home cured, a fit bride
for a man learned in the law but ignorant of life."

"And what happens to the babies?"

"They are cared for—apprenticed. I shall talk presently to your aunt—not mentioning you. Some young woman in whom I take interest and feel responsible for. Meanwhile, eat little and, when the time comes, pull in your stays, and let us not speak of this again."

Restraining my appetite was easy and for a time pulling in my stays no great hardship since the struts were no longer made of iron, as in the old days, but of a new substance, whalebone, less rigid. And everything combined to keep me for a time long and lean. I worried about Philip. He knew how I was placed, he must surely send me a comforting word; but he did not. I worried about Father, who now walked with a dragging leg and whose face was distorted— all my fault. I worried about Simon, whose education had been stopped so abruptly. Not that he cared; he was glad, but I felt that I had wronged him, too.

Father was as good as his word and there were no more recriminations. While I was still presentable he took me about with him even more than formerly and we entertained a good deal. There was talk of my paying a visit to my relatives in Devon. Father said it seemed rather disgraceful that his parents had never seen me; he regretted that he had never been back himself and that the only comfortable time for travel coincided with his busiest season; he discussed whether Simon should come with me. Everybody was well prepared for Lettice Tresize to be absent from home in the spring.

Well before I left home something had happened to me. The love I'd felt for Philip, my sense of guilt, my feeling of having disgraced Father all melted away before another emotion—concern for the unborn. I'd asked Father what happened to the babies and he had said that they were cared for and apprenticed to some trade or other and with that answer I had been content at the time; but as the weeks passed and I grew bulky within my whalebone cage other thoughts came. My child, begotten in love—on my side at least and probably Philip had not been so unloving as Father depicted him. Who'd guide that child's first steps, teach it its first words? I thought of all the love and care I'd lavished on Simon. And there was a gap between birth and apprenticeship age; how would that be spent? And what sort of master or mistress would *my* child fall to when the time came?

Masters and mistresses varied enormously; some treated their apprentices like an extension of their own families, some behaved to them as though they were slaves, and indeed a properly indentured apprentice had no more rights than a slave except that his master was not allowed to kill him because he was one of the King's subjects. He could be beaten and starved, ill-used in many ways, for it is a sorry fact of life that some people are born with a taste for cruelty and will indulge it, even to their own despite. Everybody knows that a well-fed, well-treated horse is a friend, a willing partner, yet I have seen horses—donkeys and mules, too—tethered out in the full sun, just out of reach of the water trough in Baildon marketplace on a hot day. It was the same with apprentices. Happy girls and boys must surely work better, and the miller's apprentice could have been his son, but in Baildon there was a saddler whose boys worked in fear. I'd have taken my trade—and directed Father's—away from him had there been another in the town.

Once and only once did I venture to speak to Father on this subject, and then I realised that all the pent-

up rage which had consumed him while Kate ruled
the house, and then evidenced itself in such ruthless
fashion, was now turned upon me.

"Are you asking me to recognise your bastard?
Bring some squawling brat home here and say to my
neighbours, 'Look, this is what my daughter and a
beggarly tutor begot.' Are you out of your mind? I
have with great difficulty and subtlety arranged for
you to go to Oxney, shed your load and return to my
house. If you prefer to whelp in a ditch like a tinker's
bitch, go and do it."

So I went, without further talk or complaint, to
Oxney.

# PART THREE

# Narrative by
# Lettice Tresize

# CHAPTER 1

I have never tried to describe Oxney to anyone for
the simple reason that I have never admitted having
been there; but had I tried I should have found myself
at a loss for words, and no hearer would believe me.
The one thing to be said for it is that it existed for
a purpose and served that purpose very well.

Some people think that we were isolated at Ockley, but looking in one direction one could see the
cottages of Father's labourers and in the other the
cottages of the older village across the river. But
Oxney stood on its own in the middle of a wild heathland on the borders between Suffolk and Norfolk. No
other house was visible, and there were no trees.
Just miles and miles of heath and bracken, with a
single track, too faint to be called a road, linking the
house to Brandon, the nearest small town.

The place itself was a curious mixture: part jail,

part poorhouse, part country mansion. Father and I were received in a richly furnished apartment with wall hangings, coloured rugs and furniture padded with velvet. It was March and still chilly; a good fire burned on the hearth, and Mistress Scott, one of the women who owned and ran the place, received us with wine and cake and fair words. Having a baby, she said, was nothing to worry about, her sister was a midwife of the greatest possible experience; she had delivered many great ladies in her day.

Father had never fully forgiven me but now that the moment for parting came he relented a little and said, "I leave you in good hands. I wish you a safe labour. Good-bye."

After he had driven away in the cart, Mistress Scott explained things to me. Anonymity was the keyword, she said. I was to tell no one my real name and I was to ask no other girl hers. I was to be known as Polly. There were no servants at Oxney, she explained; servants were such gossips and there were always young ladies still with a month or two to go, or recovering from the birth of their babies and waiting to go home, to do the work of the house. There was a man in the yard who saw to the horse and the cow and the pigs and went marketing when necessary, but it was inadvisable to talk to him or even see him more than was necessary. "When you leave here, the chapter will be closed."

She then asked me whether I *wanted* my baby.

"I do indeed. Oh, yes!"

"Can you or your family make provision for it?"

"I will."

"You have property?"

"No—a few jewels."

"You had better give them to me—for safekeeping—just in case something should happen to you."

I stood dumbfounded, for that was the first time

that I realised that there might be no future for me.
I'd been stupid, seeing Oxney as a mere interlude.
I'd been full of plans: trying to bring Father round,
cheating a little on the housekeeping, selling my
trinkets, assuring as well as I could from a distance
that my child was cared for and not apprenticed too
early or to a place with a bad reputation. My body,
of late too closely laced into its whalebone cage, had
grown inert, but my mind had been active and I had
thought that I had a distinct advantage over my
cousin Marian, who from Oxney had gone almost
straight into marriage and the making of another
life. I should resume my old one—or so I thought.

"One other thing," Mistress Scott said, giving my
trinkets a look as near contemptuous as she could
manage, "Brandon is twelve miles away, and rough
going for a woman in your condition. It has been
tried. With fatal results."

She then handed me over to Mistress Lincoln, who
took away all my clothes except my shift and gave
me an anonymous garment, rather like a smock
without the gay smocking, and a pair of cloth shoes.
She asked could I cook and seemed pleased when I
said that I could. I was glad, too, for the cooking was
more interesting than the endless scouring and pol-
ishing which went on all the time. And since I handled the food I took myself a tasty bite or two now
and then.

We all ate at the same table, but not from the
same dish. Mistress Scott and her sister ate large
quantities of delicate food while we made do with
the cheapest kind—even the bread was different,
theirs being white manchet and ours so brown as to
be almost black. Nobody complained, partly because
Mistress Lincoln explained that fat women suffered
more in labour than others and partly because there
was a whispered story of a girl who had just been

told to leave and thrust out in smock and slippers because she complained.

We were none of us called by our names; we were Polly, Dolly, Sally, Judy, Cathy and Maggie, all diminutives and in other places used with affection. Not here! I was Polly, and the girl I most wanted to have a real talk with was Maggie, because she had had her baby—born dead—and had therefore been here longer than the others. I wanted to know where were the children that were not born dead.

"I don't know. I think they are taken away."

"Where to?"

"I don't know. I expect these women know others who specialise in keeping babies."

Mistress Lincoln rustled up and said, "Too much idle chatter here."

I suppose the policy of restricting talk was wise; in a weak moment we might have exchanged confidences which would have destroyed our anonymity, the one thing which the place guaranteed absolutely.

Maggie left and her place was taken by a girl called Janey, who cried a great deal, thus annoying Mistress Lincoln, who when angered sounded rather like Kate: "What are you crying for, you stupid girl? You should be on your marrowbones thanking God for good parents who care what becomes of you. Go polish the pewter!"

Even the two women, watchful as they were, could not have us all under surveillance all the time. I asked everybody if they knew what happened to the babies. Nobody knew, and it seemed that I was the only one who gave a rap. Everybody else seemed to feel animosity towards what they were gestating. The girl known as Cathy put it into words: "Care what happens to it? Why should I after it got me into this mess?"

I was in the same mess, but I cared.

My plans for seeing that the poor little thing was looked after suffered a shock when one day at the table I saw that Mistress Scott was wearing my emerald earbobs. I steadied myself by thinking that perhaps she had simply had a fancy to borrow them—they were far better than the things most girls in disgrace could have brought with them. So was the ruby on its gold chain and the flat diamond. But suppose she chose to confiscate them all! I'd have no redress. Nobody in the world knew that I owned them. I had thought that by selling them I could ensure my child all that a baby needed until I could raise money somehow, or until Father came round. I still cherished the hope that he would. But if my trinkets were lost to me there might be a gap during which my child would be a pauper—and pauper babies had short lives.

I was hot from the stove when I noticed the earbobs. I'd cooked a half saddle of lamb for the privileged, with the first few peas, and to please the other girls I had served their hard cheese in a tasty way, as Jenny had so often served ours, grated into a sauce made of flour and water, a dab of butter and heaped hot onto the bread. But I had a shivering fit which shook me so severely that I could not raise the food to my mouth, and if I could have done I couldn't have chewed it. All I could do was to steady my shaking jaw with my shaking hands and think.

In a way I was a very privileged cook; other hands washed the dishes and scoured the pans—outside as well as in—and the meal over, I followed Mistress Scott and Mistress Lincoln out of the dining parlour and into the other. I was courteous. I said, "I would have speech with you if you can spare the time, ladies."

Since my coming I had built up a certain amount of goodwill, making custard and marchpane and syllabub and tarts. They even invited me to sit down. I sat and they waited. I waited too, for as I sat it seemed as though the soft velvet cushion had turned into a spike which impaled me, but only for a moment. It was a savage pain, and then nothing.

"Well, what is it?" Mistress Lincoln asked the question, but I addressed myself to Mistress Scott.

I said, "When I first arrived here you asked me if I wanted my baby. I said then that I did. And I still do. But I am anxious. Nobody can tell me what happens to the babies. Given time mine will be all right. I shall manage somehow."

"You can count upon your father?"

"Not immediately. He was angry—and had every right to be so. And if I go home—after a supposed holiday in Devon and a baby—said to be adopted—appears in too short a time, it will look suspicious. But after some months...it would seem natural, since I am unlikely to get married and everybody knows how devoted I was to my brother when he was small. I am sure I could persuade Father..." I floundered on. "But I need help. Do you know of a woman who would keep a baby, safely and kindly, until, say, Christmastide?"

They conferred together in soft voices and then looked at me blankly. The truth—and to me it was terrible—dawned. When a girl left Oxney the chapter was closed.

The spike drove into me again, but unaware of its significance, I ignored it. All I could think of was all those dead babies. Strangled at birth? Drowned like unwanted kittens?

I left the two sisters to the wine, the sweetmeats and the cards that occupied their evenings and stole upstairs. Mistress Scott was wearing my earbobs, but I had hopes of finding the ruby and the diamond. I failed to do so. But I needed clothes, too, and those

I found—not my own, which in any case would no longer have fitted me, but some of Mistress Scott's. She was a stout woman. I chose the plainest of her dresses and, thinking of the baby, a shawl.

We girls slept in cubicles made by dividing ordinary bedchambers into two or three. We were forbidden to visit each other's cubicles and now that the evenings were lighter had no rushlights. We were all in varying degrees of pregnancy and the work we had done through the day—much of it unnecessary—made us go to bed gratefully.

There was still some movement in the house. It was Cathy's turn to wash the supper dishes and to leave the kitchen spotless. I thought about her, about what I had just understood causing her no anguish at all. When she had settled I stole out, wearing my soft cloth shoes and carrying Mistress Scott's shoes in my hand. I thought of the girl in the story who had done something very similar—with fatal results.

I imagined that there would be some attempt to get me back, so I did not take the trail any girl in her senses might be expected to take; I turned in the opposite direction. I was now wearing the shoes and they fitted badly, too short and too wide. My toes were cruelly cramped and yet at almost every step the shoes slipped off, sadly impeding my progress. So I changed back into the cloth slippers, determined to wear them as long as they lasted, which would not be long, on such rough ground. Underfoot it was sandy and pebbly and riddled with rabbit holes. Gorse and bracken grew profusely for a time and then gave way to nothing where the soil was too poor to grow even coarse grass.

I had no idea where I was going or what I should do when I reached some sort of destination. I was fleeing from Oxney and for a time that was all that mattered. I'd read somewhere that people who walk without direction tend to bear to the right and thus walk in a circle, so I deliberately bore to the left.

There was a time between the last lingering daylight and the moon's rising when I was in the dead dark. I tried to keep going, but I put my foot in a rabbit hole, tripped and fell down. The wrenched ankle added its pain to the one already striking upward at irregular intervals. I thought it wise to rest, so I sat down, and then lay down, and I slept intermittently. I woke whenever the spike probed.

My last waking was to a blue morning with more larks in the sky than I have ever heard. There was a moment of joy at waking to such loveliness—and then pain. The thrusts were more frequent and deeper today and at last I realised what was happening. I was having this baby and unless I quickly reached somebody who could help me it would die and so should I.

I stood up quickly and found that in the heel-less slipper I could not walk a step; in Mistress Scott's shoe, which had a heel, I did rather better. I limped on, stooping over when the pain struck, looking about for some kind of human habitation, and almost missing it when I reached it, for I was looking for a house, a cottage. What I found was a kind of tent. It and the donkey tethered behind it were all so much in colouring like the ground and the sparse grass that I was practically into the encampment before I realised. A lurcher dog rushed out at me and then halted, realising that I was harmless, and a woman came ducking out of the low opening of the tent and said, "What do you want?"

I just managed to say, "Help. I am having a baby," and then the earth tilted and I went with it.

After that there was a nightmare of pain. The brown-faced woman kept saying, "Push! Push! There's no

more to having a baby than wringing out a cloth. I
know, I've had four. Push. Push." I pushed, as anxious now to be rid of it as one would be of a tooth
with an abscess, magnified a hundred times, but the
sun was high in the sky and it was hot under the
canvas before the child was born in one long tearing
pain that seemed as though it would never end.
"There you are," the woman said. "And a boy." Her
voice, which had been impassive when not downright
contemptuous, changed slightly at this mention of
the child's sex, and I thought that even here, in the
tinker class, boys were valued more than girls. I
remember thinking, I am glad for his sake; he will
never have to undergo such torture!

Then I must have dozed, for the next thing I knew
was that my baby, wrapped in the filthy, ragged
remains of a shawl, was lying in the crook of my
arm; the tent had been taken down and a half-grown
boy was hitching the donkey to a little low-sided cart.
A man was taking down what looked like brown
washing from several lines. They were rabbit skins
which had been drying in the sun. He was throwing
them into the cart. The woman put a broken jug with
water in it, a rabbit leg and a slice of bread on the
ground beside me. She carried Mistress Scott's shawl,
folded carefully, over one arm.

"I'm taking this," she said. "We've wasted half a
day on you, and I'm leaving the jug."

I said, "Thank you. I wish I had something of more
value to give you."

"It's a good one. Worth a shilling to the right customer."

The man gathered up the lines and the stakes
which had supported them and threw them into the
cart. The woman lifted a bundle.

I realised that I was about to be left alone. I cried,
"Wait! Please! Where am I?"

"On the heath. That way"—she gestured vaguely—"is Brandon. That way Thetford."

The man called fiercely, "Must you waste more time jabbering?" and started the donkey with a blow.

Father had once said to me something about whelping in a ditch like a tinker's bitch. I'd done just that—except that I was not in a ditch. By evening I wished that I were for I had drunk all the water the broken jug held. And I had eaten the food, straight off the ground; for the baby, after some ineffectual efforts, had learned to suckle, and no woman can feed a child unless she feeds herself.

What about tomorrow?

There must be some curious euphoria that follows a successful childbirth. I lay throughout that summer day, except for my baby surely the loneliest creature in the world. I had absolutely nothing, I was weak and exhausted, I didn't even know where I was except that I was on a heath between Brandon and Thetford. Yet each time the child woke and drank from the overflowing fountains of my breasts, I was happy, lay back again on the bracken bed which the tinkers, knowing the terrain, had brought for their comfort. Cuddling, feeding my child, I felt that I had outwitted everybody and that somehow everything would be well. All day the larks sang.

Next day was very different. I still felt weak but I told myself that that was mere lethargy. Out of the nightmare of pain I could remember some of the things the tinker woman had said when she wasn't telling me to push. She said that this was an easy birth because I had walked up to the last minute; she had always done the same and walked again the next day. Easy!

She had taken nothing but the shawl; the clothes I had stolen from Mistress Scott, who had stolen so much from me, lay there at a slight distance. I could

do without a petticoat, so I discarded the filthy rag
and wrapped my child in sound linen.

The earth tilted a bit but not as it had done when
I fell at the tinker woman's feet. My wrenched ankle
still hurt but I was now able to distinguish pain from
pain, and it seemed nothing. I carried the child in
my left arm and the broken jug in the other hand,
hoping to come upon water. And I soon did. A small
idling stream between banks of green grass. I dipped,
drank, dipped, drank again. But how long could I
live on water?

Still, I kept my head and reasoned that every little
river had its settlement. And I was right. The narrow
green banks widened out into pastures with cattle,
and there was a farmhouse, square and squat, not
unlike our house had been before Father took a fancy
to build on. I went to the back, through a yard where
a hundred chickens were pecking and clucking. The
door was open. I knocked on it and a man came, as
squat and square as his house and with an angry
red face. Before I could speak a word he said, "Be off
with you. We had some of your sort here yesterday.
They stole the very washing off the line." Then he
called over his shoulder, "Another tinker, Alice. Good
thing I was here!"

I said, "Sir, I am no tinker. I seek work. I can cook.
I know something of..."

"Be off," he said and slammed the door in my face.

Later, when I had time to think it over, I realised
that the tinker's wife had dealt magnanimously with
me—she could have taken all my clothes! People
who would steal washing from a line...

At the moment I was concerned at being taken
for a tinker. Partly the hair, I supposed, drenched
with the sweat of agony and not brushed, and partly
the fact that the baby was wrapped in a woman's

petticoat, of good quality—stolen, the man would think, from somebody else's line.

In this part of the country houses were few and far between, but there was a path, roughly following the river, and the scenery grew less bleak; there were a few trees, then more. The attitude of the people did not improve. I lost count of the houses I called at during that long day. One of them was large and there were servants about—they seemed to find my plight amusing.

I was obliged to take frequent rests, I was so frightened of falling down in a faint and hurting the poor baby. So whenever I felt faint or dizzy I sat down until the spell passed. I still managed to feed him, however.

At homestead after homestead I was told to be off and often threatened: "Be off, or I'll set the dog on you."

Some women would have died of despair, some of hunger. I stayed alive, partly because I was country-bred and partly because I had an incentive to live in my child.

I'd left Oxney on Wednesday evening; I lived on water for most of Friday and for all of Saturday, and what with the walking, the lack of food and the worry, by Saturday evening my breasts were growing flaccid, and the baby, after sucking with vigour, wailed with discontent. I saw myself in the position of a cow with a suckling calf, shut in a shed, away from pasture, and left unfed.

Cow!

As the slow dusk fell that evening I began looking about for a cow. And I found one in a meadow near the little river. Slightly too near the house of its owner, but with a calf frisking about. I knew enough about cattle to know that cows with calves were often as dangerous as bulls. I also knew that a cow who was what was called a good milker produced more milk than a calf needed. So I waited in the shelter of a hedge. Presently I saw a light in the too-near house and I imagined the cow's owner coming out, perhaps with a lantern, to do what was called the stripping off, the taking away of the surplus milk. But after a minute or two the light shone from an upper window.

I tipped what water remained in the broken jug onto the ground and laid my baby down under the hedge—not sure of the cow's behaviour. But I believed that all animals, approached gently, respond kindly. One woman with a sweet face had actually set her dog on me that day and I had held out my hand and said, "Good dog! Good dog!" and, to her amazement and disappointment, he had not attacked me. I now approached the cow in like manner. "Good cow, sweet cow," I said.

I had never milked a cow in my life and I was milking into a broken jug, not a wide bucket. I could not establish the rhythm of the milkmaid—one, two, three, four. I was obliged to hold the jug with one hand and squeeze the surprisingly leathery teats with the other. But I got enough. The first half jugful I drank immediately; the next more slowly. The third I kept for the morrow.

And the morrow was Sunday, a day which brought me another idea. Hen's eggs! Waking early to another day of blue sky and lark song and moving as quickly I could from the place where I had stolen the milk, I kept a sharp lookout for a place where there were hens. I did not go to the door and ask for charity—I had learned that at least in this part of the country charity was nonexistent. I lurked, watching the fowls, and when a hen came clucking from a nest, far enough away to be unnoticed from a kitchen window, I pounced, the egg still warm in my hand.

Raw eggs are disgusting in a way that people who have only eaten them cooked cannot imagine. So slimy. But I braced myself, opened my throat and let the disgusting but nourishing thing slide down. And my breasts grew turgid again and my child flourished, which was all that mattered to me. Hedgehogs are said to milk cows in the night and foxes are said to steal hens' eggs; probably these innocent beasts were blamed for my depredations. I lived on stolen milk and eggs until I reached Thetford, a busy town much like Baildon.

# CHAPTER 2

I'd set such high hopes on Thetford, seeing it as a place where I might find employment. I'd jib at nothing, I told myself. I'd become a night-soil carrier if nothing better offered, but I hoped for a scrubbing job. I had a muddled idea that butchers' shops and bakehouses needed a lot of scrubbing and I hoped to be paid in food. I had not found a suitable cow or a suitable nest on the previous day and the baby had been dissatisfied with his feed in the morning. The margin between semistarvation and starvation itself is a very narrow one.

Keeping to the path by the river, I had been able to maintain a certain standard of cleanliness. I'd torn the petticoat into two and sacrificed my shift so that when the child was soiled I could change him, but of course with no soap or other cleansing material his makeshift napkins retained their stains.

I came first to a butcher's shop, and the sight of so much meat, even in its raw state, was weakening—I of course imagined it sizzling on the spit. Bracing myself and trying to look less lame than I actually was, for my strained ankle was still swollen and painful and the ill-fitting shoes had raised blisters on my heels, I went into the shop and said, "Sir, I am looking for work. Have you any scrubbing I could do?"

He looked—there is no other word for it—furtive.

"You ain't local?"

"No." I wondered wildly where I should say I came from and could think only of Wymondham.

"Then you're a vagrant and I ought to hand you over. We passed a byelaw against beggars and vagrants, we was so pestered. Here, take this and be off." He turned and cut a thick slice from what is sometimes called travellers' sausage because one could carry it on a long journey along a route where the inns were known to be bad and yet eat well. It consisted of minced meat so salted and spiced that it could withstand rot and mould. It was encased in a pig's bladder.

"Not here! Not here!" the kind man exclaimed, as, my mouth watering, I was about to take a bite. "We all swore to stand by the rule..." A woman customer entered the shop and his manner changed. "Be off," he said, "before I call constable."

The woman said, "Thass right! We hev our own pore!"

I never even thanked him.

Across the road from the shop there was a patch of grass and a tree which cast wide dense shade. There I sat down and with slow deliberation, getting the utmost out of every mouthful, ate half the slice, saving the rest for what? To keep me and the poor baby alive for another day? And after that? Another?

Another? In a world where even to offer to scrub was wrong. I realised then that I had no option but to go home, brave Father's wrath and hope, just hope that the sight of the baby would soften him.

But I did not wish to put Father in an impossible position. I must not arrive home as a beggar or vagrant with a baby in my arms. I must arrive as though from a holiday in Devon with a poor child upon whom I had taken pity.

Just for once Fortune favoured me. I was wandering as purposelessly as a thread without a needle, but holding to the river, when I came to a great house, all in a bustle—the moving out for the summer cleansing of floors and drains. In our part of the country Merravay, Mortiboys and Muchanger and, since the building, our house counted as big, but not great. None of us, for instance, kept retainers or a flock of waiting women. We all, the Hattons, the Fennels, the Tresizes, managed with one house and had it cleansed and aired by moving about within it. This place, which I had stumbled upon in my anxiety to be out of a town where to beg was an offence, was in a different class altogether. I never knew to whom it belonged—probably the Duke of Norfolk.

Screened from view by the willows that dangled long green arms into the river, I watched a positive cavalcade. Two lumbering coaches, each pulled by six horses, carts, men on horseback, indescribable confusion and then a silence, so sudden as to be stunning. It looked to me as though this vast house were being left in the keeping of two old men and some dogs. Of dogs I had no fear, and the sausage had strengthened my body just as despair had strengthened my mind.

I went in by one of the innumerable doors, crossed a hall bigger than our church at home, mounted some stairs. I went through several anterooms, spacious and well furnished but stripped of all portable things. The silver and the ornaments one might have expected to find on the cupboards and buffets had all been taken away in the wagons or stored in some lockfast place.

I came at last to a bedroom. It had been left in some disarray, chests left open, some clothes on the floor. The great lady who owned the room evidently possessed a travelling set for her toilet, for there on the table was everything necessary to improve the appearance. And there was a glass in which I could see exactly how much my appearance needed to be improved.

The use of artifices such as rouge and lipsalve and false hair was curiously interlinked with rank. Decent middle sort of people were discreet, almost stealthy about their usage, and unmarried girls were supposed to use none at all lest some would-be suitor should be deceived. I was about to attempt to deceive the whole world so I felt justified in falsifying my face. The one thing I did not need was the white paste which could give even a sallow complexion the look of a lily petal. After so long in the open air, in sunshine, without so much as a sunbonnet I expected to look as tanned as a field worker, but my face was as pale as that of a corpse. So I applied rouge, rubbed it well in, wiped some away. It gave me a spurious look of health and even seemed to disguise the extreme thinness of my cheeks. I used the lipsalve in the same way.

I worked hardest on my hair, which was not merely tangled but had lost all lustre and too closely resembled the staring coat which was a sign of sickness in animals. I brushed and I brushed, but it did not respond. Then I found, amidst the clutter on the table, a flask of scented oil and applied it liberally.

Instantly my hair acquired sheen and became easy
to handle. The glass told me that I now looked healthy
and well-groomed, but hunted. As I was. Anybody
might come in at any moment, and in a town like
Thetford, illegal entry and theft could mean hanging. But nobody came.

I then turned my attention to clothes, for Mistress
Scott's gown was now far too big for me and was
soiled and creased from having been worn day and
night. The lady whose clothes I was about to purloin
was, of course, less tall than I was, but riding habits
were made long, and at the back of a closet I found
one, made of green velvet and slightly worn. Just
right. I also found a little shawl for the baby and
some shoes that fitted me much better. Presently I
was the very epitome of what I wanted to represent.

I looked like a young woman of decent family and
moderate means whose word might be trusted when
she said that she had found a baby abandoned in a
ditch. The child's makeshift napkins compared with
my own good velvet bore out the story. But I was
still miles from home and had no money. Nor in a
place like this could I use my father's name to get
credit. I wished most heartily that I was in Baildon
or even in Bury St. Edmund's where the name Tresize would have procured me anything I wanted.

I stole out of the great house and, with the baby's
rags concealed by the shawl, set about looking for
an inn. I soon found one. It was called the Bell and
was very much like Baildon's Hawk in Hand. I walked
into the yard with confidence and sat down on a
mounting block—young wife with baby awaiting her
husband. Nobody saw that inside the green velvet
there was a vagrant who must be told to be off. And
nobody could have guessed that I was waiting for a
chance to commit a hanging crime. I was planning
to steal a horse.

My chance came quite soon; three gaily dressed young men rode into the yard and the ostler ran forward. One of the young men said, "Let them drink. No need to unsaddle. We are not staying."

I hate to malign ostlers, but the behaviour of the man was typical of some. He ignored the horses completely and turned away to attend to those whose masters wanted more attention given to them and would therefore reward the man better.

Never in my life have I moved so fast. One-handed—for I was clutching my baby—and one-legged practically since my ankle had no spring in it, I was into the saddle of the nearest horse in the blink of an eye, out of the Bell yard in two blinks and out of Thetford in two minutes. I did not even allow myself to choose direction, but my luck held. I could see by the sun that I was going south and in no time at all I was in country exactly like that I had trudged through, a continuation of the heathland.

I was lucky too in that, as a young child and a hoydenish girl, I'd ridden astride and except for the pressure of the stirrup on my swollen foot my position would have been comfortable, but there was the baby. When I considered that I had outdistanced all pursuit I reined in and rearranged myself, making a kind of sling of the shawl, so that I had both hands free and the baby was suspended, almost like seamen in the hammocks which Father sometimes talked about. Infinitely more comfortable, he said, than fixed bunks.

I had hit upon—no choice in the matter—a good horse and I remembered that his previous owner had asked that he should be watered. We were now away from the river, but sometime in the afternoon we were in fertile country again and I saw a farmhouse with a duck pond. I rode past it, alighted, laid the baby in the shade and, leading the horse, hobbled back and asked of the farmer permission to water my horse.

He was agreeable: "Water, young mistress, is about the only thing to come free these days."

Surreptitiously I drank too. It was quite unlike river or well water. Quite horrible, but it served. I leaned against the horse's neck and promised him corn every day and a fresh bucket of water before the other was finished, if only he'd bear up bravely now.

I was again in a country where little farms stood like islands in the uncultivated waste, but I was in Suffolk and every stride of the horse brought me nearer home. That day I drank nothing but water, for I had imprudently abandoned the broken jug, and even had I found a milch cow far enough from a dwelling, it would have been safe from me. But the baby was satisfied that night; the horse had grass.

I had stolen the fine lady's comb and before lying down I removed my dress so that it should look fresh in the morning. Before dressing, I tried to feed the baby and failed miserably. He wailed and I felt inclined to cry, but even that turned out to be a blessing in disguise, for my figure had regained its flat-chested look, so that nobody would have suspected me of having had a child within the last few days and the baby's intermittent wailing fitted exactly with my story, which I needed rather sooner than I had anticipated.

Well before midday we rounded a bend in the road and there was a church. I had that familiar I-have-been-here-before feeling. Often this is a trick of the mind, but this morning it was real enough. I *had* been here before with Father when he came to buy cattle to turn out onto the Slipwell marshes. I remembered the name of the place—Ixworth—and, after an effort, the name of the man from whom he had bought the young stock—Master Gladwell. He lived in a black and white house, almost opposite the church.

I turned into the yard, trying over my story. Master Gladwell, hearing hooves, came out of a byre and stood looking at me, wrestling with his memory. That is one thing about having real chestnut-coloured hair; it is rare enough to be remarkable. I did not help him. I said, "Good morning, Master Gladwell. I trust I find you well."

"Ah," he said, coming to grips, "Mistress Tresize. I trust that I see you well."

"In health. In all other ways distraught. Was ever a woman in such a plight?"

I dismounted boldly and the movement wakened the baby, who had cried himself and his hunger to sleep.

"Until I recognised this place and remembered that *you* lived here, Master Gladwell, I was completely lost. And I picked up this poor thing from a ditch where some tinker had thrown it." I removed the decent shawl and showed the makeshift wrappings. My child did look like a baby abandoned by tinkers. And my story held together.

"I have been on a visit to my grandparents, in Devon. My father sent a servant and a cart to bring me home. All my baggage, everything I owned, is in that wagon. But in Devon I had acquired this horse— a good one as you will admit, having an eye to animals. Sometimes I rode in the cart, sometimes I rode the horse. And this morning, riding ahead, I lost my company and my way and found this poor little thing."

The baby, finding strength from somewhere, was now yelling.

"You went wrong at Main Cross, mistress. Five roads meet there. But come in. Dinner's about ready and no doubt my missus knows how to handle a child untimely weaned."

Excellent woman, she did. She warmed some milk from her dairy and dipped a twist of flannel into it. At first the baby refused this makeshift nipple and turned his head this way and that; but at last he settled for it and sucked lustily while she clucked to encourage him and expressed her wonder that any woman, however hard-pressed, could leave a baby in a ditch.

Manners maketh man, but clothes to a great degree make woman. I and my story were accepted here. The baby, full fed, slept on a settle while I shared the Gladwells' dinner, remembering to eat delicately, as a lady should. And although by some standards—by those of the great lady whose clothes I was wearing, whose comb I had stolen—I was just a common person, barely distinguishable from Mistress Gladwell, to the Gladwells I was a lady, the daughter of a man who owned not one but several properties.

So I restrained myself from gobbling, though the beef was the first I had tasted for months. And my horse was being handsomely treated in the stable.

Mistress Gladwell—inquisitive as women so often are—asked what my father would do with the child.

"He may call me a fool for losing my way," I said gaily, "but the baby—oh, he will accept it and farm it out to some tenant."

A crucial word. Gentlemen, of whatever degree, had tenants. It had the effect of stopping the gossipy talk, and the cattle dealer spent the rest of the meal explaining to me how I had gone wrong at Main Cross and how from here, if I followed his directions, I could get back to Ockley without going through Baildon.

Greatly refreshed and greatly cheered, I rearranged the baby in the sling and rode away. I had a story that sounded feasible to ordinary people and if I could just convince Father of that I half-believed that he would accept it, too. He would of course put the child into the care of one of his labourers' wives, and I should have to avoid any undue show of affection for it; but it would have enough to eat, and after my experience of starving that seemed a thing of the utmost importance. Still, I was nervous as I neared home, positively trembling as I crossed the bridge. The confidence inspired by the Gladwells' behaviour oozed away.

There is a saying that the thing you dread most never happens, and I need not have dreaded Father's wrath. He'd had another stroke on the previous day and it was my Uncle Thomas who met me at the door.

He said, "Thank God! Lettice, never have I been so truly glad to see anyone. He died of a heat stroke, poor man—and without pain. But nobody knew where you were. I was beginning to think I must have you cried in every Devon town.... And what is that?"

"A baby. A tinker's brat, left in a ditch." I shouted for Margery and said, "Here, take this and feed it as best you can," for it was awake and ready for food again.

I think my uncle hardly noticed, he was so relieved to see me, for I was suddenly, for the first time in my life, of supreme importance. And all because of Father's most unusual will. It granted me such complete power until Simon reached the age of eighteen that it was for me to decide whether Father went to his grave in elm or oak, decked with silver or brass.

Granted the will had been made before I so grievously offended him, but it was proof of his affection and trust—something I had always been sure of even when he allowed Kate to ill-use me, even when he sent me to Oxney. That thought brought tears; I regretted that his last thoughts of me must have been tinged with anxiety and anger.

I said, through my tears, "Where is Simon?"

"In the field, he does not yet understand his loss."

But, warned of my arrival, he came running in and at sight of me cried, "Oh, Letty, I have missed you so much. I am so glad you are back." We mingled our tears for a while, but he quickly recovered and began asking awkward questions. The grey horse, had I bought it in Devon? Yes, I said. "And there's a baby in the kitchen, did you buy that too?"

"No. I found it. In a ditch. Screaming so my horse shied."

"Poor thing."

"Poor thing indeed."

My uncle said, "Lettice, about the funeral..."

# PART FOUR

# Narrative by
# Alan Heath

# CHAPTER 1

I must have been about six when I began to question my place in the world. I was a very fortunate boy and my place was very comfortable.

We all lived in a big house: Mistress Tresize, her brother, Master Tresize, and two or three servants.

On quiet days I lived in the parlour and Mistress Tresize played games with me and taught me my letters and how to count. But sometimes, when there was company, she'd say, "Run away, dear. Find Margery." And I didn't mind at all, for everybody in the kitchen was kind to me too, though not quite with Mistress Tresize's kindness. I still think that animals and children have a special sense about such things—the kindness that comes from the heart and the kindness imposed by custom or circumstances.

I had none of either kind from Master Tresize, whose name was Simon. One of my earliest memories is of going towards him, pleased that I could walk, and being pushed over instead of being lifted and praised.

When I was six I had a pony and Mistress Tresize taught me to ride, and I remember Master Tresize saying in a very nasty voice, "That is a better pony than I had to start with." She just laughed and said, "Simon, when I am too old to ride your acres, Alan can do it, he will need to ride well."

My name was Alan Heath—but once when, much later, I went and looked in the parish register, my name was not there.

One's place in the world is reflected in how people address you—and how you address them. I always used the "Mistress" and "Master" when addressing Lettice and Simon, but in my mind I used their given names. Once, copying one of the maids, I called Lettice "Madam" and she looked startled and not at all pleased. Everybody simply called me Alan. So although I knew that I was a fortunate boy and had many advantages denied to most, there was always some mystery and, being no less inquisitive than other children, I tended to listen at half-open doors and sometimes ask questions.

Lettice and Simon talking in the parlour:

"...luckier than you had any right to expect, my dear. But he must *not* be seen in company. The hair alone..."

"Yes, I shall speak severely to Margery. You can't blame a child for drifting towards sounds of merriment."

What was wrong with my hair, except that it was always cut very close, like a ploughman's? Lettice wore hers long and pinned up; Simon's was long and curled. We all had the same coloured hair, more red than brown, the colour that in a horse is called chestnut.

Margery and Maude talking in the kitchen:

"He always struck me as a man who didn't mind overmuch what people thought and with a mad wife locked up all that time, he was entitled to a bastard or two. So why such a roundabout way of going about it? It could have put the mistress's name at risk."

"I've often wondered myself."

"Well you needn't and you shouldn't. His navel wasn't healed and she flat as a board. And on horseback, too!"

Puzzle upon puzzle.

It was far easier to understand remarks about my riding Simon's acres for him. When he was of age he would inherit a good deal of property. There was all the land on our side of the river, Top Field, Nether Field, Ten Acre and Eggar's Piece, and some pasture. There was some land on the other side of the river called Bowman's. There was a big sheep run at Stratton Strawless and a great stretch of marshland at Slipwell upon which cattle were pastured each summer before being sent to market in London; and there were two farms, both run by foremen, not let to tenants, one at Clevely and one at Muchanger.

And for all Simon cared they might have been on the moon. He was far too fine a gentleman to bother about such things. It wasn't until much later that I realised that he was extremely stupid and that his understanding was so limited that business was outside his range, so he devoted himself to what he could do, which was dressing himself up—he was extremely handsome—and entertaining people and being entertained by them. He had a passion for gambling and he was always asking Lettice to give or lend him some money, and she was always saying that he must make his allowance do and then giving in but looking pained. Once when she was more than ordinarily obdurate about it he called her a skinflint and said, "The cautious Turnbull blood runs in your veins."

She said, "And what runs in yours, Simon?"

"How can you be so unkind? I try to forget. Letty, that howling...How could you remind me?"

"Yes, how could I? It was unkind. I apologise."

Howling! When I was very small and too young to understand anything, there had been nights and days—but nights mostly—when it had sounded as though all the dogs in the neighbourhood were baying to the moon or that one of the few wolves left in Layer had fallen into a trap. I had been aware of it, and frightened until Letty explained about an afflicted woman who lived in the dovecote, a woman who was deaf and dumb so far as ordinary speech was concerned but who could at times make animal noises. They meant nothing, she said, and I was so busy growing up that I did not even notice when the noise stopped. Nor—so self-absorbed are the young—did I notice that a woman, very short but thickset, still lived in the dovecote and came every day, or every other day, to take away provisions from our kitchen.

I did not, therefore, understand why Lettice and Simon were now referring to the howling and he was calling her unkind.

It always seemed to me that she was, if anything, too kind to him. They had little disputes, always about money, or Simon's fondness for dog fights or cock fights, which she denounced as cruel as well as likely to lead into bad company. Then he'd laugh and say it was in the nature of dogs and cocks to fight and that many of the people he met at such gatherings were the same as those who came to dine or sup and play cards at our house. By and large it was true, and she had no answer.

But over and over she would try to interest him in other things.

She'd say, "They start reaping at Wood Farm tomorrow. I shall go. Come with me?"

"Do you mean Clevely or Muchanger? Every hamlet has its Wood Farm."

She'd tell him and he'd make some excuse for not going. "Deputise for me, sweet sister."

It took me quite a long time to realise how very jealous I was, because as soon as Lettice and I were alone, going about the business of the farms and the fields, we seemed so absolutely one, so much so that often we'd start the same sentence at the same time and must touch wood and wish for luck, as was the custom.

Often, when some bit of stupidity on his part made her look sad, I'd go hot all over and long to spring at him, scratch his face, kick his shins, but circumstances had made me precocious and I realised that such action would be folly—and bad for me. I was here on sufferance, a child Lettice had saved from a foundling's fate; Simon was heir to a considerable estate.

I was eight when Simon had his eighteenth birthday and came into his inheritance. It was somehow typical that whereas ordinary people have to wait until they are twenty-one to come of age, Simon Tresize should be regarded as a man while still in his teens.

The birthday was to be properly celebrated, with a great supper and a ball. Talk began about it weeks before and there was a great argument over refurbishing the place.

"Everything here must be a hundred years old," he said, "and it all looks as if it was made by the village carpenter."

"Much of it was. Not a hundred years ago, but made to last for two hundred."

"Well, I want new."

"It will cost a great deal."

"I know. But what is money for, except to spend? Anything you feel sentimental about you can move to your side of the house."

That was the first intimation I had of a situation which meant nothing to me at the time but had a great—one might say an overwhelming—effect upon my life in the future. The man who had sired both Lettice and Simon, but on different women—I cannot now remember exactly how or when I solved that bit of the mystery—had decreed in his will that Lettice was to have one side of the house for as long as she lived. She was also to receive out of the estate the sum of a hundred pounds yearly.

That man was Simon's father and Simon was stupid; his father must have been stupid, too. For no man ever left a will better calculated to breed dissension. (But of course I am now looking at the situation from a man's standpoint, not from that of a child of tender years.)

It was a grand ball and I saw most of it, crouched on the landing. I'd heard all the arguments about where the feast should be held and where the dancing should be. And Simon had decided that the dancing should be in the hall and the supper laid out in two rooms on his side of the house.

I saw ladies as gay and pretty as butterflies, gentlemen gaudy as peacocks and I heard the music. Every village in that day had its fiddler, sometimes two, and there were men who played the flute. Simon had gathered as many as possible of them together and I had heard him deploring the fact that his father, when building, had not thought of a gallery.

Simon was fortunate even in his weather. On the

whole that had been a bad summer, chilly and over-
cast, even in June. It brought murrain to cattle and
the sweating sickness to people, but that day the sun
shone and everybody said that summer had come at
last, which added to the gaiety.

Lettice looked beautiful, though she had no spar-
kling jewels; but her dress was tawny, like her hair.
She did not dance, but sometimes sat with older ladies on the new sofas that had replaced the old set-
tles, or moved about, seeing that all was well. Lady
Fennel, I remember, wore a great necklace of yellow
stones which went well with a primrose-coloured
gown and I made up my mind there and then that
if any effort of mine could procure such a necklace
for Lettice she should have it even if it meant breaking my back.

I was then so young and silly that I believed that
hard work, attention to business and care with pen-
nies could achieve anything.

Between Lettice and Simon now there were no
more disputes about money; for all was his, though
he still did nothing to earn a penny. Lettice saw to
everything, just as before, and he did not hesitate to
remind her that now she was being well paid for her
efforts. She said, "Yes, I suppose I am the best paid
hired hand in England," and managed a smile, but
the hurt look was there.

The separation of our two households did not come
about suddenly, nor was it final, and certainly it
worked to my advantage for I saw more of Lettice
when she took supper and spent the evening in her
own part of the house. The arrangement began soon
after Simon's coming of age; he wanted to have a
supper party and when he named his guests, Lettice
looked disapproving. "All strangers," she said.

"You know Nicholas Helmar and Ralph Hatton," Simon said defensively.

"I know they're both wild."

"Well, if you feel like that, avoid them. Stay in your own house."

"I think I will."

The Priory might almost have been built with some such division in mind; it was really two houses, joined by the stone hall, big enough to serve as a dancing place but now on ordinary days used only as an entry and that seldom, since each of the flanking wings had a door of its own.

I think Simon was pleased when Lettice accepted his suggestion so easily, and yet a little dismayed too, for he hastened to say, "I hope you will sup with me when I am alone, or have guests of whom you do approve."

"But of course. Whenever I am invited. And I hope you will dine or sup with me whenever you feel inclined."

It was a declaration, not of war but of division. And actually she was so fond of him and took such pains to please him when he supped with us that only I—and the servants—realised that a slight breach had been made.

Over servants Simon was truculent. Margery and Maude, he said, did very well, but a gentleman should have men to wait upon him, not two snuffly old women, helped out—as on his birthday celebration—by village women.

Lettice said, "If it pleases you to hire men, do so; but they ask more wage and I must remind you that this has been a bad year."

But for her telling him, he would not have known; the summer, so disastrous to flocks, herds and grain, had given him a fine day or two around his birthday, and for such a bone-headed fellow that was enough.

Informed, he said, "Dear Lettice, no bad season can affect you. Your annuity is the first charge on the estate. If I lacked a crust, you must be paid."

At that offensive speech she did not look hurt but momentarily angry. Colour rushed into her face and her eyes flashed.

"That was where Father was so wise! He knew that while I had a crust you would never starve!

The years, even the unseasonable ones, clinging to seasonableness, moved on, and one day Lettice said to me, "Alan, you are eleven and it is time you went to school."

# CHAPTER 2

I have heard men dwell on their schooldays, the happiest years or the most wretched years of their lives. I always think that those who speak thus are men to whom nothing much has happened in later life. Life at Baildon was spartan, very cold in winter, and not too much food at any time, but looking back I remember only the misery of being homesick for Ockley and for Lettice, and then the joy of moving steadily up the form, from bottom to top and so on to the next.

Also, because boys are great gossips, I learned about the father of Lettice and Simon, a man who came out of nowhere, bought a property with a curse on it, defied the curse and prospered. He'd had three wives, one of them a howling maniac—Simon's mother. There seemed to be a general opinion that he had fathered me too, and that I was born out of wedlock and therefore was a bastard.

A smaller, more timid boy might have suffered from this stigma, but I was big and strong and had the devil of a temper even then. Those who used the word suffered more than I did.

I used to go home every Christmas and for the long harvest holiday each summer, and on several occasions between these two happy times, Lettice would come and ask permission to take me out. We went to the Hawk in Hand and I ate myself near to bursting.

Each time I saw her I loved her more and, since love has a keen eye, noticed changes. She'd always been a very thin woman, but she grew thinner and her hair had silver threads in it. She had an ankle and a wrist which had given twinges in damp weather; now she moved as though they hurt all the time. I had noticed how soon the wives of poor men seemed to grow old, then once aged were impervious to the years' damage, but it seemed all wrong in a woman of her position who had always lived well and comfortably and not been dragged down by a brood of children.

Once I said to her, "Are you quite well?"

"Quite well, my dear."

"Then are you worried about anything?"

"I have some cares. Nothing for you to worry about."

"Is it—Simon?"

"Partially. Now, Alan, eat up or I shall feel I have wasted my errand."

It had always been a thing understood between us that if I did sufficiently well at school I should proceed to Cambridge and pursue some kind of study which would enable me to earn a living, since I had no patrimony. During my first schooldays, when I was homesick, I had little taste for such a future, but as time went on and I proved so apt a scholar, I grew resigned, even enthusiastic about it. I decided to study law, for Lettice's family, the Turnbulls, were several of them lawyers and, though not rich, substantial and respected people.

So I was sixteen, school behind me, and all that stood between me and Cambridge was an examination there, a mere formality, my masters assured me, just a precaution against some unlikely boy, favoured by his masters, getting into the university on their word alone. I had no fear of it.

It was sweltering hot weather, but when Lettice came down to breakfast one morning she was rubbing and twisting her hands together as one does on a chilly day. She was walking badly, too.

Having greeted me, she said, almost with gaiety, "They say old wounds ache in extremes of weather. My wrist and my ankle I can understand, but my fingers defeat me. I never offended *them.*"

"Let me see."

She held them out; the fingers all curved inwards, the knuckles swollen and shiny. Then she withdrew them hastily and said, "It is nothing, my dear. I consulted Dr. Standish some time back and he said it was gout and told me to avoid red wine and gave me some pills, colchicum, which did no good."

"I'm sorry," I said, remembering a time when I'd had earache and she'd comforted me, holding a bag of hot salt to the aching ear. Saying soft, comforting words.

"I'm sorry too," she said, taking the words in the wrong way. "Everything comes at once these days. The wool merchant is out at Strawless, and as slippery a rogue as ever wore boots. And the first batch of cattle—in fact the last—coming up at Slipwell.

A full two months early. But Simon sold Slipwell, and our beasts must be away before Lammas."

"He sold Slipwell! Why? It was one of the most prosperous..."

"I know, I know. But he said he needed the money and I have no power now. Only responsibility. Unless I can prove to him that the wool pays, Alan...he might sell Stratton Strawless, too. Everything that our father worked so hard for...I am sorry, my dear one....Eat your breakfast. This"—she rubbed her crooked fingers and her wrist—"wears off as the day widens. I shall manage."

I said, "Look here, my dear"—and that was the first time I had ever ventured to use an endearment to her—"just tell me what to do, what to look out for. I can be at Strawless in the morning and at Slipwell in the afternoon. And God help any slippery rogue I come across!"

She said, "If you could...This is nothing. Just one of my bad days. And Simon at Newmarket."

"As well there as anywhere. He couldn't tell a maggoty fleece from a sound one."

I half-expected a rebuke for that, but all she said was, "Then I will rest today....If there is any argument in either place, hold over the business. These attacks seldom last long."

Thus, imperceptibly, the current of my life changed. I supervised the sale of the wool, the removal of our beasts from the marshes and then it was harvesttime. Every day Lettice said she would be better tomorrow. And when our harvest was in full swing she did limp out to see the last sheaf carried home, but it was painful to see the effort it required. Dr. Standish came again and did not mention gout but spoke of an inflammation of the joints usually confined to the elderly. In so young a sufferer, he said, some remission could be hoped for.

I then mentioned, tentatively, my plan to abandon Cambridge.

"My dear, no! I will not have you sacrifice your whole future. Simon is so profligate. In a few years' time all may be lost. You would be joining a sinking ship. I cannot allow it."

I argued; she was stubborn. I lost my temper.

"And who gave you authority over me?" I demanded. "Even if your father were my father, too..."

She made a smothered noise. "Who said that? Who *dared?*"

Later, when I knew the whole truth, I understood why the idea so shocked her. She said, "That is a vile lie! Your father was dead before you were born."

"And my mother?"

"A friend of mine...There was no money and sooner than see you in a foundling home, I—I brought you here. If you had a happy childhood—I tried to give you that—then you owe me some obedience."

"But I don't wish to go to Cambridge. I never did. I was homesick enough at school..."

"You survived!"

"I know, but it is not an experience I wish to repeat."

"You are too young to make such a decision. You are too young to understand. If Simon goes on as he is doing, we shall all be ruined. My annual allowance is the first charge on the estate, but, dear Alan, *think*. If there is no estate—and that could happen all too easily—we shall have a roof over our heads and no more. Gambling has ruined wider estates than this. God help us, haven't I enough on my mind without you trying to defeat me?"

She rubbed her crooked fingers and looked so distressed that I said, "Very well, dear Lettice, I will not oppose you."

It had occurred to me that though the way into

King's College at Cambridge was a hard and stony one, the way out was wide open. I had only to fail that examination, and any boy with wits enough to pass one can fail one if he is so minded. I failed most ignominiously.

# CHAPTER 3

The next four years were almost happy. The two households under the same roof were more separated than ever, so I had Lettice to myself a great deal. Her disability came and went; there were some days when she could ride abroad and others when she could not even manage the stairs. Farfetched as it may sound, I often thought that there was a connection between her mental and physical states; she always seemed to be worse after she'd had a quarrel with Simon.

I was never the occasion of such disputes, for even while I was overseeing his affairs he behaved as though I were not there. He never offered to pay me a penny and his invitations to Lettice to sup or dine on the other side of the house never included me. Nor did the talks about business and policy, though during Lettice's bad spells a great deal depended upon me. He'd come to our side and say, "Letty, a private word with you," and wait ostentatiously for me to take myself off. And almost always after such interviews, her hands seemed more cramped and her other joints stiffer. At such times I'd lift her, light as a leaf, and carry her up to bed; she said this was much less painful than Margery heaving and Maude pushing. Then she would say, "What on earth should I do without you, Alan?" but at other times she lamented my not going to Cambridge and talked about ruin engulfing us all.

It was slow ruin at first, for though Simon was an inveterate and unlucky gambler, the men with whom he associated played for limited stakes, none of them being outstandingly wealthy. But one of them, Nicholas Helmar, had friends in London and it was he who introduced Simon to the most dangerous form of gambling—investing in vague schemes guaranteed to pay incredible rates of interest. This speculating fever had been started by the East India Company, founded in the last year of the old Queen's reign. It had proved very successful, being run by businessmen with agents on the spot. Men as simple and avaricious as Simon Tresize handed over their money to men who promised to make them rich and merely enriched themselves.

Simon had sold the marshes at Slipwell while I was still at school. Two years later he sold the sheep run at Stratton Strawless, so one of his sources of income was lost—there were no animals on the hoof for the hungry London markets—and in the next year he sold the outlying farms at Clevely and Muchanger.

Rubbing her aching neck with her bent fingers, Lettice said, "Father would turn in his grave. We are now back where he started—and he worked so hard..." She was a woman who never cried, but she looked at me with desperate eyes. "Suppose he takes it into his silly head to sell the Priory. Honestly, he is capable of it. Where then should we be?"

"He could not sell the roof over your head," I said, trying to find something comforting to say.

"I know. But imagine strangers—and almost certainly hostile—in the rest of the house. In the garden..."

I imagined it. I also assessed my prospects. A failed schoolman, which was what I was, had two occupations open to him; he could become an usher in a school or go as tutor to a boy whose father did not desire him to suffer the rough and tumble of school life. Having damaged not only my own reputation but that of my school in my deliberately poor performance at Cambridge, I could not count upon an usher's post and neither in that, nor in a tutor's, could a man provide for and look after a crippled woman.

I said, "Lettice, have you any money?"

She looked distressed and her hands cramped tighter. She knuckled her neck.

"A little, not much. Things have not worked out as Father intended. Simon has very seldom paid me my full allowance and turns surly when pressed. Also, hoping to save the sheep run, I made him a loan.... Don't look like that, Alan. It was weak-minded of me, but I know better than anyone why sense cannot be expected of him. And I was so fond of him when he was a child. I regarded him as my own."

If I scowled it was not in criticism of her. I knew how charming Simon could be when he chose. And the curious thing was that the years, ageing Lettice before her time and bringing me to full growth, had not touched him at all. He was still a golden-haired, carefree boy, living in high style with two men-servants and a maid or two, entertaining lavishly and lately making visits to London. I recognised now the jealousy that I had always felt for him, mingled with resentment for his shabby treatment of Lettice, who must have been hard-pressed, keeping herself and me and Margery and Maude and the poor deaf and dumb creature who lived in a little hut at the base of the old dovecote. She came to the kitchen door each morning for the day's supplies, and if there was insufficient meat she mouthed and made noises and waved her arms about.

I scowled, thinking of this and also of the two patches of land on the other side of the river. They'd once been small holdings, part of a village community where a plough, an ox could be shared and neighbours helped each other at busy times. The father of Lettice and Simon had acquired them somehow and made them into one cornfield, known as Bowman's.

And it would be the next to go.

Both holdings had once had a house; only one had been preserved, but if I could get my hands on that acre or so of land, and that house, Lettice and I would be safe no matter what happened to the Priory and its fields.

"I said, "Could you manage twenty pounds?"

"Oh, yes. What is more, at Christmas I shall insist upon having my allowance. Even if it means a quarrel. What have you in mind?"

"If you can trust me, I'd sooner not tell you until I have accomplished my aim. But it is something safe, I promise you."

"That I don't doubt. Oh, my dear, if only you had had Simon's opportunities—or he your good sense."

I moved very cautiously. I had a feeling, justified by no more than instinct, that if Simon knew I had my eye on Bowman's, he'd defeat me in some way—put up the price or refuse to sell.

During the time while I had worked for Simon I'd made the acquaintance of cattlemen and woolmen and butchers and it was easy enough for me to find somebody who would keep a sharp lookout for me should Bowman's Piece come on the market. And I started to swindle Simon systematically, arguing that he had never paid me and had failed to pay Lettice her allowance and might even be mad enough to sell the Priory to finance some wildcat scheme.

We no longer sent flocks and herds to London but we did send the occasional home-bred beast to market, and I began to lie about the prices they fetched. I kept my peculations within limits—a little here, a little there—and when I began I had a tender conscience about it. The first time Lettice said, when I handed over the day's takings, "So little! I thought beef always went up just before Christmas," my heart hammered. I was afraid I should blush as I said as carelessly as I could, "It was a slow market; more animals than buyers. Did I do wrong? Should I have paid the drover to bring them home?" I hoped she would think I was blushing over an error of judgement.

I soon became hardened, however—helped by the fact that when she tackled him about the money due to her, Simon shillied and shallied and gave her ten pounds instead of the twenty-five due. I thought, Never mind, my dear, we'll get even with him yet!

After Christmas came the corn selling. Men with few acres and little space hustled their grain on to the market as soon as it was threshed. We at the Priory had always been able to hold back and wait for the rising prices in February. Lettice expressed surprise again when I turned over to her less than the whole that the millers and corn dealers had paid, and I did not blush, nor did my heart hammer. I said, "More farmers are prospering now and can afford to hold on to their grain."

She trusted me implicitly, and Simon trusted her. And soon I had twenty pounds of my own to add to what she was prepared and able to lend me.

Yet the crash, when it came, caught me unawares, for I had reckoned upon another year at least, and upon the small patch, Bowman's across the river, being sold off and safe in my hands before Simon even contemplated turning the Priory into cash.

It happened in early March and I shall dislike that pleasant, promising time of the year until I die. Nose down, like a good hound on the scent, I had been following my own plan and had gone to Cambridge. Because it was there, called up for an examination and sent down for failure, I had found myself seated beside a small reticent man who taught Greek but was really a botanist and had an infatuation for a vegetable called a potato.

Even he, inspired by my interest, and coaxed into talk, could not tell me much about the origin of this vegetable. Some people, he said, gave the credit to Sir Walter Raleigh, some to Sir Francis Drake and some to the Spaniards who, wrecked when the Armada failed, had introduced it to Ireland. But he said it could be cooked in various ways and that it was prolific beyond belief. One tuber the size of a man's palm, saved until spring and then carefully divided, planted in good earth, not too damp, yielding a hundredfold.

I had eaten my portion but had not recognised it for what it was; I'd thought it a meat dish cooked in some unusual way and used to eke out the poor meat.

"A few rich people grow it in their gardens," the old scholar said. "Dug when young—which is wasteful—it is a luxury, tastier than asparagus. In ten years it will be in general use and in twenty a substitute for bread amongst the poor."

I had not thought much about this conversation until I began to rack my brain for some way of turning Bowman's into a livelihood should it ever come into my hands, which it had so far shown no signs of doing. However, in order to be prepared, I thought I would make a beginning by using part of the Priory garden. So I went to Cambridge, found the old botanist and came home with a sack of potatoes and a headful of instructions. He charged me five pounds and was rather apologetic about it. "You see, I thought that one way of getting the good tuber known was to give it away to the poor people in the Fens. It is a most remarkable plant; it grows well in the peaty soil there and equally well in the sandy soil near Newmarket. But although I am permitted to grow a row or two in some of the college gardens, nobody will agree to a patch, so I have to hire a field." He eyed the good clothes and the good horse—all provided by Lettice—and said, "You are not poor so you must pay for those who cannot."

I had always regarded the garden at the Priory as Lettice's province. Simon took no interest in it, though he liked it to look well—a gentleman's residence should have a garden. I explained to Lettice what I was about to try and she was interested. In fact, the next day being one of those March days with a feeling of summer to it, she came out and watched me set to work with a spade.

The old scholar had spoken of a row and of a patch and of a field, but I was obliged to dot my tubers— already sprouted—about in odd places, marking each spot with a twig to which I tied a scrap of rag, so that the village man who came to keep the garden tidy should not, by accident, disturb my plantings.

I ran out of space before I had disposed of my sackful and then, following my dream, I thought of Bowman's. The winter wheat was already green in that field, so nobody would need to work on the headlands where the plough oxen turned until men went with scythes at harvestime and by then the "luxury" crop, the summer dish that was better than asparagus, would be ready for digging.

The potatoes had been in the ground for a week when Simon, who had been in London with Nicholas Helmar and Ralph Hatton, came home, a changed man. His cap was without its usual jewelled ornament, he wore no rings, chains, brooches, even his shoe buckles were gone. He was completely sober and his demeanour was solemn.

At first sight I thought, He's turned Puritan! Such sudden changes were not unknown: whoremongers marry and become very hot against whoring; sober men take to the bottle; flighty girls become model wives. And Simon, with his poor mental ability and his proneness to be influenced by any stronger personality, was just the man to make such a *volte-face,* and to do so in an extreme manner. I wondered how long it would last. With him any change could only be for the better and I had nothing against Puritans as such; on the whole they were industrious and honest in their dealings and law-abiding. They tended to be dull and rather smug and to talk of God as though He were a special crony.

Simon had not turned Puritan. He came home in the afternoon, and in the evening, half tipsy, wearing a richly embroidered robe and slippers, came over to our side of the house. He said, "Good evening, Lettice. I must talk to you." His manner was now uneasy, that of a man who had no great taste for his errand but had braced himself with wine. As usual,

he waited for me to withdraw and as usual I took
my time about it, fussing over Lettice; would she
like a footstool, or an extra cushion to her back?
Despite the fine bright weather, or because she had
overexerted herself to watch me planting potatoes,
she was having a bad spell.

It was still dusk and I went around the garden,
idly visiting my potato plants though I knew that
nothing could possibly show above ground for at least
three weeks, and then only if the warm weather
continued. But the daffodils were out, and for lack
of anything else to do, I gathered some. If she couldn't
get into the garden, the garden should go to her.

Presently I saw the windows of his side of the
house begin to glow and guessed that he had gone
back to his own place, so I went in, carrying the
flowers awkwardly. I could see that something had
upset her deeply but she had the courtesy to say,
"Thank you, my dear," as I laid the daffodils beside
her. Then, in a cool, remote voice, she said, "Well,
now the worst has happened. He proposes to sell the
land, this house, everything."

I said, "Oh!" and sat down. Everything included
Bowman's, and at a forced sale, such as I imagined
this to be, it would go cheaply. "Did he say when?"

"As soon as possible. A man called Turnberry—
a mercer at Colchester—is looking for a place to
retire to. He is coming to look over it early next week.
Alan, the trouble is he wants the whole house and
Simon has as good as promised that we shall move."

Hugging my secret plan, I said, "Well you once
said how much you disliked the thought of sharing
the house with strangers."

"Dislike it or not, I shall do just that. I told Simon
so. He was most abusive. But as I pointed out, the
law is the law. Nobody can evict me."

I let my glance flick over the furniture, all old and

massive. The smaller of the two court cupboards, the gate-legged table, the fireside settle—yes, there would be room for them at Bowman's. And there was already a small garden there. I'd extend it. And I'd take some of her favourite plants—I'd steal them at night.

"Nobody can evict you," I agreed, "but unwilling neighbours can be very unpleasant."

I was willing her to say she would move if she had a suitable place to go to. I was willing her to say, "Oh, Alan, what shall I do?"

"It will be very unpleasant," she said. "A houseful of grudging Turnberrys on my doorstep, and him hating me just across the river."

"The river...?"

"Yes. He is keeping Bowman's. It needs, he says, only minor alterations to make it a suitable residence."

My heart plummeted into my boots. At the same time my mind scurried round like a rat in a box trap. If Simon wanted her out he must surely have suggested some alternative accommodation for her. Let it not be Bowman's, dear God; even for *her* sake I could not share so narrow a house with him and remain civil.

"Did he suggest that you go to Bowman's, too?"

She laughed. A sound without mirth.

"After the things we said to each other this evening! No, his plan for me has a beautiful simplicity. Since there will now be no estate and therefore no income for me, I'm a suitable candidate for an almshouse. You know the ones. One window looking straight on to the brewery wall. It is known as Blind Row!" It is impossible to describe the bitterness in her voice.

I thought of all she had done for him: riding to Slipwell, to Strawless, Clevely and Muchanger, keeping his accounts, leaving him free to play the fine gentleman and ruin himself. Rage flared in me, but I stayed cool, just as she was.

"I'm not certain that he can, by the stroke of a pen, make you a pauper. There is the letter of the law and there is the spirit. I'm no lawyer, but I think this bears looking into. If you were to have—but often did not—a hundred pounds annually from the estate, it seems to me that when the estate ends, you are entitled to a proportion. I also think that you could make a back claim for what he owes you and for the money you say you lent him at various times. Master Thomas Turnbull is your kin, and a lawyer. I think he would uphold you."

"I was careless, you see, my dear. I should have insisted that Simon paid my money to Tom and Tom handed it over to me—charging for the service. But I trusted Simon, took less than my due—which, since we are using legal terms, may have established a precedent. And I certainly lent money, time and again, with nothing to show for it. Also, although Tom Turnbull is my cousin, he is also Simon's godfather. It would be embarrassing for the poor fellow."

"Very well," I said. "But have I your permission to put this point of view to Simon and try to make him see reason?"

"You can try. And you may certainly tell him that nothing, no threats or curses or Turnberrys, will move me by an inch. Pushed to it, I will keep pigs in this parlour and fowls in the room beyond. We'll do, my dear, we'll do. I have faced worse things...."

She then said that the quarrel with Simon and the bad news had exhausted her and she would like me to help her upstairs. So I carried her and, doing so, realised that I had been edged into a position where I could give her nothing but my body's strength to bolster her frailty. Not enough!

# CHAPTER 4

Simon, who had meantime been drinking, laughed his rather high, silly laugh and said, "This is rich. A rich joke! *Your* coming here to scold *me* for my treatment of Lettice! Take a look at yourself, boy, and see what a drag you've been to her all these years."

I took a look. Quite unnecessary. I was well aware of what I owed her.

"Since I left school I have done my best to repay by taking over her work. Work connected with keeping your estate together. Now you propose to sell out and suggest that she should go to an almshouse. That is shameful. And she told me to make you understand that nothing would make her budge."

"That we shall see. One of Turnberry's reasons for moving is to get good country air for his grand-children. He has upwards of a dozen—all unruly brats."

He laughed again and I had the old desire to attack him. I battened it down and went on with some words calculated to take the grin off his face. "It was plainly your father's desire that Mistress Tresize should be safe and comfortable all her life. Any good lawyer will find a way of making you pay her out of what you get for the land. Not to mention the money you've borrowed from her."

"Even Tom Turnbull can't get blood out of a stone. I have debts. When they are paid there'll be little enough to keep me, leave alone pay annuities."

"The law may regard hers as a prior claim."

"That we shall see," he said again, comfortably wrapped about with that attitude that makes gamblers—the certainty that *this* time they'll be lucky.

He'd never looked at me kindly, either through me, or past me or, in an unavoidable confrontation, with a chill hostility. Now he looked at me with such hatred that for a moment his handsome face was ugly.

"You'd be better employed," he said, "looking about for a job. It is, after all, generally reckoned a man's duty to look after his mother!"

I was struck speechless, like the poor woman who still took Lettice's charity at the back door.

"Don't look so damned simple," Simon said. "You must have known. One look in the glass..." As though we were puppets, both tugged by the same string, we made identical movements, hand to hair. At the same time Simon's other hand went out to his wine cup and he lifted it and drank. My other hand fumbled in darkness and space, nothing to cling to. But after a reeling moment I caught hold of the back of one of his velvet-padded chairs. On it I steadied myself as he said with great viciousness, "I well remember your arrival, miaowing like a kitten and wrapped in filthy rags. She said that she found you in a ditch, a baby discarded by tinkers.... Bear that in mind when you go into who owes who. You've had a good home and everything paid for out of what was, had the will been just, my estate." Plainly he'd grudged me every mouthful.

I turned and walked away, mounted the stairs in our side of the house and went into Lettice's room. She was reading. I took the book from her and, holding her hands, said, "Now I know the truth..."

Just for once Simon had said something with which I was in full agreement. It was a man's duty to look after his mother, especially one so fond and dauntless as she had proved herself to be. So I took stock of my assets. I was young, strong and healthy; I had some knowledge of farming. I owned nothing except a few potatoes, all in somebody else's soil. I was capable of acting as somebody's agent but there were few great landowners in our part of Suffolk and agents' jobs always went to younger brothers or cousins. I could hire myself as a shepherd, ploughman or drover but I should never earn enough to keep my mother in anything but squalor. So I thought the first thing to do was to call on Tom Turnbull. He had little comfort to offer. He repeated Simon's words about the impossibility of getting blood out of a stone. He said that nothing but sheer necessity would have driven Simon to sell the Priory and he feared that whatever price he received for it would be swallowed up in debts.

"And Mistress Tresize's claim has no priority?"

"It is not so stated. She had an allowance to be paid out of the estate. No estate, no allowance." He made a helpless gesture with his hands. "It is all most unfortunate."

"For her?"

"Yes."

"In addition to everything else, she has lent him money."

"Has she evidence of that?"

"She just lent it."

"Exactly. She has no redress. No note of hand, no IOU. No witness to the lendings."

"She has spoken of them to me."

"Hearsay is not evidence. As I see it, all that Mistress Tresize is fully entitled to, under her father's will, is the right to remain in one half of the house. Beyond that I can only say that litigation is expensive and long drawn out. There are men who call themselves lawyers who would advise her to bring a claim against the estate and the suit might well last five years. With nothing to show for it at the end." His honest, red face looked genuinely troubled and then brightened as what seemed to him to be a solution presented itself. "What I *can* do," he said, "is to make sure that she has an almshouse. I am on the board of trustees." He warmed to his subject. "This Mr. Turnberry—indeed, anyone intending to purchase the Old Priory—would be willing to pay her to vacate her half of the house. Perhaps even a considerable sum. Also, beside rent-free accommodation, dwellers in almshouses enjoy certain charities. She should be—comfortable."

Maybe what I felt showed in my face, for he muttered that it was the best thing he could suggest.

What I felt was sick! Lettice, my mother, who so loved her garden, her half of the house, Layer Wood and the wild flowers. Lettice, who still, when her affliction eased up a little, enjoyed a ride on her horse. Immured in one of the minute houses in a group called Blind Row because they turned a blank windowless wall to the street.

I thought about what she had told me about the

circumstances of my birth. How easily she could have gone with the tinkers and left me there to die!

What will a man give for his life?

Another life!

Not my own; for if they took and hanged me she'd have nobody at all and would be grief-smitten. I'd got to kill Simon in such a way that nobody could suspect me. Not even Lettice herself. And I hadn't long in which to plan.

Lettice accepted quite calmly my story that I was going to Cambridge to talk about potatoes to the old professor who had first spurred my interest in the new vegetable. "I may stay two nights," I told her, and she looked pleased. I needed a change, she said, and a chance to talk to somebody who shared my interest. In fact, the more we talked about it the more enthusiastic she became. She seemed happy, though admitting that the stiffness of her joints was worsening. "But there's nothing you can do about that, my dear," she said, "and I am well looked after. So go and enjoy yourself."

I carried with me to Cambridge something that not many visitors to that seat of learning include amongst their luggage—a length of rope, measured meticulously and with loops at either end.

My old friend was glad to see me and had much to show me and to talk about; but I stayed only one night there, making—as was not my habit anywhere—the very most of my presence, so that I was noticed, both on the Friday and on the Saturday morning. Then, glad that in the first place Lettice had bought me a very good horse and that he had always been corn-crammed and well-treated, I rode at a fast, furious pace back to Ockley and Layer Wood.

Simon's household and ours were no longer on confidential terms, but our servants talked and I knew that on the Saturday he was spending the evening at Merravay. He'd be returning late, riding like the devil, and he'd be drunk. I planned to lay my trap for him on that part of the path through the woods which led only to the Old Priory.

It was growing dusk by the time I reached my home ground, but I'd gone over and over the thing in my mind so often that I could have done what I had to do in the dark, so there was no hurry and my horse was tired. It was as well for me that we were going slowly, otherwise the fate I planned for him would have overtaken me. The rope stretched from tree to tree across the path caught me by the throat and jerked me backwards out of the saddle so that I slid down over my horse's hindquarters and fell, hitting my head heavily on the path. I lay for a moment stunned. Then I struggled to my feet and realised that my horse, trained to stand in all circumstances, had found a fresh burst of energy and gone galloping off, whinnying as he went.

I stood there, too puzzled to think more than one thought: Who in the world had guessed what I planned for Simon and then laid precisely the same trap for me? And then I saw him in the middle of the path. We had both gone over our horses' tails, going in different directions, and he, riding faster, had been flung farther so that rather more than two horses' lengths divided us.

He was dead. He had fallen so heavily on the back of his head that it was misshapen. And he had been robbed. He'd come back from his last visit to London with not a trinket left, but he had others, and on his way to Merravay would have been wearing them. Now not so much as an ornamental button was left. Except for that rope stretched across the path, just at the right height to catch a horseman, it might well have been one of those attacks, growing increasingly common, when a man carrying money or money's worth would be attacked, robbed and if necessary killed.

But such attacks did not involve such planning as the slung rope indicated. And although a man of Simon's sort necessarily had enemies, they were not of a class to steal buttons.

My trap set and Simon dead, it had been my intention to remove my rope and get away, perhaps as far back toward Cambridge as Newmarket or, failing that, some village on the Cambridge road; but now everything had gone wrong. The bang on my head had done me no good—I was bleeding from the nose, and—unaccountably—from the ears. And I acted as people, hurt in mind or body, always try to do. I made for home. Dizzy-headed, weak-kneed.

My horse stood by the stable door, which was closed; but a lantern burned within, and that was highly unusual unless a horse were sick, stables being so very vulnerable to fire. Lettice's horse stood inside, saddled and bridled.

I made my way into the house and upstairs, and there was Lettice, dressed for riding and paler than death. Yet at the sight of me she turned even paler and put her hand to her throat. "What are you doing here? I thought you were safe in Cambridge! You might..." Her voice choked. "God in heaven! You might have been killed!"

"As Simon was."

"As Simon was. Are you hurt at all? Apart from a little blood?" Assured that I was not, she said, "*His* skull cracked like an eggshell!" She spoke with malice.

There was brandy and a cup on the table beside her. "Brandy," she said. "Very heartening. Drink some. They say that given enough a man can suffer an amputation without a whimper. I am drinking in order to ride again and remove the rope. You see, I dismounted to make sure he was dead—and to make it look as though he had been robbed. Then I could not remount and had to leave the rope there."

"I'll do it," I said.

"Take my horse. It is fresher. Go back to Cambridge. Pretend you never left. There'll be a commotion here for a day or two." She looked thoughtful, then merry. "No one, not even a coroner, would believe that a woman in my state could rig such a trap; and you were miles away. And Simon was certainly not the kind of man to make a will. So the place will be mine, as next of kin—and that means yours, my dear boy. Go now—and speedily."

Neither of us had said a word of pity or remorse, and that, in its way, was an epitaph.

# CHAPTER 5

I do not regard myself as superstitious, but in the
days that followed it almost seemed that that old
story about the Priory being a place under a curse
had some foundation. Happiness, it seemed, could
not flourish there for long.

The law took its course, bound to the letter, but
totally inadequate. In the distant past one constable
had been reckoned sufficient to maintain order in a
group known, whatever its actual number, as a
Hundred. Our Hundred consisted of Ockley, Clevely,
Muchanger and the two of the Minshams, and our
constable, elected for the year, was the miller at
Minsham St. Mary who had little taste for the office,
which no longer carried much prestige. Since he was
allowed to choose and pay a deputy, the fellow who
came to inquire into why Master Tresize should be
found, by a woodcutter on his way to church, lying

dead and robbed, was a very simple fellow indeed. He took it for granted that Simon had been set upon and robbed. And the coroner took the same view. Murder by person or persons unknown.

No suspicion attached to a woman virtually bed-ridden or a young man who had at, or about, the time the crime was committed been studying pota-toes with an old botanist at Cambridge.

So far, so good. And then along came Tom Turn-bull with the will which Simon had made, leaving everything of which he died possessed to Widow Thorington of the Sheepgate, Baildon. "A woman of ill repute," Tom Turnbull said, "but he was infatu-ated with her at the time and argument was useless. She has since married again, but that does not in-validate the will."

When I saw her, I could, after a fashion, under-stand the attraction she had held for a silly boy. She was sex personified. Even to Mother and me she could not talk without flicking a red tongue out of full red lips, a movement as obscene as it was sig-nificant. She said, tongue flicking, "It may surprise you that Simon remembered me, 'specially as we ain't seen much of each other lately. But I taught him all he knew."

"That is debatable," Mother said with a sneer. "But he certainly remembered you to good purpose, Mistress—it is no longer Thorington, I understand."

"Babcock," the woman said, and her tongue flicked, "but the name sticks to me. I've heard him called Master Thorington!"

The ultimate tribute to her dominance. I thought her a most detestable woman but Mother changed her attitude and became conciliatory. She said, "You have a goodly heritage, Mistress Thorington, but a great responsibility. I know because I shouldered it for some years."

"He always said he could leave everything to you." In the coarse voice there was a softer note.

"And I do not envy you at all," Mother said, "except in one tiny thing. A small holding with a neat house just across the river. It is called Bowman's."

"You mean you want to buy it? Now that'd suit me and Babcock a lot better than having you in the half the house, as I understand was the arrangement. All right; it's a deal. Fifty pounds."

"Rather much," Mother said. "But I will pay."

Afterwards she said to me, "Now, my dear, you have a house and acre. It is the best I could do for you."

"And you will share the house?"

"No. Haven't I said again and again that here I am and here I stay?"

The prospect appalled me.

"That woman understood that you wanted Bowman's to live in."

"I never said so. I am not responsible for any misinterpretation she may have placed on my words."

"Turnberry and his brood of grandchildren would have been preferable. He'd have been buying with his eyes open. The Widow Thorington will feel that you deceived her."

"As I did."

"She could be vicious," I said. But it was useless. I used every argument, including the fact that I wanted to live at Bowman's; that I should be working very hard and that it would not be easy for me to look after her if she stayed at the Priory. To that Mother replied that she was much better, hoped to remain so and that I was not to worry about her.

She certainly was much improved. It almost seemed that my fantastic idea that Simon, and her quarrels with him and her anxiety as to what he would do next, had been the cause of her affliction.

She did not make a show of her sudden betterment, but held to her room for a while. Her fingers, however, were much straighter and the tight tendons in her palms and in her neck were now hardly noticeable. Her other stiff joints had also relaxed; she moved without pain. And she was full of plans for the future.

We were sitting in the smaller of the two parlours on our side of the house when she said, "Do you remember how I once said I would keep pigs in the other room and fowls in here? I am still of the same mind. Like you with your luxury potatoes, I shall cater for people with expensive tastes. I shall rear birds for the table and kill the pigs—or have them killed—as sucklings. At the moment only the rich, with land, can enjoy such delicacies; people in towns get tough old birds who have finished laying and pork from pigs sold by weight. I shall alter all that." She gave me a look. "It means getting rid of some of the furniture. But you now have a house. You could take..." Unerringly she picked out the pieces which I, planning a home for her at Bowman's, had considered suitable.

I told her that and added, "It seems a pity that two people who see eye to eye"—I lowered my voice—"even about murder, should live apart. *Why* do you feel a compulsion to stay here?"

"It was my father's wish. He and I did not always see eye to eye. But I came to realise that so far as he understood things, he acted for my good. And he died before we were fully reconciled. That has been an abiding grief. I once thought that by looking after Simon... Let us not talk about that. Next time you go to market, buy me two sows in pig..."

I said, "Do you realise what you are undertaking? Pigs stink and stenches rise."

"Not in this house. I saw it built. Two hands' breadth between ceiling and floor and all the space filled with oak shavings. Besides, one can open the windows."

"And who will dress and singe the sucklings? And prepare the fowls for table?"

She said, "That dumb woman. She can be made to understand simple things and I have kept her in idle comfort long enough. Now, Alan, please, no more argument. My mind is made up."

PART FIVE

# Narrative by Marian Thorington

# CHAPTER 1

I was sixteen that summer when we moved out to
Ockley. Somebody whom my mother just called an
old friend had died untimely, knocked down, killed
and robbed on a lonely woodland path, and he had
made a will, when he was younger, which left his
estate to her.

Before that we had lived in the Sheepgate, the
lowest part of Baildon, and there was a feeling about
against people like my mother, who lived by whoring. Not that I blame her entirely. They were hard
times for the poor, and my father, who was a drover,
had been gored and killed by a bull that went mad.
We'd always been poor, but after that we should have
been almost starving, for women who did washing
or went out to pick over and bale up wool earned
miserable wages. So she took to whoring, and I must

say we were always well-fed and fairly well-clothed, but, of course, looked down upon.

When I was ten I got a job at the grammar school, making beds and emptying chamberpots, but that lasted only two years because I began to be pretty and a danger to the young gentlemen; so I went to pick and bale wool. Picking, which meant taking thorns and burrs out of the fleeces and cleaning out the bits which dung or tar had soiled, was, I suppose, no worse than emptying chamberpots but it was a good deal heavier and harder on the hands and I was not altogether sorry when Mother said I could leave, trim myself up a bit and take to harlotry. But I hadn't the nature for it. I wasn't ignorant, of course; I'd known for years what happened when a man came to our house and Mother said, "Out, all of you! Go and buy pies at the cookshop!" But when it came down to a man in a shirt and me in my shift, or sometimes completely naked, I felt a kind of shuddering. Mother was amused and said I'd get better with practice.

But she had her weak point, too—a craving for respectability. Nothing else could have made her marry Master Babcock, the tanner. He was such a stinking little man. I tried to be tolerant of him—after all, while I worked with fleeces I must have stunk of dirty wool, but a tanner, dealing with the raw hides and the tan pit into which dogs' dung is shovelled, smelt far worse.

He'd had an ailing wife for years and had been one of Mother's regular customers; then his wife died and he came along with an offer of marriage and Mother was delighted, as though being Mistress Babcock could wipe out the years of being Widow Thorington, a woman with a bad name. Apart from being marriageable, and willing to marry, he had nothing to recommend him. He was years older than

Mother and in height came only about up to her shoulder, and he had the bleached, dead-haired look, as though he'd been suspended in his own tan pit for ten days. Also there was so little about him that, so far from Mother being known as Mistress Babcock, he seemed to take her name and ignorant people would call him Master Thorington.

They had one thing in common: Both pursued trades of which the people of Sheepgate disapproved. Everybody in Sheepgate was very poor at that time, but most of them were rigidly respectable. Mother offended their respectability and the tanyard offended their nostrils. They could ignore their own stinks!

Then Mother had this wonderful legacy.

My stepfather owned a sound cart and a sturdy horse, for he was obliged to fetch his hides from the Shambles and they weigh heavy; so we rode out, after he had washed the cart down, and I went and fell in love with a place. To this day I think of heaven as Ockley.

Baildon is a country town and a short walk can take anybody into the country, but what with one thing and another I had never taken that short walk. The drive itself enchanted me and Ockley itself was doubly enchanting. On this side of the river some neat houses with small green patches behind them, then the bridge, the little church, a slight incline and what I thought was the most beautiful house I had ever seen. With a garden.

Mother went into the house to talk to Mistress Tresize, a relative of the young man who had left her this glorious place; my stepfather, obscuring himself as usual, went to take what he called "a look-round," so I had the garden to myself.

That March had been almost like summer and now it was April, even warmer. The daffodils were at their prime; so were the gillyflowers; there were pansies, too, edging the borders, and some small bushes covered with a pale purple flower with a delicious scent. There was grass, too, all bespeckled with daisies, and against the walls, shaped trees, tacked flat and bearing on their branches, amongst few leaves or none, flowers, dead white, bright pink or a mingling of both.

The truth was I'd never been in a garden before. In the Sheepgate there were spaces behind the houses, with here and there a tree, but the rest given over to rubbish, and citizens who had gardens walled them in. Here all was spread out to be enjoyed, and there was a stone seat upon which I sat and enjoyed myself to the full, looking at the colours, sniffing the fragrance.

Presently Mother came out of the house, full of that self-satisfaction which made her the master of everybody with whom she came in contact. Of how many whores can it be said that a regular customer offered to marry her, and another, almost forgotten, had mentioned her in his will?

We piled into the cart again and Mother said, "Then that's settled. Mistress Tresize is a reasonable woman and she is going to live there." She pointed to one of the neat houses across the river with a green field behind it. "Fifty pounds," she said jubilantly, "and none of Lawyer Turnbull's silly arguing." Master Turnbull had annoyed Mother by suggesting that *some* of the dead man's bills should be paid. Not all— that he said would be impossible—just small sums owed to people with small businesses to whom a bad debt was a serious loss. Mother held that death cancelled all debts. The lawyer had then further annoyed her by suggesting that she would be wise to hire Master Heath as overseer, since farming a hundred and fifty acres required experience. Mother

replied that, between them, she and my stepfather
had enough experience to run anything. In talking
to other people Mother always said "My husband"
and tried to make him seem more important than
he was. In private she never listened to a word he
said and called him a fool to his face.

We moved in in May. Gathered together, there
was quite a family of us: my brother Jimmy, a bit
simple-minded, who had done odd jobs about the
market or acted as potboy if the Hawk in Hand was
short of staff; there was my sister Fanny, who was
a widow, and her two boys aged seven and eight;
Fanny did plain sewing when she could get it and
the boys did odd jobs, too. They'd lived with us since
Fanny's husband had died of the weavers' cough,
and, as Mother never failed to point out, they'd have
starved if they'd had rent to pay. Fanny was too plain
for a whore. I was next, and then came the twins,
aged six. Mother hadn't wanted them but she made
the best of it by saying that they made her seem
younger than being a grandmother made her *sound*.
Not that she looked old: her hair was dead black,
her cheeks round and rosy and she had a high bosom
which tight bodices showed off.

Up to a point she was a good mother; nobody be-
longing to her should go hungry if she could help it.
But she was unfeeling—she could be amused and
she could be angry, but of finer feelings she had none
and didn't understand them in other people, so she
trampled on us all, called Jimmy a half-wit and my
stepfather a fool and reminded Fanny of what she
owed her and fetched all of us a clout when she felt
like it.

Between the April day when I fell in love with a
garden and the day we moved in, Mother had been
to Ockley once. She reported then that she'd seen
furniture being moved from Mistress Tresize's half

of the house to the house on the other side of the river, she she took it that Mistress Tresize was leaving. When we arrived and she found that this was not so, that Mistress Tresize had no intention of leaving, had in fact turned the ground floor of her side of the house into a piggery and a hen house, Mother's wrath knew no bounds. "She cheated me, the bloody bitch! I let her have that place across the river cheap. Put up to auction I might have got sixty pounds for it. I let her have it for fifty and she's turning this house into a stinking pigstye under my nose. I'll show her! I'll go and see that lawyer fellow."

My stepfather said, "He's her cousin..."

"What are you mumbling about, Job Babcock?"

"I only said he's her cousin. In any dispute he'll take her side."

"Oh, will he? Then I'll show him, too! I'll go to Clevely and see Sir Edward Shelmadine. I'll..." There was no end to what she would do, and when she was in a temper wise people kept out of her reach. I slithered off into the garden, regretting the ham which Fanny had just brought in and set on the table when Mother came down raging. Some food had been left in the larder.

I failed to see what all the fuss was about. It was a wide house and, even without the part which Mistress Tresize was clinging onto, far more spacious than the Sheepgate house.

The garden had changed. The daffodils were over and gone, and because the weather had been so unseasonable a few roses and some sprays of early honeysuckle were out.

To Mother the provision of food was all-important, the manner of taking it nothing. There was the meat, the bread, the knife, help yourself but leave something for others or risk a clout. I doubt whether Mother had ever seen a table properly set and a meal decently taken in her life. I had, having worked at the grammar school, with grace before meat, even when there was no meat, and everybody seated, handing the salt and the bread.

I sat there, breathing in the fragrance as the light faded and I thought I saw a ghost. Of ghosts it is said that they walk with a gait like gliding and that they are pale. This ghost glided and was pale and came towards me. I stiffened with terror, becoming one with the stone seat on which I sat.

Some very odd stories were told about the Old Priory. Somebody had laid a curse on it, and somebody else had performed a sacrifice to get the curse lifted, and somebody else had kept a madwoman in a cage for years and years. It was mainly servants' talk but none the less scary for that and a ghost seemed to fit in well.... And so did what this ghost carried in its hand—a sprig of rosemary.

A few feet short of me she stopped, abruptly, as though the sight of me had startled her as much as the sight of her had startled me. She said, "Good evening. I apologise for intruding." Her voice was sweet and haughty and dainty all at once. I stood up, my legs of stone turning to legs of feathers, and mumbled, "Thass orright!" Never before in my life had I heard my own voice sounding like that, coarse and rough.

"I remembered this"—she moved the rosemary— "at the last moment. It roots easily and I hope to grow a pot on my windowsill."

I'd have given anything to have been able to say that she would be welcome in the garden whenever she liked, but that was not for me to say to a woman who had fallen out with Mother. The sad thing is that had Mistress Tresize gone to live in the small house beyond the river, as Mother had expected, she would probably have said, in her carefree way, that she could walk in the garden whenever the fancy took her.

All I could say was, "I hope it grows. If not I will get you another piece."

"That is most kind. But...but I imagine that after this afternoon, relationships between the two houses will be somewhat restricted."

I imagined so, too. I said, "Some of your windows overlook the garden and I shall often be here. If I see an empty pot on the sill, I will put another piece on your doorstep."

I was now in love not only with a garden but with a person coming out of the shadows. When presently I saw her in plain view, I was not disappointed. She was not pretty—I doubt whether even when young she had been—but she had such elegance, such grace. She looked far to frail to sustain the onslaught of the war which Mother began to wage as soon as she understood that nothing, no deception upon Mistress Tresize's part, no amount of property which she obtained elsewhere by whatever means, could justify her eviction from her half of the house and what was called "reasonable access" to it.

I knew—who better?—that Mother liked her own way and that opposition simply fired her blood. And I think that the disasters which came thick and fast, just when she was feeling secure and successful, soured her temper.

The main disaster that year was the weather: April, May as hot as summer; June cold—one day it actually snowed!—and after that rain every day. Some days it cleared before evening and a pink glow in the sky seemed to herald a fine day tomorrow. That fine day never came, but during the fine interval I'd go out and pluck a few roses that had not rotted on the stem, shake the day's moisture from them and sneak round and put them on her doorstep. And I kept a sharp eye on the pot on the windowsill; the rosemary sprig seemed to flourish.

# CHAPTER 2

The troubles that year were unending, and Mother's belief that farming was a simple business, merely demanding hard work from us all for a time, did little to help.

Ockley was really two villages and they were in fact beginning to be known as Ockley Major and Ockley Minor, words which I, having worked at the grammar school, understood. Ockley Major consisted of the cottages across the river, with some land attached to each—Bowman's was one of them. Ockley Minor consisted of cottages built later, rather huddled together, near the church. They had little garden plots, insufficient to make them independent, and in most families the man had worked on the Priory land and been paid. All those families, it was said, had been brought in by Mistress Tresize's father when he bought the land with a curse on it. Some sons had gone away, daughters had married and some men had taken to specialised trades. Ockley Minor had its own carpenter, its own blacksmith, its own weaver and inside the farming business men had done their own jobs.

There was a man called Soames who was a cowman, and when Mother realised that her legacy was not the immediate money spinner which she had imagined, and that wages must be paid, she dismissed Soames, saying that Jimmy could look after the cows, being as simple-minded as they were. I was there. I heard Soames say with some dignity, "I wish your boy and the cows well, ma'am." Then he said, "There is another matter. There's that bit of land called Eggar's Piece. I'd like to hire it. Say five pound a year and I'd throw in a bit of help to the boy. There's udder trouble and calving trouble, and when to take a cow to the bull. Things townsfolk don't know. Five pound a year and more knowledge than you could put a price on."

Mother thought she had made another good bargain. But the weather was against her. In such moistness the hay grew tall and was scythed, but it could not be brought in because it never had a chance to dry, and my stepfather assured Mother that wet hay, stored in a barn, would set itself on fire.

"How could it? With no tinder spark?"

"I don't know how. I only know it can happen. Don't be guided by me ..."—my word, he had learned his lesson!—"...experiment with some small quantity. I'll put an iron rod in and you'll see how it heats up."

He was right. The rod became so hot that even mother was convinced and left the hay in the open, with all of us rushing out and tossing it about whenever the rain held off for an hour. Even so it was mouldy and rotten and quite unfit for fodder. As for the wheat and barley harvest, that was calamitous. More rain and some lashing winds had laid a lot of it flat, so it couldn't be scythed properly; a reaper had to take a handful, raise it and cut through it with a knife. As often as not the ears had already begun to sprout.

For each fresh calamity Mother blamed Mistress Tresize. "She's envious of us and envy breeds malice," she said. "She's a witch and she's overlooked me."

When she said that I took a great fright, not of Mistress Tresize but *for* her. Terrible things were done to people suspected of being witches, and a thing had only to be said often enough to convince the ignorant. In my own mind I could see how, if it ever came to the test, Mistress Tresize's whole way of life would count against her. Her refusal to go and share the house at Bowman's with the young man who must, judging by his looks, be some relative; her harbouring the deaf and dumb creature; even her keeping pigs and chickens in the parlours. And witches *were* supposed to control the weather—generally in the sense of making it bad, and although some other villages, mostly those near the great wood, had suffered similarly, the heavy rainfall had not been universal.

When Mother mentioned the word I gave a great shudder, not wholly put on, and I said, "Mother, please, never say that! You bring us all under suspicion. We're under the same roof and there has to be thirteen."

"Thirteen *what?*"

"People to make what they call a coven."

"You seem to know a lot about it."

"I have to. I'm the one in most danger." Mother goggled. I invented the next bit. "Every coven has to have somebody who looks like a virgin and isn't.

They'd examine me and say I'd been laying with the Devil."

Mother looked stunned. "But we know who you laid with. I could name every one."

"Ah," I said as solemnly as I could, "but would they admit it in court? They're all married and two at least very respectable."

"Thass true," Mother said, and I thought I'd rounded that corner very nicely.

Mother had one stroke of luck which was unexpected. Master Heath came across the river most evenings and spent some time with his relative, but one evening he knocked on our door. I went and so saw him face to face for the first time and fell in love again. He took off his hat and bowed and said he'd be obliged if Mistress Babcock could spare him a few minutes. His voice was like Mistress Tresize's, but low and deep instead of dainty. I asked him in. I was suddenly aware of how horrid our home looked and smelt. We had two parlours now, but both were in the same disorder. The only difference was that the back parlour, being nearer the kitchen, was kept as a feeding place, with some sort of food and some used dishes and mugs always on the table. I had sometimes tried to tidy things up a bit but it was difficult. Mother set some store by respectability, but none at all on what she called fussiness, and I'd grown discouraged. Everything lay where it fell and with the wet weather there were muddy boots everywhere. Still, I would have taken him into the front parlour, which was rather neater and sweeter, but Mother came to the door of the back one and said, her tongue flicking, "Ah, Master Heath. And what do you want with me?"

"Earlier in the year I planted some potatoes in what is now your garden. I have come to ask leave to dig them up."

"Potatoes. What're they?"

"A new vegetable, madam."

"In *my* garden! Then you can whistle for them. I've had about enough of your lot! Her over there with the law protecting a cheat! But there ain't no law that says you can dig in my garden."

"I'd pay."

"How much?"

"A pound." Mother laughed and her tongue flicked.

"Try again."

He said abruptly. "Three. I dislike haggling. I would point out that they are of no use to you. You couldn't distinguish them from weeds. Three pounds is too much and it is my limit."

"All right," Mother said. The money changed hands. Then she turned nasty again and said, "I'll come and see that you take what is yours and no more."

"As you wish, madam. I can assure you that shortly a man digging potatoes will be so common a sight that nobody will give him a second glance."

I was grateful to Mother for her ungracious suggestion because that meant I could go too. The rain held off for a little and we all went out into the dripping garden.

He'd counted on getting Mother's consent; he'd brought what we called a long barrow, much bigger than a wheelbarrow; and though he spoke of digging, he had a fork, not a spade.

He had been right in saying that we should have thought it a weed, some green growth of no beauty, no flowers, no fragrance, but up the roots came, bringing with them oval lumps about the size of my palm. When the wet soil wasn't clinging to them they had a pearly sheen. He took one between his hands and cleaned it, holding it out for Mother to see.

"This, madam, is a potato, not yet fully matured,

but I was anxious about the rain. I have little experience. A good root, though, ten and all sound."

"Whass it for?" Mother asked.

"Food, madam. One of the most wonderful plants in the world." He went on to say that dug even earlier, scraped, boiled and served with butter, it was a delicacy comparable to asparagus, and even now, half grown, boiled or baked, it was delectable.

"But few can taste it so this year. I will dig these and free myself of my obligation to you. At Bowman's I have some which must ripen fully and serve as seed stock."

He dodged about, for his ragged-looking plants were scattered, near a bush, near an arbour, near a clump of marigolds or lilies. Some came up bearing thready roots with little knobs no bigger than a bead; but presently he had his long barrow full. He placed the fork across it. Then he said, "So that is that! I'd have given you some to taste, but you were so damned awkward about the horse."

No denying that. Mistress Tresize had a horse and there was stabling for a dozen, but Mother, angry and clinging to her rights, had said that half a house and reasonable means of access did not include stabling. So Mistress Tresize's horse had gone to Bowman's, to share the new stable there, and when she wanted to ride she had to walk down to it, or her nephew—nephew seemed the most likely relationship—would bring it across to her.

And the horse hadn't been the only thing about which Mother had been awkward. There was access. Access to the well, shared by both households, access to Mistress Tresize's entry. The two old maids from the other side of the house would no sooner come out with their buckets than Mother would demand that Fanny's boys or even the twins should fetch water at once, and if necessary the old crones would be jostled aside with what might look like childish play-fulness but actually was not. Then there was access. Master Heath always brought his horse and cart to collect the young suckling pigs and the fowls dressed for table—all prepared by the dumb woman—and nine times out of ten there'd be some obstruction: our cart, a yoke of oxen, once a whole tree trunk waiting to be sawn into lengths.

Mistress Tresize would pick her way round the obstacle, tap on our door and ask with icy politeness for the obstacle to be removed. Mother always pre-tended complete innocence, bawling at the nearest person who could be blamed, but leering and winking at the same time.

However, with the last of his potatoes dug—and I hoped marketed—Master Heath took action and started to build a new doorway on the flank of that wing of the house. This was a spot absolutely invis-ible from any part of our house, and thus I was able to make his acquaintance.

The weather remained strange that year; once the ruined harvest was in, it became dry and sunny. The little summers of St. Luke and St. Martin ran into one another and a few late roses bloomed. Mother had gone into Baildon with my stepfather, who made the journey each day; the children were gathering apples, supervised idly by Fanny, who had brought her sewing out to the stone seat. I drifted about, plucking a bloom here and there and then vanished.

Actually the Old Priory was a splendid place for vanishing, for the ruins had never been completely cleared away; even between the front of the house and the garden there were stumps of stone, bits of archway, mostly overgrown with ivy, but some with roses and honeysuckle. I snatched a last red rose—most fragrant of all—and left the garden.

I knew all the tricks, of course. My hair was neatly

parted and smooth on the crown of my head, then it
broke into curls. I was clean and I wore a dress from
which the most defiant scarlet—the harlot's sure
badge—had faded slightly through washing and ex-
posure to the sun. I went round the house and said,
"Oh," as though the sight of him surprised me; as
though I hadn't been waiting and watching for this
opportunity. I feigned some hesitation in my speech.
I said, "A few flowers...perhaps the last but I
thought...I have often thought how much Mistress
Tresize must miss her garden...so from time to
time..." I held out the bunch.

"So you're the good fairy! Go in. Up the stairs. Tell
her I have the holes dug and shall be up in a minute
or so."

He had the hole made in the wall and all evened
off into a kind of arch and was digging holes for the
doorposts.

I went in, knowing that I was treading on forbidden ground, and I thought, If Mother knew I had
come here in friendliness, she'd wallop me, old as I
am.

At the stair foot I could just smell pigs—but pigs
in clean straw, not filthy styes. Halfway up it dis-
appeared, and in the upper parlour, specklessly clean,
and with the window open and all the green things
growing on the sill, it was different from any place
I had ever been in.

She took the bunch and thanked me. "I often wondered," she said. "Every time I watered the rosemary
I hoped you'd see that the pot was not empty. Thank
you for these—and all the previous posies. Do sit
down. Alan is making me a new doorway."

"I know," I said, keeping my voice as soft as I
could. "And he said he would be up in a minute or
so."

"Hungry and thirsty after such labour." She went

to a cupboard and came back with a clean white cloth
which she spread on the table, and from above the
cupboard, from a shelf, she took down a bowl of salt,
which had a spoon of its own so that nobody need
dip into it with dirty fingers or the tip of a gravy-
dipping knife. Such delicacy I had not seen since my
servitude at the grammar school.

She said, just as Master Heath entered the room,
"We should be happy if you would join us, Mistress
Babcock."

I said, "Thorington. My name is Marian Thorington. And thank you, but I must not stay. In fact,"
I said, all distraught and blurting, "if my mother
knew I was here now she'd have the hide off me."

I thought, What a vulgar expression! And to say
that about Mother made us sound such a rough family. And it was misleading, too. Mother raved and
stormed and dealt out clouts but she was not a beater
in the real sense of the word. Some parents in Sheepgate were.

"I don't mean literally," I hurried on, making
things worse. "It's just that you...well...got on her
wrong side and she takes time to come around."

"There was no intention to deceive," Mistress
Tresize said with instant understanding. "And perhaps there will be less friction now that I have the
new doorway."

Master Heath said, "It is to be hoped so because
I, Mistress Marian, entertain some hope of becoming
her tenant."

I thought it friendly of him to use my given name.
And spoken in his beautiful voice it sounded much
nicer than it had ever done before. I wished I dare
call him Master Alan and see how his name sounded
on my tongue. But I did not dare, which was queer
for I was generally reckoned a bold girl and in Baildon it had always fallen to me to undertake an er-

rand nobody else wanted, like asking for more credit at a place where we owed money.

"What do you wish to hire?"

"Two or three acres of Top Field."

"Mother might let it," I said doubtfully. "The harvest has been disappointing."

"Except for potatoes," he said, and smiled.

"It would be better not to mention them until you have the land you want," I said. Mother often complained that she should have charged more for allowing him to take what she called his rubbish out of her garden. "I should have stood out for five," she said. And she'd grown more bitter when, with every ordinary thing doing so badly, his potatoes seemed to thrive. "He has sackfuls, and selling at sixpence a pound. My friend at the old Hawk told me so. She bought some and made a separate course of them with an extra charge. The world's gone mad."

Out of sheer perversity, for she could have done with the money, she refused to let Master Tresize hire an inch of Top Field. She said, "A good harvest always follows a bad one and I need all my land."

"Then would you allow me to use your garden again, and pay you as I did this year?"

"You beat me down on that, too! No, I will not. What I will do"—her manner changed and her tongue flicked—"I'll buy some of this potato seed from you and grow some of my own. Name your price."

He laughed. "The potato plant has no seed," he said. And went out and hired two acres of Eggar's Piece from the man Soames, to whom his first harvest also had been a bitter disappointment.

Mother was like a hornet, but there was nothing she could do. When she bargained with Soames, in the old-fashioned way, no lawyers or papers concerned, simply twelve men standing by and saying, "To this I bear witness," nothing had been said about his not subletting. And the question of access, which the new door should have solved, arose again and more bitterly, for it was almost impossible for Master Heath to get to Eggar's Piece without crossing some part of the Priory land.

He wanted, understandably, to haul the manure made by Mistress Tresize's pigs and hens out onto his two acres after Soames had ploughed them with his own. Mother forbade it; so Soames did the carting for him and Mother could not afford to quarrel with him since Jimmy had proved as witless as a cowman as he had done at everything else, and the advice and help which Soames had promised was often needed.

Eggar's Piece was within view of the house, so that autumn I had the mixed pleasure of watching Alan Heath at work, breaking the furrows that Soames had made for him into a fine soil and mixing in the manure. "Muck spreading" it was called, one of the humblest of occupations, and when so labouring he dressed as labourers did. Even so, to me he always looked like a king. He was taller than most men and, though strong, more lightly built, and his hair was a wonderful chestnut colour. Mistress Tresize's hair was heavily steaked with white, but enough remained of the original to show that once hers had been the same; that and their profiles and their grace showed their kinship.

When his bit of land was ready, he left it waiting to receive the sprouting bits of old potato in the spring, so after that I saw him little and then driving a farm cart, which I always felt should be a coach, or on his horse. He looked splendid then.

Harlots—and I had been one for rather more than two years—are not supposed to be sentimental about men and to care only for what they can get out of them; but I was as sentimental about Alan as though

I'd been a virgin with sixteen years of most sheltered life behind me. I was in this state of mind when Mother made a move calculated to make reconciliation between the two households impossible.

# CHAPTER 3

It was the kind of action known as cutting off your nose to spite your face, yet there was some slight reason behind it.

My stepfather didn't own, he hired his tanyard, and when he paid his rent at Christmas that year his landlord warned him that next year it would be almost doubled.

"Bloody rogue," Mother said. "He only did that because he thinks I inherited a lot and you can afford a fancy damned rent. If only he knew!" She couldn't very well rant and rave at the poor stinking little man and blame him for his misfortune and this fact soured her even more.

It was bitterly cold just then but, wrapped in her cloak and with a shawl over her head, she began to prowl and prowl about amongst the ruins.

The Priory in the old days had been a big place,

and the ruins contained not only heaps and pillars of stone and some half arches but several holes in the ground lined with stone—cellars at one time. I'd done some prowling, too, being fascinated by the whole place, and I'd found at least three such ancient cellars. I'd actually warned Fanny's boys and the twins, who liked to play chasing games, to beware of how they ran, for in the summer the holes were almost concealed by shallow-rooted, short-lived plants like a pretty pink-flowered thing called Herb Robert.

I had never been near Job Babcock's tannery but I knew that the most important thing in a tanyard was the pit. In this the hides soaked and stank to high heaven. The pit had to be lined with brick or stone to hold water, and during the rainy summer three of the Old Priory cellars had held water for a time, but they'd dried out during the dry autumn.

Give every dog his due; Job Babcock, though he might be scornfully called Master Thorington by some people who knew better, had stuck to his unsavoury trade, driving in almost every day to turn his hides, scrape the hair from one surface, the fat from the other, beating them smooth and supple. He'd never for an instant been dependent upon Mother and her great legacy which had turned out so poorly. And one evening when she told him that she had the answer to his landlord—"Tell him to let it to another poor fool"—he did object, but feebly. And opposing Mother was always like spitting against the wind.

He'd save the rent, she said, and here were Fanny's boys, not yet big and heavy enough to do much farm work but capable of scraping hides and hammering them.

"But, Martha, I get my hides from the Shambles and sell my leather to Master Greston, or on the market. Hauling them to and from here would be a strain on the horse."

"Not more of a strain than the daily journey in and out."

"Maybe not. But we have to think about the dog dung. Boys collect it and deliver it to me, a farthing a bucket."

"Here surely we have dung enough—cattle, pigs. Wouldn't that serve?"

"No. For some reason that I do not understand, in the making of certain leather, dogs' dung is necessary."

"Then arrange it. Once a week you take your leather in and bring your hides and the dog muck out. If that is beyond you, leave it to me."

"All right," he said meekly, but with a certain sullenness. A man convinced against his will. Perhaps Mother was aware of it, for she smiled and flicked her tongue at him. "Come while the light lasts," she said, "and see what an excellent tan pit I have found for you."

She had chosen, of course, the hole nearest to the house, just to the right of the garden and directly outside Mistress Tresize's side window and her new doorway.

I tried. I said, "I have always watched those old holes because of the children. There are three, and this is the least watertight of them."

"A few cracks," Mother said. "We'll get it cleared and some clay slapped on." She was by this time so set against Mistress Tresize that to persecute her she was almost willing to provide my stepfather with a faulty pit. "And drying racks already made for you." Mother pointed to some clumps of ruin dotting the rough pasture near the planned pit.

I thought, Poor Mistress Tresize! Her front windows look out onto a garden as lost to her as the Garden of Eden and now her side view will be marred by unlovely hides at all stages. And she'll get the worst of the stench.

Mother said, as though answering me, "After all, *she* started it, keeping pigs in parlours!" What irked her, of course, was the thought of all those succulent little pigs, all those coddled table birds going to market with such regularity. And to do her justice I must admit that she'd tried with young pigs and fowls herself and had no luck; fowl pest took the fowls and the pigs died of swine fever. "Somebody did warn me that this place was cursed," Mother said. "I'm beginning to believe it."

I preferred that she should believe in an ancient curse than that she should regard Mistress Tresize as a witch, though she reverted to that from time to time. And that was not the only thing she reverted to.

There is a saying, "Once a whore, always a whore," but for that to be true a woman has to have a taste for it. I never had done; and now, of course, cherishing a hopeless love, the thought of having been possessed by other men, however briefly, was completely hateful to me. Mother was different; even in the old all-out-get-a-pie-at-the-cookshop days she'd always seemed better tempered *afterwards*. And perhaps a man so unsavoury and timid as Job Babcock was not quite the husband for Mother, so big and vigorous and handsome in a coarse way.

When did I begin to suspect? To be sure? Some time in that spring when, with little or nothing to sell, she began going in to Baildon whenever my stepfather went in to collect his hides and deliver his leather. She always came back in a good temper and always full of talk about the Hawk in Hand— a name hateful to me, for it was in that old, dignified hostelry that I had done my whoring. All arranged with the innkeeper's wife.

I'd reached the right age, shape and size just when Mother was beginning to look at Job Babcock "through a wedding ring," as the saying goes; so there'd been no all-out for me. I'd gone along to the inn, wearing my cheap red dress and with a bow of red ribbon on my hair. Nothing was required of me but to look amiable but I was as much on sale as the food, the liquor and the stabling. A word in the land-lady's ear and there I was.

When we talked about witches Mother said she could name a dozen men who had had me. So could I. But some of them came again and again.

I was very pretty, perhaps much as Mother had been once upon a time before she grew gross. I had the same shining black hair, the same black, slightly slanting eyes with long lashes. But where Mother was ruddy I was pale, and where she was sturdy, I was slender, and whereas I had no doubt she laughed and flicked her tongue and was enthusiastic, I was not. I was reluctant, and while that suited some men and sharpened their appetite, it repelled others. One of my customers said he'd as soon have an iceberg in bed with him. "You'll not see him again," the innkeeper's wife said; but that didn't bother me; there were enough of those who felt otherwise. And then, with Mother's legacy and her secret craving for re-spectability, it was all over until one day Mother came back from Baildon, satiated both in body and purse, and said that Joanna—the landlady of the Hawk in Hand—had told her that young Master Wentworth was back in Summerfield and had been asking for me.

"So you'll go," Mother said, "on Saturday and stay there at Joanna's special invitation."

Like a fool, I said, "No. I've done with all that."

Still good-tempered, she said, "Don't talk daft, Marian. Sometimes you seem to me little better than

Jimmy. You can't fail me now. Or Joanna. I said you'd be there on Saturday and she's getting the message to him. You must remember him, he paid so well."

"I know. But I've done with all that."

All of a sudden her temper changed; she reached out and caught me a great buffet on the side of my head. She said, "Don't you dare go against me. I promised and I will not be thwarted by my own daughter. Ask yourself, what the hell have you done since we came here? Idled about. Tossed some hay, took ale to the reapers, mucked about a bit in that garden. Nothing any lout couldn't do. But you've fed well and lain soft. Now comes the day of reckoning and you'll go if I have to carry you!

I said, "No." And she hit me again on the other side of my head. It rang like an empty tub, and out of the ringing and the dizziness I cried like a kitten, "I'll do anything else. I'll earn my keep. I'll work in the tanyard!"

"A fine lot of use you'd be there!" And not only useless, unwanted, for Fanny's boys were now helping Job. They were both at an age to be apprenticed.

"You'll do as I say," Mother said, "or I'll know why."

I knew the utter hopelessness of opposing her. I went out into the garden, still crying, and sat on the stone seat. My ears were still ringing, and the heel of one of Mother's hands had caught my cheekbone, which swelled up so rapidly that I could hardly see out of that eye.

I thought about young Master Wentworth, who had been my client three times in the past. He was clean and sweet-smelling at least and seemed not to share the common view that a bought woman could be handled just anyhow. He'd been in fact my favourite and there had been a time when I'd been sorry that he came to Suffolk so seldom. He'd inherited Summerfield from his great-uncle, but he had another, larger estate in Kent.

I sat there and thought of running away, but where could I go? How could I earn a living? There was a lot of unemployment about and I had no skill at anything. I lacked even the simplest domestic training that would have made me a good servant. And being pretty was no help. Mistresses did not like pretty maids; they were a danger to husbands and sons.

I had the mad idea of appealing to Master Wentworth. Of doing my best to please him and then, afterwards, in the good-tempered peace, explaining that I was dreadfully in love with another man and hated having to do what I had just done with him and begging him to find me a place somewhere. I knew it was an absurd thought, even as it passed through my head. He might laugh at the absurdity of a young harlot being in love and having such scruples. Or he might, having taken a fancy to me, take me to Kent and visit me regularly. I should never see Alan again and I should be a kept woman....Oddly, kept women, possibly because they were often envied, were even more scorned than people like Mother and me.

Nowadays even this fragrant, if overgrown, garden was faintly tainted by the tan pit's stench. I was aware of it, and when it seemed to increase, I merely thought the wind had shifted or that Job had been disturbing the murky depths. Then Job spoke and I realised that there he was on the seat beside me.

My champion had arrived, all unrecognised.

"She bin on to you?" he asked. I lifted my head and turned my face, red-eyed with crying and with the mark of the blow on one cheek, towards him. I'd never been more than moderately civil to him and there was absolutely no reason why he should take my part now. But I nodded.

"I reckoned that'd be the next step," he said in an ordinary voice, as though he was discussing the weather. "I ain't blind. I know what she bin up to these last weeks. And I know overripe plums ain't to everybody's taste. Mind, I ain't complaining. I went into this with my eyes open and a slice off a cut loaf ain't missed. But when that come to you, thass different. Maybe I could help."

I said, ungraciously, "I don't see how. She'd take no notice of anything you said."

"I know that. I could get you away, though. As you know, I do a lot of business with Greston; and he hev girls, making gloves. Ladies' gloves that men can't handle, their fingers being too big." He paused and swallowed. I saw the Adam's apple jump in his scraggy throat. "Once there and properly apprenticed, she'd hev no hold on you for three, four years.... It ain't much, I know, but the best I can think of. Knowing what I know." I realised that he knew more than Mother or anybody knew, for when he went into Baildon on business, he had, since giving up the tanyard there, stabled his horse at the Hawk in Hand. "Thass for you to say," he said.

Once, years ago, I'd been sent to the cookshop and come out with a pie. Cookshop pies, and indeed almost everything made of pastry, were called "coffins," the pastry having much of the durability of wood. Small pies could be held in the hand and eaten like apples; bigger ones, such as the one I was sent that evening to fetch, demanded a plate or dish. I'd taken a dish, and the cookshop man slid a pie out of his deep, hot, brown dish on to my cold, shallow, blue one; and I was hurrying home with it, thinking how lovely it would be when the coffin was cut into and the meat and gravy oozed out, when I was aware of a stray dog following me. Hoping for a crumb. Expecting a kick. I broke a piece of the crust off. It was only the ornamental, thick rim of the coffin and I thought, That shall be my share; I can live without it.

Now, all those years later, Job Babcock was looking at me with that dog's eyes, "I think it is a wonderful idea. I'm so grateful..." I cried again, thinking how I had scorned and misjudged him. "How can we manage it?"

"Easy," he said. "Leave all to me."

Smoothly, deceptively, everything went forward. On that Saturday, Job was to deliver some leather to Master Greston. I was to ride with him and stay at the Hawk in Hand, with Mother's friend and mine. In reality I was avoiding one kind of slavery for another. And all for a fancy. The truth was that Alan Heath wouldn't know—or care—whether I was whoring in the Hawk in Hand or stitching gloves behind Greston's shop. But I should know. I had the silly feeling that I was making a sacrifice for love, and that I was, in a way, cleansing myself, sloughing off the past.

Job's story was to be that he saw me into the Hawk in Hand and was ignorant of what I did after that. I could see Mother hoping that once in business again I might get into tune with it and perhaps stay there— the landlady sharing the proceeds with her. Nothing was said about my turning suddenly agreeable and nothing was said about my coming home. "Tell Joanna I may see her on Wednesday," Mother said.

Once I had seemed to give in, nobody minded how I spent my time, so I went into Layer Wood and gathered a great bunch of oxslips, which are bigger than cowslips and more deeply scented. I laid more

than half the bunch on Mistress Tresize's new doorstep. And I hoped that that evening, when Alan came,
she'd mention the flowers and they'd both think
kindly of me for a moment.

# CHAPTER 4

I suppose there is a good case to be made out for the apprenticeship system. Skills must be handed on; young people must be employed. Also I knew from working at the grammar school that even the young who were being educated were not pampered and that servants must take what they are given and be thankful. Still, the Greston household was a revelation to me and I cannot deny that there was an almost constant temptation to run across the Market Square and tell the landlady I'd bed with the Devil for the sake of a square meal.

Master and Mistress Greston were both extremely mean, and she was spiteful. One of the first things she said to me was, "We'll have that hair off, for a start." And have it off she did, taking the shears into her own hands and hacking all my curls away.

I don't know what tale Job had told Master Greston that Saturday. He left me sitting in the cart while two half-grown boys unloaded the leather and he went in to talk to Master Greston. My chief concern then had been not to be noticed. The saddler's shop was almost directly opposite the Hawk in Hand and I sat there thinking, What if the landlady sees me? What if young Wentworth should already be in the town? So I sat hunched over and with my face turned to the shop until Job came out and said, "Thass orright. Thass settled. Now they wanta hev a look at you." So I went into the shop. Mistress Greston took one look at me and hated me and said what she did about my hair.

There was one other girl glove apprentice; I'd taken the place of one who had died. The one who had survived was called Hettie, and they'd taken her out of the foundling home, and if anybody had ever come into the shop and said, "You starve your apprentices," there was Hettie, fat as a bladder of lard—and as pale—to prove that we were well fed. Actually we were fed abominably; even the breakfast gruel was thin; dinner was plain dumpling in watery gravy; supper the coarsest bread and the hardest, mouldiest cheese. Once a week, meat, the fat and lean pork with so little lean about it that it was no more than a vein; once a week, stockfish.

The Grestons could truly say that their apprentices fed at their own table; and that added to the misery, to see them.... And to think, Well, they are eating roast beef, tonight we may have dripping on our bread!

And to be thankful for that! We worked long hours, at the time when I joined the household, sunup to sundown, about twelve hours with a half off for the miserable dinner. The boys worked in the space behind the counter of the shop, and they did the heavy work, saddles and horse collars and riding boots.

Hettie and I worked in a back room, sunless even in summer, for it faced north.

From somewhere the boys found the heart and energy to go out sometimes after supper and roister about with other apprentices, but even had Hettie and I wished to do so, we were not allowed out. Mistress Greston, who was very religious, explained to me what Hettie already knew: "I am responsible for you in the eyes of God. If you need air, go to the back."

Nothing bloomed there. It was not a garden; it was a narrow space between sheds. But it was possible on some evenings to stand there and stare across the river Lark and see the one claw of Layer Wood which almost encroached upon the town. Away to the east another claw of it embraced Ockley and all that I held dear. I'd stand there and dream. I was young enough and, despite everything, unworldly enough, to feel, not a certainty, but a hope, that by clinging to what virtue I had left, I was earning a reward. It was a fantasy, a muddle of Master Heath saying that he loved me, Mistress Tresize approving of me, the Old Priory without the tan pit, with the garden restored to sweetness, and all the flowers of Layer Wood in bloom at the same season.

Mrs. Greston—there was a growing tendency with those who were in business and considered themselves up to date to use the shortened forms for master and mistress, reserving the latter for unmarried women and sometimes shortening even that to miss— was our teacher, and a strict one. There is great skill in making a good glove, and though I acquired it in time I was a bad pupil. I'd never done any needlework because Fanny was so handy. It was a long time before I was allowed to sew on the fine materials, like kid. I sewed mainly on pigskin, riding gloves for ladies and gentlemen, or plain but supple leather for ordinary folks' wear.

Mrs. Greston could not be said to lose her temper as Mother often did; she was just permanently in a low, sour humour, and in the food, poor as it was, she had the perfect weapon for discipline. Bad work meant no dinner or no supper, and in the curious way such things work out, it seemed always to be the better meals I was condemned to miss. I'd never been very plump; now I grew scrawny. My hair grew again, and was pretty for a brief time, a cap of short curls. Then Mrs. Greston sheared me again; one curl, she maintained, fell over my eye and was responsible for some bad work. Hettie's hair was mouse-coloured and without lustre and she wore it in a knot on her nape. Mrs. Greston took no interest in it.

One of the male apprentices was a fortunate fellow. His father had a farm at Nettleton and, when he was qualified, would set him up there as a saddler. There was a clause in his apprenticeship contract that forbade him setting up within five miles of Baildon. Every so often, when his father came in to market, he'd bring some kind of offering to Mrs. Greston, a pound of butter, a round Suffolk cheese, and at the same time he'd slip something to his son, whose name was Robin. That was the curious thing: almost everybody seemed to know, in a secret sort of way, that apprentices were ill-fed, yet nobody did anything about it. Except that there was a charity which once a year provided a feast for apprentices and people in the almshouses. There, in the Guildhall, the young and healthy and the old and infirm met under the benevolent eye of Mr. Turnbull and other dignitaries and ate beef and ham and solid plum pudding until they could eat no more. But it was not really a kindness. Stomachs, once full-filled, seemed to grow more

demanding, and the few days following the feast were
very hungry.

So time went on. To every glove there are ten pieces,
and presently Mrs. Greston learned that, though I
should never stitch so finely as Hettie did, I had an
eye for colour and shapes. Some of the kid gloves
were embroidered and there was a growing fashion
for the silk ones to be decorated with tiny beads. My
mind made patterns easily, perhaps because I was
fond of flowers. I could look at a jumble of beads shot
out haphazard onto a table and *see* where the pink
of the rose, the blue of the bluebell and their various
greenery should go in order to be pleasing. Sometimes, selecting the silks for the embroidery or the
beads for the encrusting, I'd know a moment of happiness—all the beauty of life running together, part
of my fantasy. Mrs. Greston never gave a word of
praise. She said, "It will do, I suppose. Get on with
it."

There'd been no hue and cry for me that I knew
of. No sheriff's man, magistrate or constable in-
quiring into what had become of Marian Thorington.
I could have been dead in a ditch. Even my name
was lost to me. Mrs. Greston called me Mary Ann,
or "you," or "that girl." Job, presumably, still supplied Mr. Greston with leather, but he never even
asked after me so far as I knew. He'd made the one
great noble gesture and was content to think that I
was safe.

Yet I—with the other—made a public appearance
once a week at church. Regular as sunrise Mr. and
Mrs. Greston led us to morning service; he rather
sombrely clad, she flauntingly. Robin and Dick wore
ordinary breeches and jerkins and little round caps
which they removed in the porch. Hettie and I wore

clean buff overalls, completely without shape, and hoods. Mother herself would not have recognized me.

In all that time, a year and three months, I had only one sign from Ockley and that by accident, not intended for me. It was July, and at the top of the communal table, Mrs. Greston said to her husband, "I have a rare treat for you this evening, a special course between meat and pudding." Our ears were trained to ignore such remarks, but the dish was brought and Mr. Greston said, "Oh, what have we here?" And Mrs. Greston said, "Young potatoes." And there they were, varying in size between a walnut and a pullet's egg, pearly white and glinting with butter. Grown at Ockley, either on Eggar's Piece or at Bowman's.

"Delicious," Mr. Greston said. "Completely delicious!" And Mrs. Greston began to explain about the young ones, such as they were now gobbling, and then later the full-grown ones, which could be boiled or baked. Mr. Heath had been selling them in the market, she said. It was daylight robbery at ninepence a pound, but he'd sold out in no time because people who had tried them last year had talked about them so much and everybody wanted to sample them. "And I thought if the butcher's wife..." she said, excusing her extravagance, for Mr. Greston's expression of delight had changed when he heard the price.

The very sight of a potato took me straight back to Ockley and the evening when I'd watched Alan reclaim his crop from the garden—though those he dug then were larger than the ones Mr. Greston was enjoying, the butter running down his chin. I suffered a great bout of lovesickness and homesickness, and when they receded they left, for the first time, a doubt as to the wisdom of my action in leaving home. Where was the point in making a sacrifice if nobody knew about it? I realised that if I had obeyed my mother I should have had some free time—the Hawk in Hand didn't need a permanent whore or the landlady would have installed one. I should have been free to go home to Ockley from time to time or, kept in Baildon by an engagement, been free to stroll around the market and see Alan when he came in to sell potatoes or anything else. Here I was, shut away like a slave, forgotten by everybody.

And beginning to have trouble with Robin.

Male and female apprentices were always kept as separate as space allowed. Hettie and I and the maid of all work, Jane, slept in a room opening off the one occupied by our master and mistress; the boys slept above, in an attic. We met at meals and that was all, and it was at suppertime that Robin had several times shown himself well disposed towards me. On the days when his father had brought him what he called "a bite," he'd slip his supper portion along the bench for me to take; all very secretly, for the pretence that we were all full-fed was kept up even at the table. And once it was not merely his portion of the hard cheese; it was a lump of ham, warm from his pocket. I could only thank him with a look.

Nobody who has not lived as we did, not starved exactly but deprived of all the pleasure food should bring, can imagine how large food can loom in one's life. There'd been lean days in Sheepgate, but there'd been full days, too. I was the girl who long ago could afford to give some of her coffin crust to a dog!

One evening—summer again—I was in the backyard, and Hettie, as she often did, having taken what she called a breath of air, had gone to her bed. Robin came climbing over the wooden fence that separated the backyard from the river.

"Tricked them all," he said. "I've been waiting for this." He threw his arms about me, lifted me off my feet, kissed me, where my hair was just beginning to grow again, on my mouth, on my neck where the ugly frock ended. His lips were warm and dry and surprisingly soft. He said, "I love you, I love you, Marian. Say you love me."

I said, "Set me down, Robin." He did so instantly, and I was disarmed partly because he obeyed me and partly because there was that look in his eyes—like the dog outside the cookshop, like Job in the garden. I said, "But, Robin, I don't love you." And yet, now that I came to look at him, he was not uncomely, with a smooth fall of straw-coloured hair and eyes as blue as a cornflower.

"No," he said, not minding what I said. "Maybe not. Like the decent little girl that you are you wouldn't think of such things. But I have. And wait till you hear what I have to offer. Listen, at Michaelmas I shall have served my time and my father..." He rattled on about what his father was prepared to do for him—set him up in a cottage near the crossroads, buy him tools and stock. "Outside the town's limit I can work as cheaply as I like. I'll undercut old Grindstone and steal his customers...." We'd have a garden, he said, and if I cared to make a few gloves and earn pin money I could, and keep it all to spend on myself.

I thought, If only I'd been heart-whole, what an offer it would have been! He looked at me so fondly.

"It's no use, Robin," I said, and there was genuine regret in my voice. "I don't love you." He refused to be dashed; he trotted out that old saying about love coming after marriage and said he loved me enough for two. He tried to kiss me again and I said, "What if Mrs. Greston looks out of a window?"

"No harm in that. I mean well by you. I know I can't marry till my time is up, but there's no wrong in making arrangements."

"What about *my* time?" I said, seeking any excuse.

My apprenticeship, the whole thing, had been so hurried and secret I knew nothing about what terms had been agreed.

"It's not the same with girls. If you married me you'd be free if you were apprenticed ten times over. A husband's rights come first."

A husband's rights—I wondered if he knew what he was talking about.

"I must go in."

"Kiss me good night."

"Good-bye, you mean. I meant what I said."

Undeterred, he kissed me again and the mild liking I'd had for him changed to disgust. Curiously, that disgust heartened me for a little while, seeming to prove that I had been right in taking my own line, not Mother's, for if I felt like this about being kissed by a kind, honest boy who loved me, how should I have felt doing the other thing with a chance-comer? In fact I went to bed that night happier than I had been for a long time, certain that I had acted for the best and sure that my fantastic dream would yet come true.

But after that Robin became a nuisance: edging up against me on the bench at table or the pew at church, venturing openly to give me food from his plate and bringing me a string of red beads from the Midsummer Fair. Mrs. Greston noticed and strongly disapproved, but now, in his last three months, Robin was independent. Short of committing some crime, he could hardly be denied his certificate of craftsmanship. If Mr. Greston denied his right now, all the other guildsmen would ask what sort of master was he if after five years Robin was unsuitable? An unlikely or rebellious lad could be got rid of up to the third year, with no shame to anybody, but not at the end of his fifth.

So Robin had his paper to tack on his wall and

left, saying to me, "I shan't forget. And don't you forget either. I'll get the house ready." And I thought, For some other girl, a fortunate girl who'd get a kind, clean-living young husband, and probably keep chickens for pin money. My own future was still a dream. But something must happen.

# CHAPTER 5

It happened all right.

A big wedding always brought a rush of orders for gloves since they were acceptable gifts.

Mrs. Greston always did the cutting out, using a metal template. Slicing into white satin, she said with as benevolent an air as she could manage, "I'm sure I wish Mistress Shawcross happy! Twelve pairs and all beaded!"

Captain Shawcross was a known customer. He'd been to sea, made a modest fortune and retired to a small estate, known as The Mount, just outside Baildon. He'd brought his saddles and harness, his driving gloves from Mr. Greston and once he had ordered a pair for a lady, rose-pink silk, which I had embroidered with paler pink roses and green leaves.

Hettie, taking advantage of Mrs. Greston's good

mood, seized the opportunity for a chatter and asked, "Who is Mistress Shawcross marrying?"

Mrs. Greston, without looking up from her cutting, said, "Mr. Heath of Ockley."

Darkness all round me and within my head a spinning dizziness. Falling, falling into a yawning emptiness. I thought, This is death.... But I did not fall, I did not die. The darkness cleared, the spinning world stopped, and there I was where I had been when the fatal words were spoken, my elbows propped on the table and between them the beads, no longer in a haphazard jumble of all colours, but in little boxes assembled on a tray. And Mrs. Greston was saying with her unusual good humour, "I can see that Mary Ann is planning patterns. Let them be good and all different," she said, reverting to her usual manner to me.

Good and all different and me without a thought in my head. Colour of rose, deep or pale, colour of bluebell, of marigold or primrose, three different greens. Quite beyond the power of my shattered mind to put together. I was in a worse state than when Mother had made my head ring with her clouts.

I had sense enough to keep my eyes directed to the beads, but as sense and feeling returned I thought, I cannot and will not bead gloves for that wedding! I must get away! Looking at the beads, I meditated the most ridiculous of actions: walking across to Hawk in Hand and telling some story of having been abducted, knocked on the head and losing my memory. Such cases were not unknown. The landlady and Mother might possibly accept it, provided they saw in my coming back a possible source of income. But who would desire me now, with my cropped head and sticking-out bones? And could I, in my present muddled state of mind, tell and hold on to so complicated a story? I said to myself, Marian Thorington, you must do better than that! And even now, with the dream all in ruins, I could not bear to think what a reconciliation with Mother would mean or how my tale would fit in with the one Job had told.

Muddle within muddle and all coiled up inside the shell of despair. Never now would the dream come true.

Then I thought of Robin. One man instead of many, and that man devoted.

I began to pick about amongst the beads.

It was the time of year when darkness fell soon after dinner, but work did not stop. Candlelight was too wavery and uncertain, so Mr. Greston had bought oil lamps, fuelled by whale oil. It was, he said, cruelly expensive and not to be used after supper, except in an emergency. That evening counted as an emergency, and after supper Mrs. Greston went on cutting and Hettie sewed and I pretended to make patterns.

At last Mrs. Greston said, "That will do for today. Get to bed." In standing up I managed to disarrange all the patterns so carefully assembled. I thought, I will have no part in this! And Mrs. Greston said, "You clumsy wench! No dinner tomorrow."

In our cold room, Hettie said, without malice, "No dinner. And no Robin to slip you a piece."

"I know. Such a dismal thought, I need a breath of air in order to face it." I reached down my cloak and hood.

"In this howling gale?" But she had already lost interest.

I went out by the back door and over the fence which Robin had climbed, coming in from the street by the back entry. I did not take that way. I went straight for the woods.

Amongst the trees it was less sheltered than I had expected; the wind came in gusts, sometimes so strong that I seemed to make no progress; sometimes after a lull, coming at me so suddenly and with such force that it knocked me into tree trunks. Within half an hour I was regretting having acted so hastily. I should have waited for daylight—but then how should I have made my escape unobserved? Although this part of the wood was so near Baildon, it was unknown to me—in my childhood there'd been no time for taking walks. I knew that on the side of the wood where Ockley was there were pools, and in winter, swampy places; this side might be the same, so despite my eagerness to reach some kind of shelter I walked with care. Once a thought struck me and I halted. Why be careful? Why not walk into a pool and have done? Nobody would know, or care. I'd lived in an idiotic dream which had been shattered that morning: what did life hold for me hereafter? Nothing that I wanted.

Yet despite the empty bleakness of the future, I could not, when I came to the first pool, walk into it. Vaguely I realised that I had made too many decisions in a hurry, but none fatal as suicide would be. I was not yet eighteen. I'd been a great fool, but while I was alive, I might do better. Meantime I was completely lost in a wood and a thin sleety rain was beginning to fall. Skirting the pool, I plodded on.

I smelt the charcoal burner's oven before I came to it—a smell of scorching, as though a woman, ironing some garment, had fired her iron too hot or not moved it quickly enough. Following my nose, I went on and came to the oven and the hut, two similar structures, and the oven not much smaller than the dwelling place. The oven showed a glow at its base, the hut a gleam of firelight through a hole in the wall. There was a little low doorway with a door of rough planks. I tapped on it, and after what seemed a long time it creaked open and an old, querulous voice said, "Is that you, Emma? I told you I'd leave the door on the latch."

I said, "I am a stranger, asking shelter." One of those gusts, laden with sleet, charged at me and I almost fell into the tiny hot room. The old man to whom it belonged said, "Come in, whoever you are, afore you hev us both blown away. God in heaven, you're in a sorry pickle!" Then he turned away and, moving stiffly but as quickly as he could, snatched a frying pan from the fire. "Just saved it," he said. "And I mighta known Emma had more sense than to be out in this. Who're you?"

"Just a lost wayfarer, trying to get to Nettleton."

"That ain't so far," he said, "you ain't missed it by much. But you can't go on. No, you must bide. Have Emma's piece. I cooked for two." The pan was full of rasher bacon, the best. He set it, still sizzling, on the plank of wood that served him as a table, and he sawed into the loaf of fine white bread, handing me a slice. "Help yourself," he said, "Emma ain't coming. Your clothes is steaming and thass bad, very bad to sit in damp steaming clothes. Give you the lung rot in no time at all. I'll hang 'em up."

He did so; then we both dived into the pan where the bacon was still hot but no longer sizzling and, balancing the rashers on our bread, ate.

I'd had no appetite for the fat pork dinner or the hard cheese supper because my heart had broken that morning, and even had I not been planning to run away from those wedding gloves, Mrs. Greston's punishment of no dinner tomorrow would not have hurt me, for I had felt then that I should never want to eat again. But now, face to face with such un-questioning kindness from this odd little man, I recovered my appetite and ate heartily.

Afterwards he said, "You can hev Emma's bed. She wouldn't mind. And don't let me disturb you. I have to keep the oven going and the logs turned. Emma 'on't to be back tonight."

I spurred up enough interest to ask, "Is Emma your daughter?"

"No. A lotta people make that mistake, she's so young-looking and pretty. No, Emma's me wife."

Emma's bed, though it lay on the bare earth, was soft and plump, filled with feathers. I sank into it, and after the day which had been endless and all the battering of the storm, I sank into a deep, dreamless sleep.

When I woke I lay for a moment, thinking. At this time yesterday I didn't know; I'd never heard of Mistress Shawcross: I was still living in a dream. Then I thought, This is a new day and Robin will be pleased to see me. And I thought, I shall make him a good wife, all the better perhaps because I do not love him and so shall always be paying off a debt.

We breakfasted off bread spread with the fat left in the frying pan. Then the old man said, "You can use Emma's box, if you like. She wouldn't mind. She's a kindhearted girl." From some hidden niche he produced a box, rather handsome, with the letters "E E" carved into the lid. For a charcoal burner's wife, Emma was well supplied: her box contained a brush, an ivory comb, a mirror of polished metal and a pair of scissors, with some other oddments for the toilet. I don't know why but I had the feeling that nothing in the box had been used very recently. Then I dropped that thought, staring at my own face. One of the tree trunks with which I had collided had gashed my forehead. I hadn't noticed and perhaps the rain had washed most of the blood away, but enough remained, congealed over the wound, to leave an unsightly mark. I cleaned it and the rest of my face with the hem of my cloak, which was still damp; I brushed and combed my hair, which was growing

out again from the last cropping. I tried to pull a
curl over the gash, but it was not quite long enough
yet.

There was lipsalve in Emma's box and I would
have used it, but the paste was dry and cracked. The
old man came back from the turf-covered mound in
which his wood was baking and I thanked him again
and asked him to point out the way to Nettleton.

"Village or crossroads?"

"Crossroads."

He knew the woods well, could even tell me of a
place where a fallen tree lay. "It ain't so very far,"
he said encouragingly. "And if you should see Emma,
tell her...tell her the door's on the latch."

It was not until some time later that I learned
that Emma had been dead for ten years.

The wind had blown itself out during the night
and it was a clear, wintry morning. The path was
thick with mud. I reached the point where, as the
old man had told me, three woodland paths met. The
one to the left led to Ockley and I stood and stared
down it for a long minute, letting the heartbreak get
the better of me again. Then I trudged on and came
to the Nettleton crossroads.

Robin's father had set him up well; the house,
rather larger than a cottage—in fact rather like
Bowman's at Ockley—had been newly whitewashed
and freshly thatched. Over the door a painted sign
said, "R. Reeve. Saddler." One of the lower windows—the one facing the road—had been enlarged
to admit more light. Immediately within it was a
working bench scattered with material and tools,
and behind it sat Robin, lining a horse collar.

I tapped at the window, and Robin looked up. Another of life's unforgettable moments. I had expected
astonishment, followed by delight. What I saw was
recognition and utter dismay.

He had mastered it by the time I reached the door, which he had come to open, and he greeted me with one of those smiles which do not include the eyes.

"Marian," he exclaimed. "Have you run away?"

Even a year earlier I might have mustered enough courage to have thought up some alternative plan, but months of low feeding, yesterday's shock, the struggle through the wind and rain had robbed me of something so that all I craved was shelter and security.

Mustering a brightness as brittle as his own, I said, "Yes. When you spoke to me of marriage, you said it would set me free."

He said, slowly, "Ye-es. I did say that. Well, come in. Give me your cloak. Sit by the fire." He noticed the mark in my forehead. "Did she hit you?"

One more smear on a chimney sweep couldn't hurt, so I said, "Yes. Ever since you left, Robin, she has been hard on me. She said I was dreamy and absentminded. And I was. You see, I was always thinking of *you*. That night in the yard when you said you loved me, I said I didn't love you. I was mistaken. When you left I missed you so much that I realised I was wrong. I was too young to understand then..."

Young! I was older than Eve!

"We'll be married then," he said, and he spoke like a man taking up a heavy burden. But I had no care for him; I had my own burden. Poor boy; afterwards I learned what he had faced at that moment. In so short a time he had forgotten me and the boy's fancy he'd taken for me, and he'd found, or his parents had found for him, a far better match. Yet he stood by his word, and I stood by my determination to make him a good wife simply because I did not love him.

Curiously, ours was a most successful marriage. Even his mother, who had disliked me on sight just as Mrs. Greston had done, came round with the birth of our first child, which was also her first grandchild, Robin's elder brother, who had inherited Curlew Farm, having so far had no child.

I worked, kept house, bore and reared three children and made uncountable pairs of gloves, for in that dismal room behind the shop at Baildon I had learned almost without knowing. And I suited Robin particularly well in the early days because I was no shrinking, cringing virgin faced with a clumsy inexperienced boy. I knew enough to make him get up from our marital bed well pleased with himself and with me. The burden which he had shouldered that wintry morning grew featherlight, finally vanished altogether. Mine never lifted.

# PART SIX

# Narrative by Arabella Shawcross

# CHAPTER 1

My father always denied that he had been a pirate, but sometimes in his cups he let slip words of places and bits of reminiscences not strictly in accord with his claim to have made his fortune by honest trading with the East India Company.

I could understand his reticence, for times had changed. In Elizabeth's day men like Francis Drake, John Hawkins and Walter Raleigh, who behaved on the sea just as sturdy beggars did on land, had been honoured and popular, but with the coming of James Stuart and his desire to make peace with Spain, all was altered. The execution of Sir Walter Raleigh was symbolic.

With Father, too, there was the family to be considered. My Grandfather Shawcross was parson at Gorleston in Norfolk, and my mother's family, the Mortons, owned Browston Hall. All eminently respectable people. Father had been destined for the Church, too—sometimes he claimed that he had actually been ordained. Then he'd run into some sort of trouble and the two families had combined to buy him a ship.

Mother and I spent most of our time at Browston, with regular visits to Gorleston; after her death, which occurred when I was about six, the process was reversed, to my sorrow, for I loved Browston and my Morton grandparents were far more easygoing. At Gorleston I became very much a parsonage child, always being adjured to set a good example, and later to indulge in good works.

While Mother lived, Father made fairly frequent visits; afterwards he came home more rarely. He had long since repaid the money he owed, with most handsome interest, and he brought extravagant presents for everyone, but he was not fully approved of. He drank, he smoked and, when angry, swore.

He never showed towards me that doting indulgence which many daughters receive from their fathers, though he was kind enough and always brought me gifts of great splendour. Once, I remember, it was a necklace—no, more than a necklace—a parure of emeralds and diamonds, huge stones linked together with gold and intended to be worn with a very low-necked dress. The green fire and the rainbow-coloured fire blazed as I tried the centre piece against the back of my hand.

Grandmother Shawcross said, with rebuke in her voice, "It is pretty and doubtless of value, Daniel. But where could the child wear it?" I was fifteen at the time and no longer strictly a child.

"When she goes to the Castle. Or are you no longer invited there?" He could say things like that without meditating them. He knew that his mother valued above all things any mark of favour from the Dunwich family. We were never invited on truly grand occasions, only when other people of a moderate sort were present, but then, as a clergyman's wife, my grandmother took precedence.

Now she said, "My goodness! If the Dowager Lady Dunwich saw that, she'd die of envy."

The Dowager Lady Dunwich was a most formidable old lady. She must have been a beauty in her youth, and though she was old now, with the help of every means known to woman, she still, at a slight distance, looked wonderful. It was said that she had modelled her appearance on that of Queen Elizabeth: false hair, padded bust and a complexion so loaded with paint, red on white, that it was like a mask and would crack if she gave even a halfhearted smile. She never managed even that, and on the only time when I was really close enough to her to see the falsity of it all, I also saw her eyes; and they were sad. As though she had known a great sorrow, or cherished some nagging regret.

Yet, from such of her story as I had heard in bits and pieces, she'd been a singularly fortunate woman. Her husband, Lord Dunwich, had died, leaving no child, and his apparent heir, a nephew, had come storming down from Lincolnshire, set to claim all, but she'd halted him, saying that a month would elapse before she knew whether or not she were pregnant. And she was. The would-be heir retired growling and suspicious, but the posthumous child—the present Earl of Dunwich—conformed in every way to the family pattern.

My grandmother always said that she detested gossip; but yesterday's gossip seemed to mellow, like medlars, and become acceptable.

I was not, as a rule, much interested in my grandmother's old stories, but in anything to do with the Dunwich family I took an interest that was morbid, yet understandable considering my near worship for all things beautiful. Lord Dunwich's son, Lord Gorleston, was the most beautiful young man, the most beautiful person, I had ever seen, or was ever likely to see. He was tall and slim, with an outdoor complexion and bright hair, midway between brown and red. He wore it in long, shining ringlets. His eyes were very blue and had what I can only call a caressing quality. He seemed to know that a smile from him could make your heart turn over.

I saw him at the Castle on what I call public occasions: Christmas, the Harvest Feast each year, and one year, his coming of age. They all ended with dancing, and as I grew into my teen-age it seemed to me that Lord Gorleston singled me out.

My grandmother, whose sharp eyes missed nothing, thought so, too, and saw fit to remind me that young lords did not seek their wives in country parsonages. Up to that moment the idea of marrying him had not occurred to me, but when she put the idea into my head I thought, And why not? My family was respectable, my upbringing impeccable and on one of his visits Father had said, "You're no great beauty, but you'll have a good dowry."

I disliked the words about my looks. In truth they were variable; when I was dull or sulky I was just a plain girl with mid-brown hair and grey eyes which took on the colour of whatever was nearest them. When I wore blue they seemed blue, but I wore blue very seldom. My grandmother favoured drab colours, grey and buff, always of good material, and all clothes made to allow for the growth of everything except vanity.

I was quite content with the shape of my face, rather triangular with a neat, straight nose and thin arched eyebrows some shades deeper than my hair. Given more colour in my cheeks and lips—momentarily attained by pinching and biting—and plenty of blue dresses, I should have looked very different.

There was really no reason why I should not have had as many blue dresses as I wanted; Father always gave me plenty of money, but my grandmother was a very dominant character and most of the time it was easier to avoid friction. She thought I should save money; she appeared to have no faith in Father's prosperity. "Easy come, easy go," she would say. "He has only to lose his ship..."

However, the time came when I decided to spend some of my hoard. I was eighteen.

Yarmouth was our nearest town, and during the winter there was always a great deal of hardship there, far more than the Poor Law institutions could possibly deal with. Yarmouth depended largely upon the herring fisheries, and if the weather were too bad for boats to go out, people starved—not the fishermen only but all those engaged in allied trades, the men who made barrels in which the fish were packed, the people who did the salting and smoking, even the net-makers. Also, of course, every winter found a lot of sailors "beached" as they called it. Gorleston suffered in the same way and from the same causes, but far less obviously, being much smaller. A certain amount of poverty can be absorbed by a community.

Charity is a Christian duty, but there are limits to it, and that year Lord Dunwich thought of a painless way of raising money—an assembly in Yarmouth Guildhall. The tickets were very expensive, twenty shillings each person, or thirty for a married couple; but as my grandfather said, sourly, "It gives every Tom, Dick and Harry a chance to rub shoulders with the nobility."

My grandmother said, "I suppose we must go. We

can afford it. But it will come hard on some who cannot and yet do not wish to appear uncharitable."

"Food and wine is included."

"So it should be, at that price."

I walked into Yarmouth to buy the material I needed for a dress. My grandfather kept a riding horse but he had never encouraged me to mount it. So I walked and I found exactly what I wanted, some velvet at the mercers. It was not quite blue—I had to think about my eyes; nor quite green—I had to think about the emeralds, which I was determined to wear come what might.

Now and then, walking about in Gorleston, doing errands or making visits to the sick, I had thought how marvellous it would be if Lord Gorleston should ride up behind me, recognise me and offer me a pillion lift. It had never happened, but the possibility lent a little flavour to my dismal errands. People who were sick or in any kind of trouble tended to send for Parson, and more and more lately my grandfather had said, "You go, Arabella. Find out what is wrong. There are few ills that a shilling will not cure." And because my father had paid and overpaid his debt, my grandfather could well afford the shilling, which did indeed seem to be a cure-all.

I bought my velvet and I shaped my dress, very low in the neck, doing most of the work in my bedroom, which was very cold, my grandmother being sparing of fires.

Lord Dunwich, to whom I had paid little attention over the years, was a good-hearted man. Well before the date of the assembly he had sent a servant to say that one of his coaches would collect us. "Most considerate," my grandmother said, but she was not pleased when she found that we were not the only passengers. A yeoman farmer and his wife, having bought tickets out of charity, but lacking the necessary transport, had been considered, taken care of, provided for.

I had emerged from my bedroom wearing my best cloak and a lacy scarf, so nobody knew how low in the neck my dress was, or that I was wearing the emeralds, until we were in the anteroom where ladies removed their outer clothing. My grandmother could not very well make a fuss here, but she gave me a look! I didn't care. There was a glass on the wall and one glimpse in it had assured me that I was looking my very best. Excitement had coloured my cheeks and brightened my eyes, and my gown, though homemade and simple, was elegant.

The main hall was far too small to contain all those who had bought tickets. Here the Dunwich family were holding court, greeting people, thanking them for coming and making the gathering such a success, and then sieving them away into the adjoining rooms. There was something for all tastes: dancing, a puppet show and, of course, the food. There were also ways of raising even more money: you could pay a penny and guess how many beans there were in a bowl or the weight of a pig, tethered in a corner.

My grandmother led the way straight into the room where the food was. It was quite unnecessary for her to hiss, "Stay close to me," for in any assembly an unmarried girl stayed with the elder woman in whose care she was, unless claimed for a dance by some man of honourable intentions or invited to join a party of young people in the charge of another chaperone.

The people in the dining room, where the buffets were all most enticingly set out, were all middle-aged or old, intent on getting their money's worth. My blue-green velvet and my emerald parure were completely wasted here. I mourned while my grandfather said, "I understand that Lord Dunwich provided this feast. Most generous of him!" and my grandmother eyed and mentally rejected ordinary things like ham and beef, cut very thin, and settled for some example of the pastry cook's art, a coffer, or coffin, filled with veal and jelly.

And then suddenly Lord Gorleston was there, smiling that heart-turning smile and bowing, calling my grandmother "Madam" and asking leave to borrow me to tread a measure with him, there being a shortage of ladies in the dancing room. She could not well refuse; in effect the Dunwich family were as much hosts here as at the Castle, but her eyes warned me.

Because, despite the great entry price, the assembly was mixed; the dances were much like those at harvest feasts, country dancing rather than stately measures. One ended with a twirl and a kiss. So he lifted me and twirled me, skirts flying, and then kissed me, and I kissed him as no modest maid would have done, with my heart on my lips. He looked, I admit, slightly astonished, but pleased, and he kept his hold on my hand while signalling to the fiddlers and flautists to start up for the new measure. In the confusion he pulled me through an archway, into a little dark room.

This was a noonday assembly because so many people had to travel to it and in late November the weather was unreliable; but everything that could be done to make this look like an evening assembly had been done, shutters closed, curtains drawn and a multitude of candles burning, but there was no candle in this small room. And there he kissed me, differently, hungrily....

Ever since I have been overtolerant of females who are not virtuous. A lustful man, if acceptable, can turn a woman's bones to wax. I was only just saved, not by my virtue or his restraint, but a voice from the outside world calling his name. He said, "I must go," and tore himself away. I stayed in the dark until I had composed myself. Then I fumbled my way out and found a stairway, dimly lighted, which led to the room where my grandparents, with others, were still eating.

My grandmother said, "That was a long dance."

"And very intricate," I said. She was still busy with what must have been her second or third helping of the veal pie; my grandfather had moved on to the sweetmeats.

Ironically, nothing came of that assembly except two offers of marriage. I had been noticed, with my bold dress and my jewels. But I was fortunate; my grandmother might dither, rather flattered, but my grandfather, whose word after all was law, said that though he and my grandmother had reared and cared for me the only person competent to make any marriage arrangement for me was my father and their suit must wait until he was ashore again.

The would-be suitors were discouraged and spread the word—avoid Arabella Shawcross.

I was nineteen, twenty, twenty-one. An old maid in an age when marriages were made at fifteen. And since, wanting only one love, I could tolerate the idea of no other man, and since Lord Gorleston now seldom came to Norfolk, I fell into resignation. Of course, I realised, young lords did not seek wives in parsonages, however ardently they might kiss daughters of the parsonage in little dark rooms.

Twenty-one is not really old except where marriage is concerned, and turning away from marriage, the prospect of childbearing, I became far more energetic.

My grandfather craved immortality through his

sermons. He believed them to be unique and worthy
of publication and he'd found a printer in Bungay
who was prepared to print them—at a price—provided a fair copy could be supplied. To make that
fair copy was my task, and no light one. My grandfather had at his best written a crabbed hand, on
papers of various qualities and sizes, and now, with
a hand made tremulous with age, he added correc-
tions, or even with scissors cut out sentences. It was
a jagged, ragged manuscript which I had to deal
with, but I preferred such work to the visiting of the
distressed, and as page after page, in a fair and le-
gible hand, was added to the pile, I took pride in it
and I was delighted when one day my grandfather
said, "Arabella, how should I manage without you?"
My grandmother never said anything quite so direct,
but as day crept past day she too relied upon me
increasingly, would I see to this and that, could such
and such a duty be left to me? Gradually I became
a kind of housekeeper to my grandmother, and a kind
of curate to my grandfather. I put away all frivolous
thoughts, and no one watching me upon my daily
round would have dreamed that I had once worn
green velvet and been kissed by Lord Gorleston in
a small dark room to the tune of "Greensleeves."

Into this placid, orderly and deadly dull life my
father burst like a hurricane.

# CHAPTER 2

This time he was home for good; he'd made his fortune and sold his ship and was negotiating for a house on the outskirts of a Suffolk town called Baildon. "Not an estate," he explained. "I wanted no tenants. Too much like crews, always needing coddling or whipping. But for all that it's a gentleman's residence. There's a lodge each side of the gate. One for the groom, one for the gardener."

He professed himself dissatisfied with my appearance. "Have you been ill?" he demanded. I told him that I was in perfect health. "Then what's happened to you since I last saw you?" I couldn't very well say that I'd had an imaginary love affair and got over it by the exercise of good common sense and keeping busy. So I said, "I suppose I've grown up. It is, after all, almost four years."

"Yes. I have been neglectful. But we'll make up

for all that! Do you have a dress that is not the colour of Orinoco mud?"

"What colour is that?"

"The colour you're wearing."

"I have a beautiful green dress..." I'd laid it away, with lavender and rosemary, rather as one lays away the body of a loved one.

"Let's see it, then. And while you're about it, put a bit of curl to your hair and a bit..." He broke off, realising where he was and to whom he was speaking, but I knew what he meant. A bit of colour.

All that was available to me just then were the petals of a flower that came out of Africa but could be coaxed into almost perennial bloom if kept indoors and not watered too freely: it was called the geranium. He had himself brought the plant to England. It had red flowers.

I disinterred the green dress. A painful business. We had, of course, been invited to the Castle on the ritual occasions, but I had gone clad in the drab of resignation. And Lord Gorleston had been there, I think, only once, for a relative in Lincolnshire had died childless and left all to him. And had he been there every time it would have meant only pain to me. There is that story of Cinderella and Prince Charming. Just for a few moments I had been Cinderella, but nothing had come of it. Prince Charming had said, "I must go," and had gone and that was that.

It had not been really necessary to put the green dress away with rosemary and lavender; moths do not attack velvet. The herbs had dried and fell about like ashes as I took the dress from the press and shook it. All that remained were ghosts: ghosts of fragrance, ghosts of feelings. And where had I put Father's emeralds? I had not worn them since, either.

Curls. Very easy, for although my hair might lack

something in its colouring, its texture was good and it curled easily. And the crushed geranium petals gave my cheeks and lips a steady colour.

"That," my father exclaimed when I presented myself, "is more like it," and something happened to me. In fact I was like my eyes, affected by what was nearest. I had lived in the shadow of my grandparents, now I was moving into the orbit of a very different character, exuberant, earthy, rather coarse. "Buy yourself a poor scribe," Father said, dumping down some money when my grandfather said mournfully that his sermons were only half copied. Now that I was to be taken from them, my grandmother admitted that I had been very helpful both in the house and in the parish. "Yes," Father said, "she was beginning to get that maid-of-all-work look."

"Better that than the way she looks now," my grandmother said tartly, eyeing the green dress with disapproval. "And if you must smoke that disgusting pipe, Daniel, you would oblige me by taking it outside." Understandably, Father was anxious to move as soon as possible, and with this in mind had bought The Mount as the house was called, with the furniture, just as it stood. We moved in April, to my mind usually a sweet month, and this no exception.

Father was disgusted to learn that I had never learned to ride. "Surely to God," he exclaimed, ignoring the rule about taking God's name in vain, "I paid enough. She should have had a pony and a groom, and by now a good horse."

"And been free to roam the countryside at will?" my grandmother asked. "Arabella has been brought up correctly."

"I have ordered a coach, but they take time to make." He turned to me and said, "You'll have to ride pillion with me."

I remembered my girlish dream of Lord Gorleston

coming up behind me and inviting me to ride behind him. A green dress, a parure of emeralds, can be disinterred, as good as new; a dead dream is dead forever.

The part of Suffolk in which Father had chosen to make his home was less flat than most of the rest of East Anglia. The Mount deserved its name. Baildon lay in a saucerlike hollow, all roads running down to it and then up again. The Mount stood on its eastern side, on the rim, as it were, with a good view over the river, which threaded through the town, and the jumble of roofs, two church towers and great sweeps of woodland. The house was large and solid and well appointed, the grounds well laid out, a gentleman's residence indeed. It had belonged to Sir Edward Shelmadine of Clevely.

Silly young girls are not the only people who dream dreams. I came to realise that hard, grown men like Father could indulge in flights of fancy, too. He wanted to be a country gentleman and assumed that he could accomplish this because he was rich, lived in a fine house and kept a coach and four as well as several saddle horses. He could hardly have chosen an area where such things made less impact.

The whole area of South Suffolk of which Baildon was the centre was occupied by what, reared in the shadow of the Dunwich family, I could only consider petty country gentry, but they were all prouder than Lucifer and they'd all been there since the Flood, and much as they might differ and bicker among themselves, to an outsider they presented a united front, all reinforced by blood kinship or by marriage. Father and I were rank outsiders and, worse than that, rich. The true country gentleman, dependent upon his own harvest, or upon his tenants for rent— and all of them dependent upon the harvest—had an inborn distrust of money gained from some other source. Later on I learned that there had been a run of unseasonably wet weather, which in an area which grew wheat and barley, or where the ground rose slightly was devoted to sheep, meant that all around us there were families rather poorer than they had been in the immediate past.

One would have thought that in the circumstances a young woman, and only daughter of a rich man, would have attracted some attention, but as Father's choice of place was bad, so was his timing. There was a dearth of young men, younger brothers, younger sons, the kind of men to whom I, for all my lack of pedigree, might have been a godsend.

Father commented upon this coarsely, and I, learning to trim my sails to the prevailing wind, answered him in the same way. I said—imagine my grandmother's horror—"Perhaps *you* should be the one on the marriage market." He roared with laughter and said, "Once was enough. Your mother, God rest her, was a good woman. I have no wish to replace her. And the bad ones come ten a penny. No, we're in the doldrums now, but there'll come a wind and we all set to take advantage of it."

I said, matching coarseness with coarseness, "I want no man. I'm quite happy as I am." And it was true. I positively revelled in the comfort and freedom this new life offered me. As for the loneliness which Father seemed to feel and resent so much, hadn't I always been lonely? A little set apart? Here it was much the same, but without the penny-pinching. A fat cook in the kitchen, positively affronted at the very suggestion of any economy; a waiting man at table; an upstairs maid.

Father, of course, was not lonely quite in the sense that I was; he could always take the short ride down to the Hawk in Hand and there be a man amongst men—and I sometimes suspected that there he met some of the bad women who were ten a penny. I saw one once, wearing the ritual scarlet and with a great mass of black hair.

During this time Sir Edward Shelmadine called, stiff and punctilious, to ask was all well, was Father satisfied with the state in which the house had been left and was Meekings, the groom, proving satisfactory? Father forced hospitality upon him. Dinner just about to be served: saddle of lamb and salad—Father, having been a seaman and so often deprived of green-stuff, could never have enough of salad—strawberries from the garden and cream. Father also opened a bottle of brandy, and Sir Edward became almost human. He said, "You are not the first man to come out of the sea and take foothold here. I was very young but I remember the talk..."

Father was not much interested, but I was. A story after my own heart, curses and charms and good luck changing to ill and two women contending for the possession of a house, a deaf and dumb woman who spent most of her time killing young pigs and a mad-woman kept in a cage.

Sir Edward lacked personal knowledge and had no idea of chronological order; also he had enjoyed the brandy. I asked whereabouts all these dramatic things had taken place and he said at Ockley, not so very far away if one avoided the road and went through the woods. I decided to go next day. He was capable of telling me which path to take where two or three met.

After he had gone Father said, "There now, didn't I treat him royally? The best of food and liquor and didn't I listen patiently to all his meanderings? He's bound to invite us to Clevely now." I almost said that I'd bet him a crown against such a thing happening. Father liked a bet, even with me, even about a triviality, but I felt that to him this was too serious a matter, so I held my tongue.

The woodland ride debouched into open farmland, green with winter-sown wheat and in one place darker green with some low plant which I did not recognise. To my right stood some cottages, and on a mound, lower than that of The Mount, a house, at first sight imposing, with a stone centre and porch and half-timbered wings on either side. There was a slightly defined track and I kept to it, becoming as I drew near the house aware of an unmistakable odour—the stink of a tanyard.

Sir Edward had called the place the Old Priory and ruins were plentiful, even in the garden, which I saw was ill-kept. I remembered Sir Edward's words about two women contending for possession of the house and concluded that neither of them wanted the garden.

Beyond the house and at a lower level there was a small church, a loop of the river with a bridge over it. Between the bridge and the rear of the house the track was far more clearly defined, and, my curiosity satiated, for nothing of the drama was evident here, I was making for this track when a woman emerged from the house.

Except that she now wore a wrapper instead of a red dress, she was—or could have been twin sister to—the bad woman I had seen at the Hawk in Hand. I thought that and then hastily changed my mind; this was the madwoman who by Sir Edward's account was kept in a kind of cage. She came straight at me, shouting, "Whaddyou want?" She frightened my horse and I spent a second or two in soothing it. I had come late to riding but I already knew that there should be sympathy between horse and rider.

I said, "Steady, girl! Steady, Bess," and patted her sleek neck.

The madwoman said, "You're on my land! I don't allow no trespassers! If you want Mistress Tresize, go back the way you come and use the bridge."

Perhaps I was better equipped than most people to deal with the demented. The good works which my grandfather had gradually shuffled off onto me included visits to the asylum for the insane halfway between Gorleston and Yarmouth. Also, in a rage, my father could shout and gesticulate much as this woman was doing. I said, "I meant no offence. I was taking a ride and just happened..." The golden rule in dealing with the demented was, I knew, to pretend and speak calmly. This lunatic woman was not assuaged. She said, "And if it's Mr. Heath and his rotten potatoes you're after, they're across the river. People who want leather know the way to come."

I said, "Well, have I your leave to go to the river?"

It worked. She said, "Just this once. Don't make a habit of it. You might make something called right-of-way. And I've had enough trouble with *that*."

Then, by one of those unaccountable flicks of fortune, I looked up and saw, inside an upper window, another woman, very thin and pale, almost ghost-like. Was she the lunatic and this angry incoherent woman her keeper? If so, I thought, God pity her! But it would explain the red-faced woman's dislike for trespassers. At the public asylum which my grandfather or his deputy were authorised to make visits to the keepers liked to be informed beforehand.

To be honest there was not much that could be done to help the insane. Looking after them is such distasteful work that only the roughest, hardest people would go in for it and all the visitors could do was to see that *some* of the funds allocated for their feeding and clothing were used for the proper purpose.

I rode on towards the bridge. I understood what the rough woman had said. Behind the house the path forked; and then I remembered part of Sir Edward's muddled story about two women contesting for the possession of the house. The good-works, busybodying person which I thought I had done with forever got the better of me and joined hands with a natural curiosity. What name had the harridan used? Mistress Tresize. Curious name. But if she lived in part of the house she should know something of the poor madwoman and how she was treated. Without really considering what exactly I was doing or what I hoped to achieve, I turned my horse onto the other path and followed it to the back of the house and round to the side.

I was by nature rather shy, yet my upbringing had given me a kind of confidence. In and around Gorleston I was Parson Shawcross's granddaughter and always treated with some respect. And spurred by any emotion—however silly, like my infatuation which had expressed itself in green velvet—I could be fairly resolute.

It was all rather like one of those crazy dreams in which everything is displaced. On the ground floor of this part of the house there were pigs and fowls. Who was mad enough to keep such stock in panelled parlours?

Yet my rap on the door resulted in nothing more unusual than a maid, rather old, but tidy and nimble.

I said, "I would like to speak with Mistress Tresize."

"She is here, madam. Dummy will hold your horse."

I said, "My horse will stand." That was one thing I had achieved by kindness. I don't say that Bess would have stood through fire or flood but ordinarily when I said, "Stand," she stood, patiently.

The maid, plainly well-trained, said, "Madam, may I have your name?"

"Shawcross. Mistress Shawcross."

She led me up some good stairs, which seemed to have nothing to do with the pigs and fowls below, and flung open a wide door and said, "Madam, Mistress Shawcross to see you," and coming forward to greet me was the woman I had seen at the window; very thin, very pale, but very obviously not a person to whom one could say, "I thought you were a lunatic, possibly ill-treated."

My embarrassment was absolute, but she had that smooth, sophisticated manner which overrides such situations with the ease of a good horse taking an easy fence.

"You are new to this district, Mistress Shawcross. Do sit down. May I offer a glass of wine? It is a warm morning."

Cooler in this upper room with the windows closed and the scent of the potpourri with which she was busy scenting the air. She said, "This is the first year that the red roses have flourished in their new home, so I am making the best of them....I saw you from the window. It is such a mortification to me to be obliged to keep windows closed, but that tanyard..." She spread elegant hands, shrugged elegant shoulders, and then, because I was momentarily tongue-tied, said, "Well, is it the young pigs or the fowls that interest you? I must warn you—I have a rather long waiting list." Thus forced into the open, I tried to explain, clumsily trying to make her see that at least I had been activated by goodwill. She listened gravely, and when I ran out of words said, "You have great courage!" and then laughed. "No, Mistress Babcock and I have the house between us and probably an impartial observer would say we were both lunatic. Me with pigs in the parlour and she poisoning her own air in order to persecute me. Tell me, how do you like Suffolk?" Somehow she contrived to smooth over the awkwardness and make it seem like a morning call which any lady might make upon the other.

I stole little glances around the room; the furniture all old and heavy but well-kept; no display of any kind; both windowsills full of plants in pots. "My makeshift garden, for a time," Mistress Tresize said, "but now I have some plants across the river."

Then the door opened and Lord Gorleston walked in!

# CHAPTER 3

It was not, of course, Lord Gorleston, but the likeness was uncanny—shape, size, everything; the rare dark red of the hair, the blue of the eyes. Dress this man in satin and jewels or put Lord Gorleston into working garb and the two would have been indistinguishable. As he said, "Good morning, Lettice, I have brought you some early potatoes," there was even in his eyes that caressing look which was Lord Gorleston's specialty. But with this man it was not a habitual look; it faded as Mistress Tresize introduced us.

"Mistress Shawcross," she said, "this is a young relative of mine, Alan Heath. Alan, Miss Shawcross, a newcomer to Baildon—and a most valiant young lady!" She made rather much of my very natural mistake. "Mistress Shawcross actually braved that terrible woman," she said. "And doesn't it show how old stories linger on? That poor lunatic dead so long ago!"

He gave me a glance, quite approving, but cool, and then turned back to her. "You invite such mistakes," he said. "If I've said it once, I've said it a thousand times. Your place is at Bowman's."

"Oh, no. Here. Here for as long as I live."

In a way they were being unmannerly, discussing in the presence of a stranger something which concerned only themselves. I was beginning to feel shy and awkward, and then, just for a second, I saw them both in profile and their likeness to one another and to the Dunwich family was so great that I forgot myself.

Alan Heath was carrying a reed basket. He set it on the table and it yawned open, showing three red roses and some whitish, roundish objects the size of a large plum.

"Since you will not come to Bowman's," he said, "Bowman's must come to you. The rose transplanted well, and here are the first potatoes."

"Thank you, Alan, my dear." She said that seriously and then, reverting to the near flippancy with which she had recounted my mistake, said, "Maybe you are missing an opportunity. Mistress Shawcross, are you familiar with the potato?"

"I am now hearing the name for the first time," I said. "What is it?"

They explained; a new vegetable which seemed to have every virtue possible to a plant; easy to cultivate, very versatile, a luxury when young—as those now in the basket were—and when mature a worthy addition to any dish, or, baked and buttered, a dish on its own. They urged me to take some. Alan Heath said that he was in the habit of giving samples— people always came back for more. I accepted, thinking that one gift would justify another and give me a reason for a further visit and that I wanted, for, quite apart from Alan Heath's appeal to my over-susceptible heart, I found the situation fascinating. Two such elegant people with beautiful voices and beautiful manners living in such unlikely circumstances. I felt that even the horrible woman whom they called Mistress Babcock needed some explanation.

I had the potatoes served to Father as a surprise; and he *was* surprised to find them in England though he said he had eaten them in Port Royal, Panama, and in Ireland. "And once a smooth rogue sold me three sacksful as a guard against scurvy. They were all rotten by the time we reached Barbados!" It was in such casual speech that he betrayed the fact that all his voyages had not been to the East. I was not particularly well-educated—my grandfather had only given lessons enough to make me useful to him—but I was observant and could read a map.

On that evening Father was not greatly interested in what I had to tell him about Mistress Tresize, Alan Heath and the place called the Old Priory. He was not intrigued, as I was, by a woman so obviously superior, keeping a neat parlour above a pigstye, or a man—Lord Gorleston's very image—wearing working clothes and growing potatoes. He did agree, however, that it would be a suitable gesture for me to go to Ockley again with a bottle of choice wine. Such company was not what he wanted. Nor indeed was the company he was forced to keep—that of gentlemen temporarily relaxing in the rather raffish atmosphere of the Hawk in Hand, willing to drink and gamble with an outsider who could pay his way and was in fact open-handed, but unprepared to invite him—and his daughter—into their sacrosanct dwellings. And that was what Father wanted above all, to be accepted by country gentlemen, as a country gentleman. Poor man; compared with that which he had not attained all that he had seemed small; all his wealth, the comfort and service he could command. He fretted and began to talk of moving to somewhere where people were more easy. When he spoke of moving I always felt a little pang; I liked Baildon and all the countryside around, and I was entranced with my new friends.

The beginnings of a friendship, its development into intimacy are hard things to trace. I remember that I waited, deliberately, for two days before taking back the basket they had lent me and presenting the bottle of wine and then stayed on, talking, until it was dinnertime and Mistress Tresize asked me to stay for the meal, simple but well-cooked and properly served by one of her two elderly maids. Alan Heath joined us, wearing his working garb, for which he apologised: "I'd have changed had I known you had company." I gathered that he lived across the river, in a small house called Bowman's, made his own breakfast but, unless away on business, ate his dinner and supper with Mistress Tresize. He kept no servant, which argued poverty as distinctly as the napery and furnishings of the table argued wealth at some time or another.

I wondered about their past and about their relationship; they were so much alike, not only in appearance, that they could have been mother and son. That day I learned something of their circumstances. It began, prosaically enough, with a talk about washing. Every so often one of Mistress Tresize's maids carried all her washing down to Bowman's, did it, with Alan's there, and tidied his house while articles dried on the line or bleached on the bushes.

"This may all sound very puzzling to you, Mistress Shawcross, but it is in strict accordance with my father's will. A typically *male* will, I may say. These apartments are mine, with reasonable access, but Mistress Babcock chose to interpret that in her own way, *not* to include a linen line just outside the back door. The first time Margery strung one up, Mistress Babcock cut it through and all the clean things slid off into the mud!"

Working as my grandfather's assistant, assessing the case in which a shilling was a panacea, had given me a sharp ear for the thing which was not said and I sensed a time lapse. Between the making of that well-meant but inept will and the dominance of Mistress Babcock there had been an interregnum about which neither of them would speak. Once Mistress Tresize said, inadvertently, "When Simon was very young..." and stopped, looking at Alan and Alan looking at her as though she had been on the verge of the ultimate blasphemy.

One day Father said, in the discontented way that was setting in on him, "You seem to be getting very thick with these people at Ockley. Maybe I should take a look at them."

I said, "It would please me if you asked them to dinner. I have eaten with them many times. But..."

"But what?"

"They're a curious couple. Self-contained. And although I understand that Mistress Tresize was a great horsewoman at one time, she no longer rides."

"I'll send the coach," Father said grandly. It was a kindly gesture, but about it and about all his preparations for the visit there hung the slight but unmistakable air of patronage; was it worthwhile, he asked, to produce his best wine? In such a manner, I felt, had Lord and Lady Dunwich prepared to entertain my grandparents and similar people. I thought to myself, Wait till you see them. And when they arrived I was proud of my guests. Mistress Tresize was very grand indeed, though in the fashion of

an older day, and Alan, in good broadcloth, was un-
believably handsome.

It was a merry meal; Mistress Tresize had the
right, light touch: quite grave when she admired the
house and garden, but completely without envy, and
then reverting to what I deemed—perhaps wrongly—
to a kind of wry flippancy. Sometimes I had thought
to myself that she was a woman who had borne whatever Fate chose to fling at her and had survived with
her talent for mockery unimpaired. When she wished
she could make even Mistress Babcock's petty tyr-
annies sound amusing. Father laughed and then said,
"But could she not be bought off?"

"Eventually. With my little pigs and my poultry
and Alan's potatoes, we hope to do so. But it takes
time—and meanwhile Mistress Babcock is spoiling
the house and ruining the farm."

"I could buy her off tomorrow," Father said. It was
one of those things which came naturally to his tongue
and in communities like this one did not endear him
to people; but Mistress Tresize merely laughed and
said, "If only you would! A worse neighbour than
Mistress Babcock would be hard to find."

"And I'd rent it—if you regarded me as suitable
tenant, sir," Alan said eagerly. "I pin my faith to the
potato but I should feel happier with the backing of
a good, mixed farm."

"I'll think about it," Father said. I could see his
mind working. Straight from the sea, he had shunned
the idea of owning land and being responsible for
tenants and had then found himself in a community
where status was very largely dependent upon
acreage and, of course, on ancestry, which in its turn
relied upon acreage. New money was in fact not acceptable until Suffolk soil had rubbed off onto it. "I'll
think about it," he said again. "How much do you
think it would take to dislodge this harridan?"

"Rather more than the place is worth at the moment," Mistress Tresize said. "It is horribly mismanaged but her standards are very low. All she wants is enough for food—and taxes. And there is the tanyard to be considered."

"The tanyard?" Father sounded amazed though actually, in my talk about the Old Priory and the conditions there, I had mentioned it. His mind had simply brushed the information aside; nothing to do with him, therefore easy to ignore and to forget. And to tell the truth I was, just then, almost as completely self-absorbed. Head over heels in love with a man who had never shown me anything but friendly courtesy.

Older people liked to pretend that love between man and woman was a new and rather regrettable thing fostered by poets like Shakespeare, but it is at least as old as the Bible—look at Jacob serving seven years for Rachel, being cheated and serving another seven years. What was true was that lately slightly more attention was being paid to individual preferences, and marriages like that of my grandparents, who before they were betrothed had barely exchanged a dozen words, were becoming rather more rare. Parents still arranged marriages and self-interest was still lively, but on the whole, all other things being equal, young people were allowed some choice.

I'd made mine and I knew it was good. My first attraction to Alan Heath had been superficial and perhaps sentimental, based on his looks, so akin to Lord Gorleston's. Later I had realised his sterling qualities: the way he worked, his behaviour to Mistress Tresize, more filial than many a son's. Even his behaviour to me was admirable, if one accepted the fact that he did not find me attractive, which was, I feared, the sorry truth.

I'd done my best, aware that I was no longer in
the full flush of youth; I'd used cosmetics freely and
had never presented myself at the Old Priory looking
anything but my best. I'd tried to reach him through
Mistress Tresize, who still felt the loss of her garden.
Ours at The Mount was prolific in everything, from
marigolds to apricots, and I'd never gone empty-
handed. She'd always thanked me extravagantly and,
if Alan came in, would draw attention to my offering
and he'd say, "Very pretty," or "How kind of Mistress
Shawcross," smile at me briefly, making my heart
turn over, and then change the subject. On the rare
occasions when he was at the Old Priory when the
time came for me to leave, he would come down with
me and help me into the saddle, the touch of his
hands rousing feelings in me which were partly delightful and partly painful. Sometimes I cried over
the hopelessness of it all, but generally I was becoming resigned. I should die an old maid, since marriage
to any other man was unthinkable.

After that visit Father pursued his notion of buying
the Old Priory, but he was not a man to buy a pig
in a poke, so he must see it, and on a warm August
day he and I went to dinner there and afterwards
Alan showed him round as well as possible without
encroaching upon Mistress Babcock's ground. About
agriculture Father knew little, but he was impressed
by the house, damaged though it was by the Bab-
cocks' occupation. What a large, careless family can
do to a house in a short time is remarkable. They'd
even contrived to break several windows, and the
garden was a wilderness. Over all hung the stench
of the tanyard, and in Mistress Tresize's part of the
house, on the ground floor, the less aggressive but
still noticeable odours of pigs and poultry. Upstairs,
however, there was that sweet air of serenity which

I had noticed from my first visit, although even on such a warm day all windows were firmly closed.

During that meal—suckling pig and the inevitable potatoes—Father asked in his blunt way, "Do you entertain much, Mistress Tresize?"

"No longer," she said. "There was a time...You see, my father's second wife was a Hatton, so everybody came and we went everywhere. Then things changed." Her face took on the look that had convinced me that somewhere in her past there were things she did not care to think about, that look of having faced the worst and survived, but not unscathed. I often thought of her as a book in which you could read a page or two in plain English and which then veered off into some unknown tongue.

"A Hatton, eh?" Father said, his eyes widening. With his unusual insensitivity he added, "But he was a new man, too, like me, wasn't he? And for my part I find the people around here a damned unfriendly lot."

"I agree," she said lightly. "But there are ways of wooing them. Marriage. Being ostentatiously charitable. I believe Baildon is in great need of almshouses. And important people are always eager to administer such enterprises." It was a hint upon which Father seized. I could see his mind at work. The Shawcross Foundation, and all the people, the Shelmadines, Hattons and Helmars, who had ignored him being impressed and willing to hobnob with him.

I was rather afraid that, facing this new expenditure, Father might lose interest in buying the Old Priory, but he held to that, especially after his first interview with Mistress Babcock during which she said flatly that she had no intention of selling. She admitted that she'd had no great success with crops or cattle, but things could only get better; and she had persuaded her husband to move his place of business, she couldn't upset him again; but most potent argument of all was sentiment. The place had been willed to her by Mistress Tresize's half brother, of whom she'd been very fond.

"That I doubt," Father said. "Women like that don't get fond of their clients. He must have been fond for her, but then soft young cubs often cherish tender feelings towards their..." He broke off, becoming aware of whom he was talking to, a female, unmarried and so supposedly innocent. Not that anything which he could have said just then would have affronted me. I was remembering that one reference to Simon, so hastily cut off. I thought, Well, of course they wouldn't want to talk about Simon, who had left so much to that old shrew.

During the next week or two Father showed his mettle and—fortunate man—was able by a quirk of luck to combine his two aims. In Baildon there was a place called Hawk Lane, running down from behind the Market Place towards the river. On one side of it stood eight cottages in poor repair, and opposite them a sawmill at which most of the inhabitants of the cottages had been employed. The owner of the sawmill, an ageing man, was anxious to sell out and retire. "Ideal for my purpose," Father said. "Some of the cottages are already empty, the rest can be cleared by Michaelmas. They all need rethatching and given at least one glazed window and there we are. My almshouses. As for the sawmill, there is a saw pit there, easily converted into a tan pit."

I managed to tear myself away from my own predicament and remember what I had learned when I was doinq a curate's work for my grandfather. One of the problems was homelessness and the ritual shilling didn't go far towards solving it. I said, "And what happens to the people at present in the cottages who will be homeless at Michaelmas?"

"Easy," Father said. "If they cannot find anything better, they can be the first tenants of the almshouses." There was no arguing with that. And bearing in mind that he must be ostentatiously generous, Father arranged that no almshouse inmate need starve, all were to receive a weekly allowance of bread, and meat twice a month as well as a shilling at Christmas, Easter, Whitsun and Michaelmas. Such a generous endowment was a nine days' wonder, and Mistress Tresize's advice—given so casually—had been sound. All the country gentlemen wished to appear as vicarious public benefactors, meeting in solemn conclave once a month in order to plan the spending of Father's money to the best advantage.

Progress with the Old Priory was slightly slower for Mistress Babcock was stubborn, bent on extracting the last possible penny. Father began by offering her four hundred pounds for the house and land, and the tenancy of the sawmill and the house that went with it rent-free for ten years. This again was extravagantly generous considering the state of her part of the house, the derelict garden and the fact that some acres of the best land were already let to a tenant, who in turn had leased two acres to Alan, but Father was stubborn too and greatly strengthened in his fight by the knowledge that all his newfound friends wished him well. They considered it iniquitous that a fine house should have found its way into the hands of a woman of low repute. Even Sir Edward Shelmadine, the first thwarter of Father's ambitions and now a lively member of the almshouse board, said that some thirty years earlier he'd known the Old Priory well and would be interested to see what sort of mess it was in now. Father took him over and Mistress Babcock, in a bad mood, came out and shouted at them, "It ain't yours yet!" and made them keep to the right-of-way. Then, perhaps as a gesture of sympathy, Sir Edward invited Father to dine at Clevely. Father's cup of happiness was full.

Through all this I continued to make my visits to Ockley, seeing less and less of Alan as the year aged. The potatoes kept him so busy. They'd grown from plum-size, pearly white to the size of a man's clenched fist and buff-coloured, and he had more customers for them than he could supply. He was interested in and anxious about the tussle between Father and Mistress Babcock because when planting time came round he must have more land. It was inadvisable to grow potatoes on the same plot year after year. It would be ideal if Father bought the Old Priory and allowed him to hire it, but failing that he must get his foot in elsewhere. Whenever we met, this kind of prosaic conversation took place and I'd listen and say, "Yes, I see," and "I understand," and "I'm sure Father will win eventually," while all the time a turn of his head, a glint of light on that wonderful hair and the sound of his voice set my heart turning somersaults and my mind evolving the craziest ideas.

Perhaps I had inherited some of Father's forthrightness. I longed to say, "Look, I know you don't love me, but I love you. I love enough for two. Why not marry me? I shall have a good dowry; you could buy acres of land for your precious potatoes."

I could never say it, of course; even the thought of doing so was so shameful that I could feel the blood rush to my face and then drain away, leaving a pinched wanness behind the paint and powder.

Mistress Babcock capitulated in late October when Father made his final offer, five hundred pounds and a life tenancy of the Hawk Lane property. She gave as a reason for conceding the fact that since moving to Ockley her husband's business had dwindled. She then struck a separate bargain. There were things in the Old Priory which she couldn't possibly fit into the humbler house in Hawk Lane: massive furniture, wall hangings, rugs. Father asked what she expected them to fetch if sold by auction and she said, brashly, at least two hundred pounds. Father said rubbish! Fifty. So they haggled some more and settled for a hundred on condition that she moved within a week. Which she did, leaving such near devastation behind her as to be almost unbelievable. Banister rails were loose, or missing altogether, filthy hands had wrenched at the wall hangings, mud and remnants of food had been stamped into the rugs. "Heathen Africans—slaves—keep their quarters cleaner," Father said in disgust. "Still, there's nothing here that a few sailor men couldn't put right in a fortnight and there're plenty of them, beached for the winter down at Bywater. And as Sir Edward says, it was once a fine house and could be again." Father never missed an opportunity of mentioning his new friend's name.

He invited Mistress Tresize to come down from her clean, sweet-scented eyrie to view the damage. She said, "Just what one would expect," and then showed a little emotion at the sight of an armchair, its padding ripped and the stuffing protruding. "That was my father's special chair," she said in a voice I had never heard her use before. But almost immediately she mastered herself and went and opened a window. "That horrible pit is less offensive now that it is quiescent," she said. "And now that you have achieved possession, what do you propose to do with the house?"

"Bless my soul, ma'am, I never gave that a thought. I was so intent on ousting that old hag."

"Would you allow me to hire it? With an outbuilding or two? Yes, yes, I can afford it. My young pigs and table birds have done very well and with more space I can do better."

"There's nobody I'd sooner see in it," Father said. He meant it; he knew that he owed her something for her hint about almshouses.

So—or thus it seemed to me—everybody within my immediate circle was happy. Even the destitute sailors, scrubbing and scouring, painting and hammering, whistled as they worked, glad of a wage, however derisory, and regular food, the provision of which Father entrusted to Mistress Tresize, she being on the spot and we suddenly so busy, entertaining and being entertained. Alan was busy and happy with his newly hired acres; Mistress Tresize was happy with her newly hired house; Father was happy with his newly acquired popularity. I, and I only, was left out, unhappy, longing for something that could be neither bought nor hired.

Over and over again I would firmly make up my mind to avoid Ockley altogether or to confine my visits to Mistress Tresize to such times as I knew Alan would not be with her. Then I'd compromise, ride over in the morning, meaning to stay only an hour and be home for dinner. Then it was as though my will became paralysed and I'd linger, accept the inevitable invitation to dine, and sit there, outwardly calm but inwardly seething with excitement, waiting for Alan to appear and inflict more hurt. Even on occasions when Mistress Tresize said, "Do stay and eat with me, Alan will not be back until late,"I'd stay for the dubious pleasure of hearing her talk about him. On one such occasion she mentioned Bowman's. "Alan could have sold it," she said, "and although he could have used the money, he said he

dare not. Poor boy, he lacks confidence and there has
been little in his life to inculcate it."

"I miss the connection," I said after a moment's
thought. "What has Bowman's to do with his confidence?"

"He regards it as something he could fall back
upon if another disaster struck."

"What would Alan regard as a disaster?" (That
was one of the attractions of these private talks. I
would never have made so bold as to call him Alan
to his face or in any company but this, yet when
Mistress Tresize and I were talking about him not
to use his given name would have sounded stilted.)

"The potato is susceptible to blight," she said. "A
really bad year might result in failure to pay his
rent."

"Father would not be harsh," I began. Then I wondered. Being lenient with a nonpaying tenant was
not the kind of generosity likely to be admired by
other landowners. I saw my doubt reflected in her
eyes.

"Your father, my dear, was very generous in setting up the almshouses, in saving this house from
Mistress Babcock and making good all her depredations before letting the place to me. But...well, the
truth is that Alan will never feel really secure until
he has a place of his own—preferably this one, of
course. To that end he is working—and saving—
very hard indeed."

I thought, And he could have it for the asking! He
had only to marry me and I'd ask for the Old Priory
as a wedding present, as part of my dowry. I had
reached such a state of hopeless infatuation that I
shouldn't have minded in the least if Alan had married me merely for security. Nothing in my life had
been likely to inculcate confidence, either, and I had
learned to be content with very little. Yet I was *sure*

that given one chance to break through that façade of amiable courtesy the very force of my passion would rouse a response.

So, with the days growing colder and shorter, the year ran downhill towards Christmas.

# CHAPTER 4

Christmas that year was very merry. I could not avoid thinking of my grandfather, who held that the birth of Christ should not be associated with gourmandising, drunkenness and tomfoolery, and he was thinking only of what went on at the Castle. South Suffolk, where so many men were little lords, would have been outside his comprehension.

It began, the Christmas around Baildon, with a feast in the Guildhall for all occupants of almshouses and people on parish relief. Roast beef, plum pudding and as much beer as anybody could drink. After that the private parties began, each host trying to outvie his neighbour not only in provender but in entertainment. Father, always wishing to be go-ahead, provided turkeys, relatively new to England. I had two new gowns, one blue and one rose pink, and Father dug into his hoard and produced a necklace of sapphires to wear with one and a collar of garnets to go with the other. My only regret was that Alan could not see me so finely arrayed. I did, however, attract some admiring—and some envious—glances and, to my grief and embarrassment, a suitor.

At Christmas all the big houses kept open house for relatives and old friends, and at Clevely, on the third day, we met Sir Francis Beaumont, a cousin of Sir Edward's, a man who would have seemed eligible to someone much younger than I. He was a widower in his late thirties, slightly too plump but otherwise not bad-looking, exquisitely dressed, beautifully mannered and a skilful dancer. Sir Edward's after-dinner entertainment took the form of a dance, far less countrified than those I had known when I was young, rather stately in fact. Like Lord Gorleston, in a past which now seemed infinitely remote, he sought me out; he stayed with me between dances, fetching me wine, plying my fan. "Dancing attendance" as the saying goes.

Father, of course, noticed, and in the coach going home used the obnoxious words, "You seem to have acquired an admirer. And about time, too!"

And it is true that if I had met the man and he'd shown a preference for me before I made my first fatal visit to the Old Priory and lost my heart to Alan, I should have been pleased, flattered and, God forgive me, prepared to marry him. As it was my only feeling was of repugnance. That old fat man, I thought, comparing him with Alan. And following the repugnance came fear. If Father thought this a suitable match, what defence had I? I was of age, but as completely in Father's hands as a child. He fed, clothed, housed me. He was in a position to bring a vast amount of pressure to bear. I had one resource: if things became too unpleasant at Baildon I could ask my grandparents for refuge and return to drudg-

ery, if they would have me. Which they might not.
They were quite likely—now that they were accustomed to doing without me—to fall back on a strictly
literal translation of the commandment about hon-
ouring one's parents.

Clumsily and quite ineffectually I thought up ways
of making myself unattractive at the next party,
which was at the Hattons' place, Mortiboys. I used
no cosmetics, scraped my hair back unbecomingly
and made the cold day an excuse for wearing a high-
necked dress. Such devices are now amusing to look
back upon, for afterwards we learned that Sir Francis was not drawn to me as a person but as an heiress
to Father's wealth. Despite his title and an estate in
Wiltshire, Sir Francis was perpetually short of money.

At Mortiboys, to which as a member of the Clevely
house party he had been invited, Sir Francis was as
attentive as before. Father was jubilant. "Lady
Beaumont," he said. "Think of that!"

"It may be just an idle fancy," I said. "And if not,
Wiltshire is so far away. We should meet so seldom!"
I put all the sentiment I could muster into my voice,
aware of the falsity of it.

"Oh, travel becomes easier all the time," Father
said heartily. "After all, Sir Francis could get to Suffolk for Christmas. We could make frequent visits."

I knew he was not thinking much about the visits;
he was hearing himself say to all and sundry, "My
daughter, Lady Beaumont..."

Yet, knowing all this, I could not say that I did
not wish to marry the man until he had expressed
a wish for me to do so. I felt helpless and trapped
and miserable. Adding to my depression was the fact
that in this hectic round of party-going and party-
giving, I was able to get out to Ockley only once.
Alan was not there and I didn't know whether to be
glad or sorry. The contrast between the man who

seemed to be attracted to me and the man who was not was too cruel. Alone with Mistress Tresize, I felt an impulse to take her into my confidence, tell her what was happening and how I felt about it. At this crisis of my life I was aware of loneliness; I'd never had a female friend.

I liked Lettice Tresize very much, I admired her elegance, which had triumphed over circumstance, her wit, her down-to-earth approach to life. And she had always seemed to like me. But between us there was the gulf of years and on her part a definite reserve. I always had the feeling that a great deal more had happened to her than showed on the surface. I really did not feel I could talk to her about my troubles. Also I had a fear that once started I might not stop; I might betray myself if once I began talking about love and marriage.

On the day when it was our turn to do the entertaining, I noticed that in the middle of the bustle Sir Francis and Father stood a little aside, talking earnestly with an occasional glance in my direction. By this time my distaste for an apparently harmless and well-intentioned man had developed into loathing and I stood there in the midst of the merriment making the most desperate resolutions. If Father insisted, I thought, I should just run away. I'd try my grandparents first and if they didn't want me I'd find some humble domestic job.

Actually I underestimated Father's shrewdness and overestimated his social ambition. In the evening of that day all our guests departed, and, the after-party sadness and flatness setting in, Father said, "Arabella, I want to talk to you."

My control snapped. I said, "I know what about. And I don't want to hear it. I wouldn't want to marry Sir Francis if he were the last man on earth."

"He feels warmly towards you."

"I know. And the thought makes me sick!"

"God in glory! Such vehemence! Naturally, as any man would, I should like to see you married and established, and I pay no attention to girlish whims. Though you are no longer a girl exactly. I bear that in mind. All the same, I don't want somebody to marry *you* for the sake of *my* money."

That touched my vanity and I said, perversely, "And why should you think that? Have I no value as myself?"

"Come, come," Father said. "Don't pretend that you were not suspicious, too. Didn't you try him out? Going to that dinner party, swathed to the chin, barefaced and looking at least forty and sick into the bargain. Enough to make any man run for his life. But your Sir Francis did not, and that roused both my hopes and my suspicions. In any case, I shall soon know. I have friends of a sort, not grand but with sharp eyes and ears, in many places. Within ten days I shall know as much about Sir Francis's financial position as he knows himself—probably more. And if he cannot match your dowry with a marriage settlement I shall give the matter no further consideration."

It was a temporary reprieve, but some of the things he said fell on my heart like stones. No longer a girl exactly; looking, without cosmetics and in a plain dress, at least forty and sick into the bargain. Naturally I thought of Alan: how did he see me? The answer was disheartening in the extreme, and I began the sad business of resigning myself once again, just as I had over the far less practical dream of Lord Gorleston. Twice in my life I had mentally chased the will-o'-the-wisp. Now I should end as a spinster, unable to get the man I desired and unwilling to accept any other.

I was relieved, but at the same time depressed,

when Father's mysterious friend reported from Wiltshire. Sir Francis was a man on the brink of ruin; his gambling was notorious, his debts colossal. His only hope of financial salvation lay in marrying a woman with money.

Father was disappointed and allowed his feelings to take a curious form. "Look what I've saved you from," he said, speaking as though I had wanted to marry Sir Francis. In my misery I looked back, remembering two would-be suitors at Gorleston, unacceptable to my grandparents because of their humble status; now there had been a man of rank, interested only in my money. What further proof of undesirability could a woman have?

For the first time my wretchedness took physical form. I lost my appetite and grew thinner, in itself an unbecoming process. Now, even with paint and powder and lipsalve in place, I did look forty and sick into the bargain.

Early in January I made up my mind to avoid the Old Priory in future and forego the dubious pleasure of seeing Alan if he were there, of hearing and speaking his name if he were absent. This meant that I should also forego the company of Mistress Tresize, of whom I was fond, and it was poor comfort to think that I should miss her more than she would miss me. She was a very self-contained person and at the moment absolutely intent upon restoring her garden. However, I thought it only civil to make one more visit and just hint that I should come less often in future. I thought that I could say with great truth that now that Father and I were entertaining and being entertained a great deal I had less spare time. I would also say that through the almshouses I had become interested in the state of the poor and intended to take up good works—the traditional occupation of the spinster!

Making tucks in the bodice of my riding habit, I thought that in time—say ten years—I might forget, outgrow the lust of the eye and the heart's desire.

I chose Wednesday for this visit, thinking that Alan would be in Baildon. For January the weather was exceptionally good and open; there had been night frosts and an occasional flurry of snow but nothing to render the woodland path impassable. I took that way and, where the wood ended and Top Field began, I halted Bess as I had done once before and looked out over the cultivated ground and the house. Since that day I had seen many of the semi-great houses and I still thought the Old Priory the most appealing. Then I looked at the land and heard, in my mind, Alan's words about the desirability of the one crop—the potato—being backed up by mixed farming. In the short time during which he had tenanted the place he had put his theory into effect. The winter wheat was already showing through, a green fluff just rustled by the wind. In other fields the ploughs were out, and down by the river, thanks to the open weather, there were cattle.

All at once my sore heart took a kind of comfort. This was, in a way, my doing. Had I not almost forced myself upon Mistress Tresize, none of this would have come about. The Babcock woman would still have been in charge here, ruining both the house and the land, and Alan would have been managing with a mere four acres, two at Bowman's, two on Eggar's Piece. I thought, I have not lived in vain! In all this there is nothing for me, but it has been of benefit to a woman I respect and a man I love. Because of my parsonage training I had a mystical thought—it was good that one man should suffer for the benefit of others. I nudged Bess into a trot.

Mistress Tresize, hooded and cloaked, was in the garden, happy because so many plants had proved resilient to neglect and ill treatment. In a sheltered spot she had found, at this unlikely season, two little flowers of the kind which some people called hearts-ease, others pansies. She held them reverently and said, "I have never known them so early. And to have survived at all they must be very tough."

And because of my present mood and my present errand I realised that toughness was the quality she valued most highly, because at some time in the past about which she was so reticent toughness had been her salvation.

As it must be mine.

I had intended only a short visit, but without seeming to insist she insisted in my going round the garden with her, marking the gaps where plants had perished and the places where they had survived. And I had a new thought—she also was an unmarried woman who had devoted herself to a variety of interests outside the meaning of love. I wondered had she ever been in love? Been frustrated? Impossible to ask, of course.

She said, "You will stay to dinner? Madge is making broth. And you look"—her cool eye measured me—"as though you could do with a bowlful. Child, you've grown thin, despite all the Christmas festivities. But I remember how they go—the strongest get to the trough first." In a way it was true, but at every gathering Sir Francis had kept my plate replenished. So I said, "If I look thinner it is not for lack of food. It is the result of trying to be in two places at once." With that as an opening, I could go on to explain how busy I had been lately, how busy I should be in future.

I must have done it clumsily for she said with dignity, "I have always set store by your visits, my dear, but if you come less often, I shall quite understand."

I was not a tearful woman but tears were near then. I thought, Oh the irony of it! When this is the place where I long to be; when your company and Alan's is all I seek! I swallowed hard and blinked and maintained control, and then, to refute the idea that I was rejecting her, stayed on. The afternoon was darkening when the deaf and dumb woman who acted as yardman brought round my horse.

"It will be darker in the wood," Mistress Tresize said. "Would you not be wiser to go round by the road?"

"The woodland way is quicker," I said. "And Bess knows the way."

"Then I'll say good-bye," she said, and unexpectedly she leaned forward and kissed me, a thing she had never done before. That came near to upsetting me again. I told myself sternly that painful though it was I was doing the right thing, the only thing. All my visits to the Old Priory except the first one had been akin to a penniless child hanging about a cookshop window.

It was considerably darker under the trees and, contrary to custom, colder. I was glad of my fur-lined, fur-edged cloak, glad of the warmth my horse exuded. I tried telling myself that I had much to be grateful for, all the comfort that money could buy and a father far less ruthless than I had expected. I thought, Poor Father, I have not been very lively company for him lately. I will do better!

I was riding carelessly; Bess was as steady as a hobby horse and she knew the way. I trusted her absolutely and was quite unprepared for what happened. We were still on that piece of path which led only to the Old Priory and to Ockley when she suddenly stopped, stock-still with a jolt that almost unseated me. And she began to tremble. I peered into the gloom ahead and could see nothing, so with one hand still careless on the rein I used the other to pat her neck. And I spoke soothingly. "Come along. There's nothing to be scared of. There's nothing there. Come up, Bess. Come up, old girl. There, there, there!" I gave her a gentle nudge with my heel. She responded in the most extraordinary fashion, rearing up on her hind legs and letting loose a squeal of sheer terror. I slid from her back and fell heavily, hitting the left side of my face, my shoulder, elbow, hip and knee. I was hurt, but not injured, for the side of the path onto which I had fallen was thick with the leaves of many autumns.

I gathered myself together and stood up and was immediately engulfed in such terror as I have never known—the terror which had sent Bess galloping off. I could hear her hoofbeats receding in the distance. I stood there paralysed with fear, with something dark and cold and evil rolling down on me. I knew I must move or be lost forever, and what I did when I forced myself to move was something of which my grandfather would have disapproved. My shaking hand made the sign of the cross and I said, "In the name of the Father, the Son and the Holy Ghost, *go away.*"

Whatever it was, it went. I could breathe again, reckon my hurts, think ahead. And—it sounds a strange thing to say—I could cry, give way to all the tears which I had not shed over the years. Everything that I had found hurtful, clear back to leaving Browston Hall for Gorleston Parsonage, came pouring out. The shames, the hopes, the disappointments, all I was, all I had experienced, pouring out, far beyond my power to control.

Yet some small nub of sense stayed with me. I knew that I was incapable of walking home. My bruised knee, my bruised hip made such exertion quite unthinkable, and the chill, which had persisted, presaged a night of frost. I must renounce all my resolutions and go back to the Old Priory and beg hospitality.

Though growing dark, it was still early and there was just a chance that Alan would not yet be back. I might, with any luck, get put to bed without even seeing him. But then, I asked myself dismally, when had I ever had any luck? For me the pretty dresses had come when I was just too old to wear them, and the social life, the chances of marriage had come when I had lost my heart irretrievably to a man who cared nothing for me, who looked on me as a pleasant visitor for his elderly relative! Could anything be more hopeless, or more ridiculous?

And even now, when I had made what I hoped was a dignified exit and Mistress Tresize—how much had she guessed?—had kissed me, here I was, made to look ridiculous again, hobbling back to crave hospitality. The bruises on my hip and knee eased slightly, but the pain in my ankle grew worse. And somehow I'd lost my hat and my hair came tumbling down. Yet I was not crying because every step was torment—I had sprained my ankle, no doubt about that, but a sprained ankle healed. This sudden, unstemmable burst of tears came from a broken heart.

I tried to use sense, to prepare what to say: "Bess threw me and I fell awkwardly and sprained my ankle."

The house was in clear view now; the two small lighted windows on either side of the door—they were in the hall and there was the wider one where Mistress Tresize might be busy with her books—or perhaps talking to Alan, listening to his market news, or merely waiting for his arrival. Instead she'd have to deal with me! The thought made me cry harder and I remember thinking that I should go on to the end of my life, one of those dreadful lachrymose women who cry as easily as they breathe.

In this state I reached the door and seized the handle, supported by it with my weight on my sound leg, easing the other, but the handle yielded, the door opened and I fell into the hall, literally at Alan's feet. He was on his way through the hall from kitchen to parlour. He hauled me up and said, "Darling!" rather as a man might use an epithet when taken unawares. But he used the word again, this time allied to my name: "Arabella, darling! What happened?"

I forgot my bruises, and now that he was supporting my weight the pain in my ankle receded. I said, "I have had a most terrible fright," and shuddered again at the memory.

His clasp on me tightened, pressing me close. "You're safe now," he said. "Safe with me."

I lost the last vestige of my control. I said, "Alan, I love you. From the moment I first saw you. More than I can say."

And now that I had said it, I'd said the wrong thing. There was a settle in the hall and he carried me to it and sat me down, remaining standing himself and looking stern, divested even of the casual, civil friendliness with which he usually treated me.

"I love you, too," he said, with no fondness in his voice. "God alone knows what I have suffered! What could I offer? And you a rich man's daughter."

"I can't see..." I began.

"You would after five minutes' talk with your father! 'Fortune hunter' is the kindest expression he'd use. I may be poor, but I have my pride."

"Is that all? Then you don't love me."

"I do. I always have done. I swear. I've suffered tortures and, since nobody else would do, condemned myself to celibacy for the rest of my life."

I thought quickly. I said, "Alan, you have it all wrong. I am poor, too. My father cannot long withstand the arguments that he should remarry and get himself an heir. And if he tries to marry me to any other man I shall refuse absolutely, and be disowned and become a dairymaid or some such."

Alan then said some loving things—he actually thought I was pretty, which shows how blind love can be. He even went back and praised my courage in trying to make certain that Lettice was not being ill-treated by Mistress Babcock. "I knew then that you were a girl of rare spirit," he said, and I tried to explain that it was all a matter of training.

"Girls from parsonages are brought up to mind other people's business!" I tried a rather tear-smeared smile but it evoked no answering glimmer from him. In fact he looked even sterner and more glum. "There's another thing," he said. "You have family behind you. I have none."

"You have Lettice."

His face jerked. "Yes, I have her and she has been kinder than God..." He seemed about to say more, but checked himself. "The kindest story—when I was young—was that she saved me from a foundlings' home."

"Even if it were true what difference would it make? And what a damned poor excuse for making me miserable for the rest of my days. I tell you, I love you. I shall never love anyone else." I cried some more. "You're breaking my heart," I said.

He said, "Darling, don't. You're breaking mine." He took me in his arms again and we kissed; that first tentative, inexperienced kiss that stays sweet while memory endures.

Then, with beautiful timing, Mistress Tresize opened the parlour door and asked what all the hullaballoo was about.

We explained—but only about my accident.

There was a loaf on the table, and while she got busy with cold-water presses and bandages for my ankle, Alan cut himself a slice and announced his intention of going at once to Baildon to inform Father about my accident. "Imagine the poor man's state of mind when Bess gets home with an empty saddle," he said. But his face informed me that there would be talk of other things. And it was typical of the man that he went as he was, no donning of best clothes, oiling of hair or other preparations.

And strangely enough that simple action turned the scales in his favour. "Not a man in a thousand would have given a thought to my feelings at such a moment," Father said. "He's poor, but he's honest and kind and he'll make you a good husband."

I had expected every possible objection, but my father was a very unpredictable man. "I shall give him the Old Priory as a wedding present, and you a thousand pounds against the day when the blight strikes."

Happy ever after is a fairy-tale ending. Happy now is more within the scope of mere human beings, and I try to savour every passing moment.